CURSE OF

The crowd cheered as the soldier's head rolled into the street. Bagsby turned to acknowledge the cheers, then noticed that the body atop him had not collapsed. It remained rigid, still pinning him to the ground. Bagsby pushed upward with all his strength, and the headless corpse tumbled over on its side.

"All idiots who desire death will be pleasantly served," Bagsby crowed.

The laughter from the crowd suddenly died out.

Bagsby spun in time to see the decapitated body, now standing, grasp its severed head by the hair, lift the half-rotted trophy up, and set it atop its neck.

"Bagsby," the thing wheezed, "you will die."

Other AvoNova Books by
Mark Acres

DRAGONSPAWN

DRAGON WAR

MARK ACRES

AVON BOOKS • NEW YORK

DRAGON WAR is an original publication of Avon Books. This work has never before appeared in book form. This work is a novel. Any similarity to actual persons or events is purely coincidental.

AVON BOOKS
A division of
The Hearst Corporation
1350 Avenue of the Americas
New York, New York 10019

First AvoNova Printing: August 1994

AVONOVA TRADEMARK REG. U.S. PAT. OFF. AND IN OTHER COUNTRIES, MARCA REGISTRADA, HECHO EN U.S.A.

Printed in the U.S.A.

RA 10 9 8 7 6 5 4 3 2 1

DRAGON WAR

Prologue

THE LONE WARRIOR sat motionless on his white mount at the top of the grassy knoll, his ebony armor casting off sparks of brilliant white light as the first rays of the cold morning sun touched its carefully fluted plates. The toes of the black steel boots curved forward to sharp points; a kick from them could pierce a man's flesh. Black greaves and leg plating covered the fighter to his waist, the metal seemingly flowing up his form in countless subtle twists and curves, accented by short, sharp steel spikes protruding forward from the knee joints. The same fluted black steel covered the abdomen and torso of the forbidding figure, with fine designs and jarring, jagged patterns raised from the smooth surface of the plates. The horse's reins were held in the flexible black gauntlets that covered the fighter's left hand. The warrior's head was hidden in the recesses of a great helm, the beaver and bottom of which jutted forward sharply, giving the impression of the beak of a giant, black bird of prey. Black, too, were the saddle, stirrups, bridle, and reins of the white horse. The only relief from the stark black-white contrast was the shock of brilliant red plumage that towered from the top of the helm, looking like an enormous spray of blood erupting toward the heavens.

The warrior gazed out on the plain that extended before him to the distant horizon—a grassy plain filled with the combined host of the Holy Alliance drawn up in full battle array. More than a hundred huge banners, over six feet on a side, snapped stiffly in the cold wind. A cacophony of colors assaulted the warrior's hidden eyes, each colorful

1

emblem competing with its peers for precedence and glory. And the troops! Rank after rank of mounted knights, each armored more gloriously than the rank before it. Spearpoints, lances, and upraised swords gleamed with armor in the early light, and the snorting, puffing and pawing of the countless horses was like a muffled thunder—how glorious would be the sound of the charge! There were footmen, too, in their countless thousands, the pawns, the senseless sacrifices, the grist for the mill of war: some professional mercenaries in their suits of chain mail half hidden behind their full length, narrow shields; some common peasants, armored and armed as best they could with spears and bills, wooden shields, and leather padding; some half naked savages, with nothing more than slings, stones, teeth, and nails with which to assault their hated foe.

To the rear of the enemy host, in a single thin line, mounted on the finest horses in all the kingdoms of the Holy Alliance, were the rulers of the Alliance lands: kings, princes, dukes, and earls—all sons of kings, with royal blood coursing quickly through their veins as the thrill and fear of the approaching battle quickened their various spirits. Golden crowns and shining silver coronets adorned their heads; behind each ruler's horse, a richly dressed squire held lance and helm at the ready, should the noblest of the nobles decide to actually participate in the death struggle about to explode across the plain.

The lone warrior turned to face forward, directly toward the countless throng. His head lurched backward, and he laughed aloud—a slow, guttural, evil laugh that rumbled and rolled across the plain, assaulting the ears of every man assembled there. The neatly arrayed blocks of infantry flinched, their front ranks surging back several steps to collide with the masses to their rear. The ranks of knights began to lose cohesion as the warriors' mounts reared and whinnied, turned and pawed the earth and, with tails tucked and teeth bared, implored their enraged masters to leave this place of impending death before the final peal of doom was tolled.

The lone warrior laughed all the harder at the discomfiture of the host. Then, with a sudden movement, he threw both arms upward and outward toward the white-gray sky, fingers fully extended. "Behold!" he cried, "the power of him whom you would conquer!"

Two tiny black dots appeared high in the white glare of the heavens, and from each emerged a stream of brilliant color hurtling earthward. The stunned host watched in silence as the small, mysterious balls of color plummeted earthward faster than any falling object, increasing in size and brilliance until . . .

"Fire!" one peasant fighter screamed.

"Fire! Fire! Fire!" The chant of fear was taken up by hundreds, then thousands, of voices. The masses of color revealed themselves to be great gouts of flame, propelled with unerring aim toward the very center of the assembled host, growing in size until, combined, they blocked out a full quarter of the sky itself.

"Not fire," the lone warrior shouted, laughing again. "Dragonfire!"

The center columns broke as the heat of the falling flames first reached them. The thousands in their neat ranks and columns became a milling, roiling mass of armed, panicked animals, slashing, spearing, and trampling one another in their haste to fly from the flaming death that would inevitably consume them. Vainly did the line of kings and princes scream at their underlings to hold against the inhuman forces hurtling toward them. Desperately, they signaled their ranks of knights to charge—not at the lone warrior whom they had come to fight, but rather at their own men, the rear ranks of whom were already approaching the rulers with deadly intent, determined to eliminate anything that would make them stand and face the burning death.

A few bold knights galloped forward, lances leveled, and were lost to sight in the swirling mass an instant before the flames hit. Men and horses burst spontaneously into flames from the heat of the great blasts alone. Then the fires struck the earth with a hideous roar that drowned out the screams of men and beasts, and soon there was nothing to be seen but the fiery display that stretched out toward heaven itself, and reduced everything in it's path to ash and molten ruin.

In the next instant, all was silence.

Where once had stood the countless footmen of the Holy Alliance host, there now was nothing but a vast, flat sea of black earth, scorched with heat so great that the bedrock, exposed in places, glowed red.

The kings gazed in silent horror at the burnt emptiness that moments before had been the assembled manpower of their realms. Now only the knights were left, and their lines, already in disarray, were weaving and snaking backward from the knoll where the lone warrior still sat, his arms motionless in extension to the sky.

"Now," the warrior shouted into the stillness, his voice louder than even the roar of the flames had been, "let us nobles fight!" He lowered his arms. With his right hand, he drew from its scabbard a great, two-handed sword, its blade of gleaming obsidian traced about with the pulsing blue glow of powerful enchantment. This huge weapon he hefted above his head with his right hand, while his left gripped the reins of his charger. He gave a great shout, spurred his mount, and surged forward, the horse building speed rapidly to a full gallop.

The line of kings broke and fled, shouting instructions as they did for their knights to engage the foe. But their knights were no longer loyal subjects with stout hearts. They were frightened men, no less than the footmen they so despised. The knights galloped toward the rear, and for a moment it appeared the kings themselves would be trampled by their own fleeing nobles, so great was their haste to retreat.

The lone warrior prevented any such fate, for his steed was faster than any demon, and the rider was upon the mass of knights long before their merely mortal beasts could carry them to safety. Up and down the obsidian blade flashed, its magical blue fire obscured by gouts of blood as the lone warrior felled his foes three and four at a stroke. With a speed beyond comprehension, his mount carried him up and down through the length of the fleeing lines, and death, blood, and screams flowed in his constant wake. The pursuit and slaughter went on and on, yet never did the warrior's arm tire or even hesitate. How many miles were covered in that race of death no man knew. In time, the knights were slain; then came the royal deaths. The kings died like all other men—some well, some not, but all with finality.

The lone warrior lopped off the last royal head, swung a heavy leg over one side of his mount, and leapt to the ground. He strode forward toward the one human figure remaining on the field of slaughter, one who had watched the entire battle in reverent silence. The warrior stopped directly in front of this man, sheathed his sword, and stood still, with his arms at his sides.

Sigurt, high priest of Wojan, the god of war, surveyed the silent form before him. The priest's mind was blank; no thought disturbed the purely sensual process of visually studying this tyro. At length, the priest extended his hands gently toward the beaver of the warrior's great helm. He grasped it, paused a moment, and then lifted it.

Deep within its recesses was an eyeless skull, covered in places with thick chunks of peeling, rotten flesh. The stench of rot filled Sigurt's entire being; his gorge rose, and he feared he would be sick.

Then a cold shock, like sudden death itself, surged through Sigurt's body. A voice that he heard only in his mind said quietly, "Heal him. But make him pay the price."

Sigurt awoke sitting bolt upright, his body rigid. Instantly, his years of self-training came to his aid. Reflexively, he inhaled deeply, then expelled the breath slowly while his locked muscles gradually relaxed. He shook his head violently from side to side for a second, as if physically shaking the last of the dream images from his mind. Then he breathed deeply again, allowing the thick, scented smoke of burning incense that always filled his Chamber of Visions to eradicate the memory of the stench at the end of his dream.

"Master . . . ?" A quiet voice timidly sounded from the dark recesses of the chamber, which was lit by a single, sputtering torch.

"Prepare the temple for a ceremony of healing. It will require the full compliment of our priesthood," Sigurt replied, not bothering to look at the humble acolyte who guarded his vision-sleep. "Wojan has spoken to me."

1

A Gang of Thieves

BAGSBY SAT ON a carpet of brown evergreen needles with his back to a tall cedar tree. The rough bark scraped his flesh through his coarse tunic, but Bagsby didn't mind. He was so preoccupied with his confused train of memories and more confusing lack of plans that he didn't even notice. His short but nimble fingers bent and tied a thin branch of green wood into knots, while he tried to put some order to his thoughts. The presence of the greatest treasure known to mankind, the legendary Golden Eggs of Parona, lying conspicuously on the forest floor, directly in front of him was a constant distraction.

"Oh, a thousand hells of a thousand gods," he finally muttered, tossing aside the mutilated branch and leaning back fully against the tree, folding his hands behind his head. "At least I stole them. I succeeded." A stab of pain from the large lump near the crown of his head reminded him of the price he'd paid for his theft. But Bagsby knew a few bumps were nothing compared to the ardors he would have to endure if he wanted to discover exactly what it was he had managed to steal.

"Wot's that?" called George, stamping noisily through the trees to the clearing, his gnarled, bruised, fighting man's body still dripping water from his bath in the nearby River Rigel. "I thought you said somethin'."

"I'm trying to understand an ancient mystery—life, love, women, ethics, and practical problems—all at the same time," Bagsby quipped, a wry smile forming on his squarish face, which was just beginning to show the first lines of age.

6

"Oh," George replied with a shrug, using his filthy brown tunic to dry the backs of his legs. "Never saw much use in all that, myself. Except the women part—and them's not for understandin', mind you, not at all." George winked a broad, stage wink in Bagsby's direction. "Like Marta, there," he said, pointing toward the river with his thumb. "She ain't for understandin'—she's for sportin' wit'."

Bagsby chuckled. "I've thought so myself for most of my life," he answered.

"Well then, what's so particular right now?" George pressed, slipping the stained, bedraggled tunic over his head. "It's that elf woman, ain't it? By the gods, you sound lovesick, that you do." A note of genuine concern crept into George's voice. He had followed Bagsby loyally so far because Bagsby had taken him where he wanted to go, was a good fighter, and an even better thief. But what if love was going to cloud his mind?

"Maybe I am," Bagsby admitted. The short man stood, brushed the tree bark from his back, and began to pace slowly, his gaze downcast. "Is that what it really sounds like to you? Do you think I'm in love with Shulana?"

"Couldn't say, guv. I just said you sounds lovesick, not that you necessarily is," George responded, cocking his head to one side and studying Bagsby intently. No doubt about it, George thought, he's as lovesick as a young boy.

Bagsby had not been a thief and a leader of thieves all his life without learning something about how to read the thoughts of fellow ruffians. The guardedness of George's reply could mean only that he was holding back. Bagsby stopped pacing, turned on his heel, and directed his gaze straight into George's small, dark eyes. "Be honest with me, George. What's on your mind?"

George turned his head, avoiding Bagsby's prying gaze. He spotted his linen breeches, dirty as his tunic, lying beneath a tree. "Well, guv," he began, walking over nonchalantly to retrieve his pants. "You asked me a question, and I answered. Now, if you really want to know wot I thinks . . ."

"I do," Bagsby interjected, a cold tone in his voice.

"Well, then," George said, puffing just a bit as he worked his bruised, gnarly legs into the breeches, "wot I think is this:

We got that there treasure there. We got one damned mad wizard, who the elf says is some kind of undead thingie ready to breathe fire down our backs for stealin' it from 'im. And we got a long way to go to find a market where we can sell it and where I can get me cut; that's wot I think."

"Have I ever cheated you on a cut?" Bagsby demanded, suddenly indignant.

"No, can't say you 'ave," George replied, his grizzled, weatherbeaten face becoming calm and thoughtful. "Can't say we've ever 'ad a cut before, either, 'cause these here golden eggs is the first thing we've stolen together. But you've always been straight with the food, right enough, and you've done your fair share of the fightin' and the risk takin'. I ain't sayin' I don't trust you on the cut. I'm sayin' let's get our bloody arses out of 'ere and get 'em somewhere where that Valdaimon fellow can't find us, and turn them eggs into cash, that's all."

Bagsby nodded affirmatively. George was right. *I must be losing my edge*, Bagsby thought. At any other time, he would have known instinctively what was on George's mind. He would also have known that no thief will trust his life to a leader who is distracted by love—especially not a soldier who's just turned thief, as was the case with George.

Bagsby scowled, and grimaced again at his own thoughts. Why couldn't he think straight? Was it the mystery of the treasure, the trouble with Shulana, or just fear and the first—the very first ever—twinges of the advancing years? But whatever it was, he'd better put a good face on it, because he needed the loyalty of George, Marta, and Shulana, at least for the moment.

"Right you are, George, right you are. Soon as the sun's down, we move from here."

"That's more like it, guv," George replied, a broad smile revealing his strong, yellow teeth. "Where we goin' to?"

"Yes, where are we going? And don't think I don't mean to have a say in this," fat Marta shouted from behind a clump of bushes where she was busily hiding her bulk in the folds of a plain, gray, ankle-length tunic. "And none of your smart mouth, George. I want to hear what Sir John has to say."

" 'Ere now, where you get off talkin' to me like that, wot showed you such a good time in your bath?" George shouted back, his eyes alight with the teasing game. "Ain't you got no respect for one what loves you and fights for you and feeds you and . . ."

A ball of wet brown mud flew from between two tall trees and thudded squarely against George's mouth, turning the end of his sentence into a series of surprised sputters, gasps, and spits.

"Don't you go on at me, George Miller's son," Marta called back, shaking her hand to fling off the clinging droplets of the mud ball. "You're nothing but a deserter, and from Heilesheim at that, the most evil kingdom in the land. Not three days ago you was ready enough to kill for that Valdaimon, whatever he is, and for that demonspawn king, Ruprecht, may he rot in the hells of a thousand devils," she spat for emphasis, "and just because I choose to take my pleasure with you, don't think you can talk familiar to me!"

Black fire flashed in Marta's eyes as she lugged her bulk into the small clearing during this diatribe. George, far from combative, had flung himself to the ground and lay on his back, alternately chortling with laughter and using his callused fingers to dig bits of mud from his mouth.

"By the gods, Bagsby, ain't she a fine one for sport?" he asked.

"And don't you be talkin' to Sir John about our private moments. It ain't no business of his, even if he is a knight," Marta snapped. Indignant, she cast about the clearing for the mail shirt and sword she had stolen from a dead trooper days ago, and which had become a part of her normal wardrobe.

" 'E ain't no knight, 'ow many times 'e got to tell you, wench?" George shouted. "That was a ruse. 'E's a thief, 'e is, and a damned good one at that."

"Well he's Sir John to me. That's how I met him, and that's how I call him," Marta replied, donning her chain-mail shirt. "He's led an army, and that's more than the likes of you can say. And if he stole that treasure from Valdaimon, with the help of us all I might add, then I say may the gods bless him." Marta struck a heroic pose, her sword raised high toward the heavens. "May the gods bless any and all who strike a blow against Heilesheim, Ruprecht, and Valdaimon!"

Then, seeing she had silenced George, who stared at her in bemused astonishment, she put down the sword and went about the mundane task of gathering the long tunic in bunches inside her thick legs, converting its bottom half to improvised breeches.

Bagsby, too, stared for a moment at the amazing Marta. He had first seen this woman when she was brought before the council of the king of Argolia, where Bagsby had sat in his guise as Sir John of Nordingham—an identity he had created for the occasion out of thin air. She had appeared to show the council the wound inflicted on her by Ruprecht himself: her back was branded with his coat of arms, a dragon with wings spread wide. Her husband had been slain and herself thus treated when Heilesheim's army had first begun its campaign of conquest against the numerous kingdoms of the Holy Alliance, a campaign that still continued and had thus far been unmarred by any major defeat. From that day, Marta had vowed vengeance on Heilesheim, Ruprecht, and Valdaimon, the undead wizard who guided Ruprecht's hand in most affairs. She had disguised herself as a man and fought with the Argolians at the dreadful battle of Clairton, the outcome of which had put that kingdom under the heel of Ruprecht. Then, after meeting up with George, a Heilesheim deserter, she had joined Bagsby and Shulana and helped them steal the fabled Golden Eggs from Valdaimon. She was a woman with a single passion, Bagsby knew, though it seemed to him now that George's attentions had softened her a bit.

"The wars of you humans are a matter of little concern," a soft voice spoke into the gathering. Silently, the lithe, thin form of the elf Shulana slipped into the clearing. From whence she came not even Bagsby's keen eye could tell, for like all elves she could move almost invisibly in any natural forest. "Whether the gods care about such things I know not," she said matter-of-factly to Marta. "But I do know we must decide what to do next." Her eyes took in all three of the humans. "Valdaimon will not be long in trailing us with assassins worse than any human he could hire. He wants the Golden Eggs, and he must not have them."

"Why is that?" Bagsby asked quickly.

George rolled his eyes; Marta averted hers. The old quarrel was about to begin. In the few days the foursome had been together, George and Marta had heard more than enough times that Bagsby wanted to know the true nature of the Golden Eggs, and that Shulana knew but would not tell him.

"I cannot tell you," Shulana said. She strode over to Bagsby, embraced him tenderly, and stared into his eyes. "They must be destroyed before he is able to recover them."

"Destroyed!" George shouted, leaping to his feet. "Now just wait a minute. I didn't risk life and limb and 'angin' to get me hands on that treasure just so's you could come along and destroy it without so much as a 'by your leave.' I wants me cut. I know wot's right, I do."

"Shulana won't destroy the treasure," Bagsby said softly, pushing her from him. "She can't."

"If you think my affection for you will prevent me from carrying out the mission entrusted to me by the Elven Council, you are much mistaken, Bagsby," Shulana said directly, her soft eyes meeting his with a mixture of affection and defiance.

"I know that," Bagsby said. "When I said you couldn't destroy the treasure, I did not mean that any affection for me prevented you from doing so."

"What did you mean?" Shulana asked, turning her back on the short thief.

"Right, what did you mean?" George demanded.

"I meant," Bagsby said softly, "that if Shulana had the power to destroy this treasure, she would already have done so. She does not have that power. This elf, my friends," Bagsby went on, explaining for the benefit of George and Marta, "can cast a marvelous variety of spells. She can even call forth a magical fire that consumes men, beasts, swords, armor, almost anything." Bagsby turned back around to face the elf. "But it cannot consume the Golden Eggs, can it, Shulana? For if it could, you would already have cast the spell."

"True enough," Shulana admitted.

"Well, that's a mercy," George muttered. The elf was a pretty little thing, at least as pretty as an elf could be, and George would have hated to have had to kill her, especially since Bagsby was obviously fond of her.

"All the more reason we must take the eggs at once to the Elven Preserve, where the combined magic of my race can once and for all destroy the threat they pose to this world," Shulana said decisively. "Yes, that is what we must do. We must take them to the Elven Preserve."

"If the elves wants 'em, let 'em pay us for 'em," George challenged flatly.

"That was the original agreement," Shulana said. "The Elven Council has agreed to pay its entire treasury for the delivery of the Golden Eggs."

"Well then, what are we waitin' for?" George asked. He started gathering his scattered weapons and pack. Then he paused. "How much is in the treasury of the Elven Council?" he queried.

"More than two hundred thousand gold crowns," Bagsby answered. "But I don't think we ought to give the elves possession—just yet."

"Why not?" George demanded. "Where else we goin' to sell 'em? Everyone in the world will recognize 'em and know they're stolen."

"Nonetheless, at the moment they are mine—I stole them," Bagsby said.

"You led the group that stole them," Marta interjected. "Still, I'm interested to know what Sir John is thinking. Why shouldn't we sell them and use the money to aid the fight against Heilesheim?"

"You spend your own money, sweet'eart. I'll spend mine," George countered.

"Because we don't know what these two things really are," Bagsby said. "How do we know that even the entire treasury of the Elven Council is fair value?"

"For a fourth part of two 'undred thousand crowns, I'm willin' to take the risk," George said, strapping on his pack.

"Maybe you are, but I'm not," Bagsby declared. "If the Elven Council's offer is fair, why won't Shulana divulge the secret of what these items really are? These two objects have been the subject of legends for thousands of years. Why does Valdaimon want them so desperately? Why do the elves want them so desperately?"

Marta strode forward to stand directly in front of the Golden Eggs of Parona. As the red rays of the sunset streaked through the forest, the two huge, egg-shaped nodules of gold, each nearly three feet from base to crown, gleamed in the dying light. Flashes of countless colors reflected from the hundreds of gemstones set in their gold finish, and the strange patterns worked into the gold coating looked to Marta like some strange, foreign writing—the writing of ancient, mystic prophets, foretelling doom for a world. The bulky woman stared at the eggs, then at Shulana, then at Bagsby.

"I see what you mean," she said slowly. "It may be that these things are . . . more than just a treasure."

"Well, what do you propose?" George said, staring with flat, dull eyes at Bagsby.

Bagsby ignored George's gaze. He kept his eyes focused instead on the man's hands. This was a dangerous moment. Nobler men than George had killed for much less gold than was here.

"I propose . . . ," Bagsby began, then paused. What could he propose? How could he learn the secret of this treasure? How could he prevent George from cutting his throat in the middle of the night? How could he keep Shulana satisfied? How could all of them escape Valdaimon, who no doubt was even now using magical means to seek them out?

"I propose that this question is important enough that we take it to the head of the Elven Council," Bagsby said at length, a friendly smile forming on his face.

"Well, okay then, we take 'em to the Elven Council. That's wot me and the elf there been saying," George replied, smiling broadly.

"Not exactly," Shulana said, "although I accept Bagsby's proposal. If the head of the Elven Council agrees to divulge the secret to you, I will be in complete agreement with him."

Bagsby's smile grew broader. He knew that the one thing that might divert Shulana from her mission to bring back the Golden Eggs would be a chance to rescue Elrond.

"Then we're off to the Elven Preserve," George sang out merrily. "C'mon, get your gear, mates. Sun's down now, and we can move more safely."

"It's not quite that simple," Bagsby said, walking about the clearing, gathering up his own belongings. "The head of the Elven Council, a fellow named Elrond, is not at the Elven Preserve."

"Where is he?" Marta asked.

"In the dungeons of Ruprecht of Heilesheim, in the king's palace in his capital city of Hamblen," Shulana said. "We can follow the River Rigel for part of the way, at least until the cover of the forest gives way to the open land."

"Ten thousand hells," George muttered. Somehow, he'd been hoodwinked.

"George!" Marta bellowed, bending over a large pile of furs, blankets, swords, daggers, spears, slings, and stones she had salvaged from the battlefield of Clairton. "Help me with this lot."

"Ten thousand hells," George muttered again.

Shulana, with her natural abilities to move in forests and her magical cloak which could afford her partial or even total concealment under some circumstances, took the lead as the group struck out under cover of darkness. Shulana was glad to have the point position, some fifty yards or more in advance of the three humans. She needed time for her own thoughts.

She was glad, of course, that Bagsby had suggested going to free Elrond, even though such an adventure seemed, at first blush, hopelessly beyond the capabilities of their small band. To strike the most powerful kingdom on earth, in the palace of its king, in time of war, with a force of four—most of whom had known one another only a few days—seemed the height of folly. Yet she had seen Bagsby do the impossible more than once. He had risen in a matter of weeks from a petty street thief to become the most respected knight in the now-doomed kingdom of Argolia, and he had masterminded the plan that put the Golden Eggs of Parona within her grasp. What was more, he had become her beloved, a fact that Shulana acknowledged, but did not understand.

The rescue of Elrond was a brilliant idea, actually, for it allowed her to continue her strange, growing relationship with Bagsby, while also remaining true to her mission to the

Elven Council. The Council could hardly be displeased if she returned with not only Golden Eggs, but also the very head of the council itself: Elrond, the oldest living elf, who had personally slain the Ancient One, the Mother of Dragonkind, some five thousand years ago.

Many times in the past few months, Elrond had communicated with her from his hideous cell, using the strange communion with plants that the most powerful elves had developed to a true psychic art form, to penetrate her mind with his most urgent thoughts. Haste had been foremost among these—haste to obtain and then, she presumed, destroy the Golden Eggs. Now she would bring the Golden Eggs to him, since she could see no way to destroy them herself. And in the process she would win Elrond's freedom from the tyrant Ruprecht and the tortures of his dungeon.

What, Shulana wondered, would Elrond think of Bagsby? Would the acknowledged leader of all elves approve of her strange and growing affection for this human? Love matches between humans and elves had occurred in the past, but usually with disastrous results—and for that reason they were frowned upon by elves in general. Yet Shulana could no more deny her feelings than she could her duty. Despite herself, she was drawn emotionally to this human. She thrilled at his touch, wanted to care for his wounds and pains, share his worries and woes, and take part in the brief adventure of his life.

Instinctive reaction suddenly froze both Shulana's thoughts and the movement of her body. She stood stock-still in the dark, moonless woods, her skin tingling strangely. Slowly, she raised her right arm, extending it from beneath the protective covering of her cloak, and motioned with her hand for the group behind her to halt. She heard a few rustles of leaves and branches as the three humans let down their burdens, went to their bellies on the forest floor, and readied their weapons. For a brief instant, Shulana wondered how humans had managed to survive—their movements were so noisy! Any good elven patrol would have heard them from hundreds of yards away.

But the men ahead, whose approach Shulana's very skin had sensed before she heard or saw them, were not listening for the rustling of a few leaves. They tromped loudly through the forest, talking as they came, mindless of the dangers that might lurk in the darkened wood.

"It's no good, I tell you," a gravelly voice grumbled. "We don't know nothing about the east country. For all we know, there may be stinking elves to the east."

"We know what's here and what's behind us, don't we," squeaked a second man with a shrill, high voice. "Hanging is what's here. Hanging for desertion—not to mention murder, rape, pillage and thieving!" The high voice broke into scratchy, irritating, high-pitched laughter.

"Shut up and march, you two," boomed a third low voice, one Shulana judged was accustomed to command.

"You ain't no leader of a hundred now," Gravel Voice challenged. "You ain't no leader of nothin'."

"Yeah," Squeaky Voice added, "you ain't no leader of . . ."

Shulana heard a soft swishing sound followed immediately by a wet slicing and cracking sound. An instant latter she heard a soft thud, followed by a loud crash.

"I'm a leader of one now," Command Voice boomed.

Gravel Voice breathed heavily, then replied, "Didn't have to chop his head off. But a nice swing. And your point is well taken. East is just fine with me. Even if there are scum and elves there."

"Hmmph," Command Voice grunted.

Shulana slipped forward through the darkness until she had the two men clearly in sight. They had interrupted their march and their conversation to rifle the dead man's pack and clothes, stuffing their own bags and packs with anything of value on him. The decapitated corpse still twitched occasionally, as if protesting the robbery, and his spilled blood glowed brightly in Shulana's elven vision as it trickled over small branches, fallen leaves, and countless thousands of brown pine needles. At length, satisfied that their former comrade had nothing else of value, the two stalked on eastward, passing within ten yards of the three humans behind Shulana, who wisely maintained that degree of stillness that among them passed for silence.

Shulana doubled back and followed the murderous pair for nearly a mile, then returned, running at a medium pace as silently as a very soft breeze through the evergreen and hardwood trees. She uttered not a word, but by gesture alone indicated to the threesome that it was safe to move forward. Then she hurried ahead again, resuming her place on point.

Three more times that night the intrepid foursome encountered stragglers from the Heilesheim army, renegade soldiers turned plunderers, murderers, and thieves. Such, Shulana realized, were always a by-product of human wars, and it would be years after peace was restored before the last of these were tracked down and killed by what the humans called "lawful authority"—which from her point of view was little more than a group of murderers and pillagers whose actions were for some reason approved by the majority of men. At the moment, these small parties of renegades, infected with Heilesheim's anti-elven propaganda, presented little threat as long as her group was vigilant and remained hidden. But the encounters did retard their already painfully slow progress.

The Golden Eggs, of course, were a major impediment to their movement. Their sheer bulk meant that it was all one person could do to carry one of them, and their weight made that an arduous task. Bagsby carried one of the eggs in an enormous cloth sack slung over his shoulder. Marta carried the other in similar fashion, while George was laden with the cache of furs, blankets, weapons, and clothes that Marta had collected from the dead (and sometimes the living) of the recent battle. Moving quietly through even light woods thus encumbered was slow, trying work. So, on the first night, they covered less than twelve miles before dawn peeped over the horizon, the signal for the party to find a remote clearing, camp, and post guards.

The second night's march brought them still closer to the edge of the forest, the open fields of Dunsford, and the main road that crossed the Rigel at Shallowford—the very village where Marta had once been revered as the wife of the commander of the Count of Dunsford's Yeoman Border Guards. They came closer, too, to the operating rear area of the Heilesheim army. Though the main force was still far to the north in Argolia, its principal route of reinforcement, communications, and supply ran up the Shallowford Road. During the second daylight period, the foursome had to move their camp twice, and quickly, to avoid detection by wandering bands of soldiers straying from the road to hunt, carouse, and generally seek a day's leisure from the more demanding brutalities of army life.

Marta snapped on the third night. Shulana, as usual, was on forward point. The three humans saw her suddenly halt, and moments later give the sign to which they were so accustomed. Like the two men, Marta went to earth, sliding her large sack onto the ground beside her and cradling a twelve-foot stabbing spear in her right hand. After what seemed a very long time—it always seemed like a very long time to Marta—the threesome could hear the voices of the men whose presence Shulana had detected.

"Shallowford—what a dungheap!" one man exclaimed.

"Glad I joined the army, so I could see fair wenches like those cows!" a second giggled.

"Even a cow needs a good bull once in a while," a third offered, chortling lustily.

"They didn't seem to care for your company much," the first teased.

"Isn't like they have much choice, is it?" the third voice responded, his laughter growing uproarious.

Marta's mind flashed back to her fine wooden house with a manservant and a maid, now a heap of ashes in Shallowford. She saw in an instant the plump daughters of the prosperous farmers of the village, now also put to ruin by the soldiers of the demonspawn Ruprecht. And she saw again the night when, within sight of her dead husband's severed head, soldiers just like these had held her while Ruprecht personally burned into her back the dragon insignia that was his coat of arms. Then Marta thought no more.

"Death to Heilesheim!" she screamed and rose from her position, charging forward before her full bulk was off the ground. "Death to you beasts and bastards, one and all!"

The party of green recruits, five in number, turned their heads toward the light woods behind the open field where they stood. Shulana saw their expressions—the looks of men who are about to burst into laughter at the sight of something at once hideous and ludicrous. Fat Marta charged ahead out of the woods, straight at the knot of men, her war cry one continuous, wailing scream, her spear leveled in her right hand while in her left she brandished a small dagger drawn from her belt on the run.

Alarmed, Shulana looked back at Bagsby, who looked forward to George, who stood, shrugged, took up two short swords, one for each hand, and began to run forward. Bagsby groaned—there was no point in silence now. Shulana shook her head in disbelief.

So ridiculous a figure did Marta cut in the course of her charge—her long tunic flapping around her ankles beneath the short shirt of chain mail, her long hair flying in tangled globs behind her head, and her chubby flesh jiggling with every thundering step—that the soldiers didn't react seriously in time. The three farthest from her managed to step back when they realized the madwoman was serious; the two nearest her stopped laughing and went for their swords, but it was too late.

Marta's spear struck the first man square in the chest. The point rammed through his chain mail and leather padding, ripped through his ribs, lungs, and heart, and poked out his back, besmirched with gore. The man flew up and back, blood spouting from his mouth as his just-drawn sword dropped from his dead hand. Marta did not drop the spear, but rather carried it with its bloody trophy on into the cluster of three, swiping with her sword at the remaining man as she passed him. It was a glancing blow that bit into the top of the man's shoulder, slicing off a chunk of leather, armor, and flesh as Marta continued forward, ripping the sword free. Her charge did not end until the burdened spear knocked into a third soldier, sending him sprawling, with the impaled corpse of his friend dropping atop him.

The fallen man screamed—his dead companion was the first man he'd ever seen killed—and thrashed about violently to get the bloody corpse off him. The wounded man was stunned, his breath coming in horrified gasps as he realized that the blood spouting from his shoulder, a source of fiery pain, was in fact his own. The remaining two, however, still untouched, were made of sterner stuff.

"Die, you fat behemoth from hell!" one roared, raising his sword as he lunged forward. He let fly a downward blow, aimed at the top of Marta's head. But the enraged Marta possessed a quickness belied by her bulk. Raising her sword, she was able to strike upward awkwardly—not with enough strength to stop the man's blow, but with sufficient effect to cause his wrist to turn. So what would have been a skull-splitting deathblow with the edge of the soldier's blade became instead a blow with its flat that glanced off the side of Marta's skull, hardly the softest portion of her anatomy.

"Kill that sow, Heinrich," called his friend. He had drawn his sword and was about to step into the fray when George yelled a battle cry as he, too, charged into the open field. The remaining soldier turned to face this new threat, which appeared to be the more dangerous of the two; but unfortunately for the green fighter, he had not the slightest idea of how to meet a pike charge—especially when he carried no shield and was armed only with a longsword. In the heat of the moment he decided to plant his feet, extend the sword, and try to either parry the pike or, failing that, leap aside at the last moment.

George was more experienced than that; he had killed more than one highly trained knight on the battlefield. The only question in George's mind, as he ran forward, was which way the man would dodge. He knew the blow of a longsword would not be strong enough to deflect the weighty pike shaft, and he knew from long experience that his own momentum would ram the weapon clean through his lightly armored foe.

George quickened his pace to his top speed. The soldier struck. Not only did his blow not deflect the pike, the vibration from the blow traveled through the hilt of his sword and stabbed his hand with terrific pain. The surprise of this caused him to hesitate, less than half a second. That was too much time.

The business end of George's pike sliced through the man in an instant, cleaving him from sternum to backbone. George let go of the pike as the soldier stumbled forward and off to one side, dead before the pike point hit the ground. He flopped about piteously as his body slid down the shaft to crash against the cold ground. But George had no time to admire his handiwork. "Marta, behind you!" he shouted.

Marta spun around from her recent attacker to see that the man she'd sent sprawling was now not only up but swinging a level, neck-high sword blow at her. She ducked and then launched herself headfirst at her foe, screaming in rage as she flew through the air to crash into his chest. At the instant of impact, she grabbed his neck in her bare hands and wrapped her mouth around his nose, biting hard. She both heard and felt a satisfying crunch, and the taste of blood was in her mouth before the twosome hit the ground, for the force of her attack had sent the man falling over backward.

George, meanwhile, seeing that Marta was being taken from front and rear, waited until her second attacker was ready to strike her from behind and then hurled himself onto the man, wrapping his scrawny but strong legs around the man's waist, and his arms around his head and neck. His left hand dug at the man's face until his middle finger located an eye socket. George poked and gouged. His foe screamed in alarm as half his field of vision suddenly disappeared, and his one good eye saw its recent companion drop to the ground, trailing bloody tissue. The shock was too great for the soldier, who momentarily ceased his struggle. George grabbed his jaw and twisted hard. He heard the crack of the man's neck, then rode the corpse as it fell to the earth.

Marta, meanwhile, had spit the Heilesheimer's nose back into his face while her fat fingers clamped into his soft throat. The would-be warrior thrashed helplessly on his back, legs kicking, hands tearing at Marta's hair, but he had not the strength to force her bulk off him. In less than a minute, the last of the life was choked out of him.

"Heilesheim scum," Marta muttered, as she spit another mouthful of the man's blood into his dead face. "You won't be enjoying any more of our Shallowford cows, will you?"

"Well done, Marta! You're a wonder, you are," George exclaimed, climbing off the corpse beneath him and glancing about to find his pike. "By the gods, you're a wonder!"

"The wonder is how we will ever be able to move undetected now," Bagsby said dryly. George and Marta turned, startled by his voice.

"Guv! Didn't know you'd joined the fray!" George sang out cheerily.

"I didn't—there was no need," Bagsby replied. "However, that fellow running for his life over there will start halooing for the rest of the company before long, and I suggest we be gone from here before they come." Bagsby's pudgy face was screwed up into a scowl of disapproval. "Once we get to safety, we'd better have a chat about the advantages of not being seen," he added, turning to stride angrily back into the woods.

"I couldn't help myself," Marta explained, as the foursome held conference in a shallow depression surrounded by piles of rock on the very bank of the River Rigel. The big woman sat on a water-smoothed, flat rock, her gaze cast down at the shallow pool where she was washing off her large feet. "That village ahead was my home once, and those beasts did such things there that . . ."

"Yes, yes," Bagsby interjected. The little man squatted on another rock, perched high enough above the others to accent his position of leadership. He gazed impassively out at the swift, rolling current of the Rigel—eighty yards wide at this point—with the enemy land of Heilesheim on the far side. "We're all aware of your pain from your past experiences, and no one here blames you for your hatred of Heilesheim. But your actions have put us at serious risk. One of those five men has escaped. Right now, a swarm of Heilesheim troops will be combing the north bank of the river, looking for a big, crazy female and her deserter companion," Bagsby explained.

" 'Ow would they know I was a deserter?" George challenged.

"Where else would you have learned to use a pike? And if you weren't a deserter, why were you attacking regular troops in the company of this crazed . . . lady?"

"Unnhh," George grunted.

"The soldiers will be searching for us even now," Shulana said. "At the rate we've been traveling, they'll overtake us within a few hours—a day at most if we're very lucky and try to go back the way we came."

"Then," Bagsby said, suddenly cheerful, "we'll lighten our load and go where they'll never think to look for us."

Marta flinched visibly at the mention of lightening their load. "Those goods," she said, pointing to the bundle that inevitably became George's bane on the march, "are all I have left in the world. If you think I'm going to give them up without a fight . . ."

"Not at all," Bagsby said, leaping to his feet. "You can carry all your loot, Marta, and we can carry treasure, too."

" 'Ow?" George asked.

Bagsby leaned over and placed his face squarely in front of George's, a twinkle in his eye and a good-natured smile on his face. "Magic," he said.

"Of course," Shulana interjected. "I could diminish some of these things."

"I thought that only worked for a little while," Marta said, still suspicious.

"That particular spell lasts until it is canceled—usually by using a command word," Shulana explained. "I can shrink the Golden Eggs down to the size of pebbles and then, when the command word is spoken, they'll return to their normal size."

"Excellent!" Bagsby shouted, clapping his hands. "Let's get going. With the Golden Eggs no larger than pebbles, there'll be no need to shrink any of your things, Marta." He began grabbing items off the rocks and tossing them toward Marta's precious pile of goods. "You and George can easily share the burden now." He stopped in midstride then suddenly turned to Shulana. "Wouldn't it be a good idea if we all knew the command word, in case one of us is killed or captured?"

" 'Ere now, that's good thinkin'!" George agreed. "If anything 'appens to you two, I wouldn't want to be stuck with little gold pebbles instead of the greatest treasures in the world."

Shulana's brow creased in a small frown. It was dangerous, involving novices in anything magical. Indeed, that was the reason she had not used the spell earlier to ease their journey. But, still, it was only one word, and it would have a very limited effect, she reasoned. "Very well. Gather round and listen closely."

In the waning moments of darkness Shulana taught the three humans one word of elven magic, the word that would break the spell she then cast on each of the Golden Eggs of Parona. Bagsby held the two shrunken treasures in the palm of his hand, then slid them into a tiny purse attached securely to the leather strap around his waist. Secretly, he felt an enormous sense of relief. Now he alone could carry the treasure. It was a wonder to him that Marta hadn't noticed the strange warmth that sometimes emanated from the eggs. Nor, apparently, had she noticed that, from time to time, there were strange vibrations from deep within them. Now, he no longer had to worry about her making such a discovery. He wondered if Shulana had pried around them and noticed these strange facts, but he dared not ask. No matter. His plan was working. Now it was time to be off.

"It's done. Let's march, before those troops are on to us."

"Wait a minute," Marta asked, puzzled. "You never said where we were going."

"I said we were going where the troops would never think to look for us—and we are," Bagsby replied merrily.

"Where?" Shulana asked.

"There!" Bagsby said, extending his arm and pointing straight out across the River Rigel. "We're crossing the river into Heilesheim."

2
A Healing

VALDAIMON STAGGERED BACK from the window of his tower room at Lundlow Keep, his mind so filled with pain and rage that he could neither think nor speak. Incapable of intelligibility, he emitted an animal scream of pure hatred.

With the one eye that remained to him he surveyed the ruin of what, only moments before, had been a major magical laboratory and study. Still screaming, he strode across the circular room, kicking this way and that the charred remnants of tables, chairs, shelves, and reading stands, shattering further pieces of glass that were already burnt shards, completing the destruction of ancient tomes whose price was beyond naming—now all consumed by the flames and lightning that had engulfed the room.

Through the greasy, stinking smoke that still filled the chamber, he perceived the form of a man who appeared in the doorway—a man in chain mail and shield. It was a guard . . . one of the guards, one of the entire company of guards . . . one of the imbeciles whose sole reason for existing was to have prevented this intrusion and destruction from happening!

"Lord Valdaimon! Are you harmed?" the man called, vainly waving at the smoke that assaulted his face and lungs.

Valdaimon turned to face the man and screamed his rage.

"By all the gods!" the man exclaimed, his face growing visibly pale even through the black smoke. "Oh, by all the gods!" The man staggered backward, turned, and stumbled out the door, visibly ill.

"Come back here, you coward! Come back and face the wrath of Valdaimon!" the ancient wizard shrieked. At least, that's what he thought he had shrieked. There was no response from beyond the door, only the sound of a single man being sick. "Answer me!" Valdaimon called, listening carefully to the sounds of his own voice. The words! The words were not right. He tried again. "Guard," he called in softer tones. To his own ear, it sounded as though he said something more like "groourd."

Horrified, Valdaimon raised his right hand to his face—or at least, he thought he had raised his hand—until his remaining eye informed him that his right arm and hand were gone.

In the main hall of Lundlow Keep, far down the great spiral staircase that led to the tower room, the assembled guards listened with fear to the animal bellowing of the man they had been assigned to protect by no less a personage than King Ruprecht of Heilesheim himself. Only the most stupid among the men were worried about their future as soldiers; most were certain that the penalty for their failure to stop the intruders who had ransacked Valdaimon's private chamber would be death.

The captain of the guard was nonplussed: he didn't know how the thieves had gotten in; he couldn't comprehend how they could have defeated his skilled guardsmen in combat, and he hadn't the slightest notion of what they might have stolen. Normally, he would have ordered a quick pursuit, but no one had seen the plunderers leave. Worse, he feared that any men he sent out in pursuit would immediately desert rather than face the penalty for failure.

"Caaaannn," a firm voice called from the stairway.

The captain ordered his men to fall into ranks, then turned to see the source of the sound. His horror was complete when he saw the form of Valdaimon on the steps—but a much modified form. The old wizard had always been an ugly devil with his shrunken, shriveled old body, wrinkly, jaundiced face, and a mouth that held only a handful of pointy yellow teeth. But now the hideousness was, if anything, more complete. The entire right side of the wizard's face was terribly burned.

Flesh peeled from the bony ridge above the right eye socket, revealing the white of bone, and beneath the empty socket, even larger strips of flesh drooped downward, peeled away from the scrawny, stringy muscles of the right cheek. There were burns, too, in a bizarre, random pattern down the old wizard's chest. His tattered robe was charred, and great, gaping holes revealed the flesh beneath—and at times, more hints of bone. But worst of all was the mouth. The entire right side looked as if it had simply melted, the lips and flesh forming one bulging mass that had dripped obscenely onto the narrow chin, then hardened and clung there.

"Caaann," the nightmare figure called again, waving with its left hand and arm for the captain to approach.

"Lord Valdaimon," the captain replied, walking slowly toward the base of the stairs, "you are . . . injured. What can I do?"

Never had the captain seen more pure hatred in a face as Valdaimon's one eye burned into his soul. But then the old wizard released his gaze and hung his head shaking it slowly from side to side.

"Is there nothing I can do?" the captain inquired cautiously.

Valdaimon gestured vaguely behind his legs and squatted as though to sit. He looked inquisitively at the human cretin—had he understood?

"A chair, a chair!" the captain shouted. "A chair for Lord Valdaimon!"

Valdaimon nodded affirmatively, pointing back up the great spiral staircase. Then he turned, without attempting to speak further, and trudged laboriously upward, lifting his scrawny yellowed feet with their long, hardened nails one at a time onto the next step, and then the next. Two guards followed his slow progress, carrying a large wooden chair and several pillows for the wizard's use in the tower room.

"My lord," the captain called, "is there nothing else we can do?"

Valdaimon waved his hand in the air with a gesture of dismissal. There was nothing any human could do for him.

He wanted revenge, but first Valdaimon decided to get some much-needed rest. A portion of his life force had been poured into the corpse of a guard and sent on an errand to the far eastern reaches of Heilesheim; the rest of his "soul," as men would call it, had been stored in the special gem that still hung from a chain around his neck. His body reverted to dead dust as he lay in his special wooden box, filled with earth from his native soil.

It had been Bagsby, of course. Valdaimon knew that as soon as his rage had cooled enough to let his keen mind function. Now he sat in the chair, alone in the tower room, seeing and smelling the damage from Bagsby's attack. From the bits and pieces of evidence available and what he had seen of the guards in the main hall of the keep below, he deduced the sequence of events that had led to his own sorry state.

Clearly Bagsby had distracted the guards in some way, causing the mass confusion. Then he and his group—at the end, Valdaimon had seen the elf woman and two other humans fleeing with Bagsby, even though they were much diminished in size by the elf's spell—had somehow tricked one of the guards into breaking down Valdaimon's locked door, the only entrance to the tower room.

The still-lingering smell of smoke and the thorough destruction wrought by the fires told Valdaimon what had happened next. The first guard through the door had triggered the magical trap that Valdaimon had set—an explosion of fire sufficient to destroy any force bursting through the door. But the wizard hand anticipated that a thief might push someone else in first to set off any magical trap, which was why he had set a second trap—a lightning bolt trap—to incinerate a second group coming through the door. How that imp Bagsby was clever enough to escape the second trap Valdaimon wasn't sure; yet somehow Bagsby had set off the trap while avoiding the destruction it entailed.

Then the little thief, with the help of that elf, had found the Golden Eggs of Parona, even though they were hidden by an invisibility spell. The elf had shrunk herself, the thief, and the eggs, and all had made their getaway down a rope out the tower window. But not before they had found a vial of holy water, blessed by the human god of love and fecundity, which had somehow survived both the fire and the lightning. They had poured it over Valdaimon's resting body, and as a result, he had lost one eye, his right arm and hand, and the use of his mouth for intelligible speech. He had no hope of being able to cast spells without the ability to speak clearly, nor could he use any magic of real power without the ability to gesture. In addition, the explosions and fire had destroyed his roomful of magical components, many of them quite rare: bits of mandrake root, the blood of a vampire long since destroyed, eyes, bladders, dried feces and dried brains from over three dozen rare creatures, and a collection of body parts from humans known to history for their . . . misbehaviors. Some of these were replaceable, but some were not. And that did not take into account all the priceless books, scrolls, and parchments the wizard had accumulated in this, his second-best study.

The worst of it, though, Valdaimon realized, was that now Bagsby had the Golden Eggs of Parona—with the secret of all-powerful fire from the sky hidden somehow within them— and he, Valdaimon, was momentarily powerless even to pursue this puny mortal who had so offended him!

Then, there were the political repercussions to consider. Valdaimon dreamed back over the past century—how, at the height of his powers as a wizard, he had maneuvered for decades to bring Heilesheim to its present pitch of military and political development, and the forefathers of the present king, Ruprecht, to the Heilesheim throne. He remembered the countless plots and ploys, the endless string of minor spells and enchantments, the thousands of insults, impolite stares, sneers of disgust, and royal rebuffs he had suffered—all from mere mortals who were not worthy to be his slaves. He remembered his great goal—the conquest of the Holy Alliance through the power of Heilesheim, and then the unleashing of the unbelievable power of fire from the sky when he had solved the secret of the Golden Eggs. At last he would dominate the entire earth, and there would be no power of human, elf, or god that could stand in his way.

But now all this was cast in doubt. He could not even appear in the presence of the king in his current state. The young egomaniac would sneer, laugh, and despise him—and the Baron Culdus, general in chief of the Heilesheim armies, would take Valdaimon's place as the decadent king's most trusted adviser.

Powerless! He, Valdaimon, powerless! The old wizard's face contorted again with the pangs of unbearable rage.

A fluttering of wings sounded from the narrow window that peered out from the tower room. Valdaimon did not turn around to see what caused the sound; he knew. He closed his one eye and let his mind wander—only a short distance—over to the window. There, his mental essence entered and merged with that of the fat, filthy crow whose landing was the source of the sound. Through the eyes of this, his familiar, he saw his own decrepit body slumped in the chair—deformed, defiled, and powerless.

Of course the crow had returned as soon as its master was wounded. The magical force that had bound it to the wizard remained intact, and the spell remained in force, even though the wizard could cast no new spells. Now, Valdaimon's mind blended with that of the cunning creature, recovering it's memories. It had followed and followed and followed Bagsby, right until the little thief had taken his booty and headed south. No doubt he would make for the River Rigel, Valdaimon realized, and the cover of the forests on its banks.

The lowly crow dared to think a thought.

The master, it thought, in the vague form in which it could think, tilting its head to one side to study more carefully the unfamiliar cast of the familiar body of its lifelong owner, feeder, order giver, and veritable god.

A god! The thought struck Valdaimon like a thunderclap.

As fast as thought, Valdaimon forced his mind back into his hapless body. Of course, the obvious solution to his dilemma was to possess another body with his own life force and then, with his powers of speech and gesture restored, perform magic as he pleased. But the higher magic would still be denied him. The correct pronunciation of the words, the subtleties of the hand movements, the balance of tensions throughout the body required for the casting of truly great spells, required a lifetime—or several—of training. No mere borrowed body, no matter how tightly controlled, would be capable of the tasks that would confront Valdaimon in the weeks to come. Only his own body would truly do. But a god could heal that body.

Valdaimon shuddered. As a wizard he had, even in mortal life, eschewed religion; and in his present undead form, he was considered an abomination by almost all the gods of the Heilesheim pantheon. And certainly no god of the Holy Alliance would assist him.

But there was one god who was not so . . . particular. There was one god who reveled in the cracking of skulls, the shedding of blood, the destruction of life, and the desolation of entire countries—a god who would tolerate any evil so long as his own power was enhanced, a god to whom even the undead could turn, so long as they had some bargaining chips: Wojan, the Heilesheim god of war. He would strike a bargain with the god of war and get his body back. And then he would engulf the damnable Bagsby and his elf—and the whole mortal world—in fire from the heavens, and become himself an immortal king!

"Caaaannn uh goourd," the old wizard shouted. "Caaann uh goord!"

There was a clank of metal footsteps on the cold stone steps up to the tower room, and in due time the panting captain of the guard presented himself, carefully averting his eyes from the unbearable sight of this disgusting creature who had the king's favor. Through a series of violent gestures and unintelligible exclamations, Valdaimon made the lowly human understand that he should prepare the guard troop to move out. Valdaimon was returning to Hamblen, to the palace of the king.

Ruprecht of Heilesheim gazed down from the window of the great council chamber in the palace of the former king of Argolia. He watched with amusement the curls of black smoke, seeking the sky above the burning city. The pitiful squeals of civilians, many being beaten or worse by his rampaging army, brought a smile to his thin lips. The booty of Clairton had been given to his army as a reward for its great victory—a move calculated to improve morale and inspire love for the man who would soon be the ruler of the entire known world. Still smiling, the thin, pale wastrel turned from the window and shook his long, greasy black locks.

"You see, my dears," he said to the assembled female prisoners, "your fate could be much worse than providing entertainment for a man who is nearly a god."

The women had been carefully selected for His Majesty's pleasure from among the fairest of the ruined city by loyal officers who, knowing no favors would come from their general-in-chief, were only too glad to court them from their decadent king. In response to his words, the women nodded fearfully.

"Take them to be prepared for us," Ruprecht snapped to the captain of the guard, who kept a wary eye on the chained Clairton wenches. It was easy, the guard knew, for a petticoat to hide a dagger. "We will have a great feast tonight, thanks to the stores of Clairton, and these will attend our pleasure."

The guard nodded, turned, and with barked order ushered the prisoners from the king's presence.

"And send for Culdus," the young king called out, flopping over the arms of the great chair upon which the king of Clairton had once sat while dispensing his wisdom and justice.

"No need," the deep voice of Baron Manfred Culdus thundered from the doorway. "I am here. Sire, a word with you . . . ."

"Indeed, Culdus, I would have a word with you," the king snarled, his lips twisting into a sneer. "I gave the booty of this city to the army . . . ."

"Which I begged Your Majesty not to do," Culdus snapped back. "This behavior undermines discipline, which has been essential to the success we have so far enjoyed." The stocky, grizzled warrior removed his great helm, tucked it beneath his left shoulder, cradled it in one arm, and bowed from the waist. "I, of course, intend no disrespect," he added quickly, seeing the familiar gleam of cruelty rising in the king's eyes.

"Then do not offer what you do not intend," Ruprecht screeched. "When I offered booty, I did not give leave for the destruction of this city. It may yet be a source of interest and pleasure for me. You will stop this destruction."

"Nothing, Your Majesty, would bring me greater pleasure."

"Except, perhaps," Ruprecht teased, "the conquest of the Duchies and the occupation of this land up to the borders of Parona? And the investment of the borders of the Elven Preserve?"

"Indeed, Your Majesty. I had come to report that once we are finished with our . . . duties here in Clairton, the army should move at once to consolidate the Duchies. And Valdaimon must proceed with his promise to establish civil administration in all these lands. With your permission. . . ."

"Granted, granted," Ruprecht said with a casual wave of his hand.

"I thank you, Sire," the general-in-chief replied. The old warrior turned and strode quickly from the room. For once, an interview with the king had gone better than expected—probably because Valdaimon wasn't around. Where the old wizard might be only dimly worried the general. He had fresh conquests, and growing difficulties of morale and supply, to occupy his mind.

The Temple of Wojan was the largest of the temples of Hamblen. Its smooth, gleaming, white marble walls soared over ninety feet, curving slightly to give the overall structure—some three hundred feet square—the appearance of a huge marble box that was bulging at the sides, ready to explode. The flat roof was crowned with a massive marble sculpture of the god himself, that reared another forty feet toward the heavens. The construction had taken three hundred years; the sculpture had occupied the talents of two generations of the kingdom's finest artists.

Wojan appeared in battle array, his muscular legs protected by grieves, his loins girt about with a simple leather skirt, and his rippling chest protected by a small, round shield made of wood and banded with metal. But his right arm was raised high, the muscles so taut that even the carved veins could be seen from street level, the right hand grasping the deadly battle hammer with which he was about to strike the imaginary enemy to his front. The god's face was a portrait of barbarian rage. His large eyes glared out from squinted lids, his wide nose was capped by flared nostrils, and his lips were drawn back in contortions of anger to reveal the broad, divine teeth. The god's hair, a thick mane longer than shoulder length, flowed backward, blown by some invisible wind. Clutching the enraged divinity's sandaled feet, two sharp-toothed, grinning demons gazed out with glee upon the anticipated destruction of the god's foe.

This imposing structure, which dwarfed mere men to nothingness, sat at one end of the largest square in the capital, the Square of the Gods—a huge open plaza surrounded by the principal houses of worship of all the deities of Heilesheim. The sole approach to this vast, holy area was the Royal Road, which linked the square to the royal residence and fortress, slightly over a mile distant. The entirety of this paved way was lined with sculptures of the kings of Heilesheim, extending back to the kings of legend who hand-forged the realm from the internecine squabbles of numerous barbarian tribes whose very names were now forgotten save in the appellations of these ancient kings.

The front of Wojan's temple faced across the square to the Royal Road; its outer courtyard, which was all the average worshiper ever saw, occupied one full side of the square. From the courtyard, a series of thirty low steps rose gradually to the great flat doors, themselves twenty feet high, which were the only entrance to the massive structure. The doors themselves were of polished, dark hard-wood, of a type not known in the land but imported from the forests of the far north. The wood had been transported by sea to the great port of Hamblen, where its arrival had been the occasion for a municipal holy day. The wood was later overlaid with gold leaf, on which panels of friezes depicted scenes of Heilesheim's battle glories from the days of old—when the kingdom was young, and many lands that now considered themselves loyal portions of the heartland were recent conquests.

The gold did not glitter in the moonless sky of the early summer night—not this night, as Sigurt stood alone in the empty square, a tiny, solitary figure gazing upward at the mass of stone erected to the glory of destruction. Normally, the sight of the temple was enough to absorb Sigurt's spirit; his very being would be caught up in the contemplation of something so much greater than himself that any personal worries were simply no longer possible. But that particular calming magic did not work for Sigurt tonight.

The priest lowered his gaze to the worn flagstones of the great courtyard. His eye caught the wide, thick, fancy strip of gold brocade that ran along the hem of his holiest white robe—a robe of heavy linen laid over with pure silk. A simple belt of similar material was tied in a single knot at his waist, while his chest was ornamented with the great, broad, purple-and-gold surplice studded with rubies, emeralds, and diamonds, which could be worn only on high holy occasions or at the command of the god himself. Beneath these ceremonial vestments, Sigurt wore the traditional garb of the god: sandals, greaves, and a short leather skirt. His own hair was short, but a wig created a black, flowing mane for the high priest. On the left arm of the white robe, the figure of a wooden shield was cleverly created by a combination of embroidery and tiny gemstones, and in his hands the high priest carried a ceremonial silver war hammer—the symbol of the divine weapon with which Wojan had conquered the Olden Ones and brought glory, order, and the mission of empire to the great kingdom of Heilesheim.

Thus adorned, the high priest was said to be the visible presence of the god himself. If that were true, Sigurt thought, then great Wojan himself must be uneasy tonight, for I surely do not trust the course the god has laid out before me.

Of all the citizens of Heilesheim, only the temple priests were aware that tonight their high priest stood in the vast, empty square in holiest garb, prepared to perform a series of rituals granted by the god so seldom that two generations had been born and passed away since the last such ceremony was held. That ceremony, a ceremony of healing for the then-king Wilhelm the Great, had been a scene of great public ritual and the occasion for a three-day holiday when the king's health was recovered. Tonight's ceremony was a secret, a secret that could be divulged only at the risk of one's life.

Sigurt had reluctantly made the necessary preparations. The entire interior of the temple, down to the last cell occupied by the lowliest acolyte, had been ceremonially cleansed. Secret offerings of vast treasures in gold, silver, jewelry, weapons, and gems had been anonymously donated to the temples of all the gods whose rank was sufficient to earn them a place of worship on the great square—for the power to heal was not one of Wojan's usual powers, and the war god was forced to call upon his siblings for the divine words that could restore health and wholesomeness to flesh.

Then there had come the dreadful sacrifices. Beasts of every type and description—from the lowliest creeping thing to a great ape reared from birth in the bowels of the great temple for just such an occasion—had been taken in the dark of night to the small, modest temple of the war god's most powerful brother, Raggenolm, the god of the dead. There they were sacrificed, one by one, a gift from Wojan to his proud brother's realm. This was not part of the usual healing ceremony: these special sacrifices were intended to secure Raggenolm's cooperation in transmuting the healing magic of the other gods so that it could apply to the flesh of one who was not alive—and not entirely dead. At the climax of these ceremonies had been the human sacrifices, warrior prisoners taken from Argolia: a dozen Argolian knights. These had required the participation of Sigurt himself, making him the only high priest of Wojan to personally slay a warrior since the worship of the god had begun in the mists of the past.

Inside Wojan's temple, while Sigurt stood his lonely vigil, the three hundred priests were gathered in ranks like a holy army in the great hall of worship, prepared to offer the supplication to Wojan and the other gods that would restore the flesh of the unusual supplicant who was to present himself tonight.

Sigurt shuddered suddenly, even though the summer night air was mild and warm. Always, always, the way of Wojan had been hard. Wojan demanded sacrifice of self to the good of the army, the good of the kingdom, the glory of war. But always, always, the worship of Wojan had been a very human thing—not humane, not kind, not even desirable from the point of view of lazy men who loved prosperity and peace more than danger and celebration in the immortal songs of the faith—but always human. Tonight. . . . Sigurt shuddered again. Tonight,

Sigurt thought, Wojan does not overcome the power of death with courage that leads to glory, as has always been his way. Tonight Wojan forges an alliance with death, death for its own sake, death that is so powerful that it itself lives. It did not seem right to the priest. But who was he to question Wojan? His duty, like every loyal soldier's, was to obey.

Sigurt's dark thoughts were interrupted by the faint sound of bare human feet padding gently down the Royal Road. The high priest raised his eyes; in the distance, he could make out a moving, dark mass in the darkness of the night, a mass that slowly came closer and resolved into the images of men bearing a litter. In that litter was the supplicant for whose sake all these preparations had been made—none other than Valdaimon, the wizard, the undead thing who could call forth more magic than any human and, some claimed, knew incantations undiscovered even by the elves.

The litter-bearers came straight ahead, clearly visible now, even in the darkness of the night. They did not slow their pace until they suddenly stopped less than ten feet in front of Sigurt, heads bowed even as they held their heavy burden.

Sigurt raised the ceremonial hammer and dipped it once in the ancient gesture of Wojan's blessing. "The power of Wojan be on everyone here who loves war, hates slothful peace, and seeks glory in Wojan's kingdom," he intoned.

The litter-bearers lowered their burden without looking up. Then, as one, they scattered back down the road the way they had come, to await their summons out of sight of the temple.

An incoherent, high-pitched howl of greeting came from within the lowered litter.

"Step forward, supplicant, to beseech the favor of Wojan," Sigurt called, in a loud voice.

The yellow-and-red silk curtains of the litter parted. With much panting, wheezing, and struggling, the withered, naked form of Valdaimon slowly emerged into the night. The old mage cut an almost comical figure as he wobbled and staggered in his attempt to rise, waving his one arm wildly for balance. Sigurt grimaced. This was sickeningly comical, obscene in a particularly hideous way. Then, as the old man steadied himself, the priest saw clearly the extent of the damage to the disgusting body. The visual assault was combined with the legendary stench that always accompanied Valdaimon—and for a moment, the high priest fought hard against his natural tendency to gag. But the dignity of his position and his duty to Wojan forbade any such reaction.

Valdaimon stared at Sigurt with his one rheumy eye. He wondered if the priest could read the hatred on his face, the utter contempt he felt for all priests and the gods they represented. Religion was a poor substitute for the real power of magic, and nothing but indomitable necessity had driven him to seek this priest's help. And the cost! The cost! No doubt, Valdaimon thought, that was what the priest would next address.

"Valdaimon, servant of the king of Heilesheim, and thereby servant of Wojan," Sigurt bellowed in a deep voice, choosing his words carefully so as never to imply that Valdaimon was a willing servant of the god, "do you come as a humble supplicant seeking from Wojan that which is beyond your power, that which only a god can bestow?"

Valdaimon was required by the form of the ritual to respond. He released a low, hate-filled growl that the priest, if he were wise, would take for assent.

"Then know," Sigurt responded, "the sacrifice that Wojan demands of you."

Sigurt paused. It was this part of the ritual that gave him the greatest difficulty, that aroused his deepest feelings of revulsion. Had the supplicant been a mere human, say a king of Heilesheim, the god would have imposed a heavy duty in gold—always useful for paying continued building and maintenance expenses—and perhaps a quest to go and recover this gem or that artifact and donate it to the holy temple of Wojan. The temple had a number of small chambers filled with such treasures, the gifts of supplicants who had sought much less than Valdaimon sought tonight.

"It is the will of Wojan," Sigurt continued, "that you shall be his instrument for bringing endless war to all the earth. In all you do, you shall foment strife. No king, no soldier, no man shall ever hear from your lips counsels of peace, but always and only counsels of war. Your powers, once restored, shall be used solely to this end. This shall be for the fostering of courage, of glorious deeds in battle, and the worship of Wojan above all other gods to the very ends of the earth," Sigurt chanted in his deep bass.

Valdaimon again grunted his assent. All this was according to the agreement he had painstakingly negotiated with the high priest. That process had required the cooperation of two of his most powerful underlings from the League of Wizards, of which he was the titular head. Their spells of telepathy had been used to translate Valdaimon's agreement to the outrageous terms demanded by Sigurt. Sometime soon, once his powers were restored, the mages involved in the negotiations would have to die, lest they divulge their knowledge of this secret pact.

"And know this!" Sigurt exclaimed, continuing in the same tone. "In the day that you violate this sacred oath, you shall certainly be destroyed. For on that day the High Priest of Wojan shall cast upon your name the spell of life, and you, being dead, shall be annihilated, reduced to less than nothingness, your being not even a memory among men."

Treachery! Valdaimon croaked his anger, but to no avail. Sigurt had mentioned no such condition in the course of their negotiations. He had tacked on this condition of punishment only at the decisive moment, when Valdaimon had no choice but to accept it. Without the power to counsel peace, the old wizard's ability for political manuever was crippled. Valdaimon could only stare, fuming, at the face of the hated high priest. Sigurt smiled. It was this part of the ritual, and this part alone, that would give him some satisfaction from this night's work.

Valdaimon waved his one arm impatiently. *Get on with it, then, you treacherous priest,* he thought. *Perhaps someday I will find a way to pay back you and your god.*

Sigurt smiled again, and nodded. He turned his back to Valdaimon and began pacing slowly toward the great doors of the temple, passing between two rows of low columns. Atop each column was a silver bowl, and in each bowl was a small amount of blood. At each column, Sigurt stopped, raised high the bowl, and poured the contents over Valdaimon's nearly bald head.

"Be cleansed in the blood of a warrior blessed by Wojan," he chanted with each such ablution. This was repeated seven times, until the naked form of Valdaimon, ritually cleansed, slowly mounted the steps that led up to the temple doors. At Sigurt's signal, those doors swung silently open, and the strange pair disappeared into the mysterious interior of that vast edifice which was the embodiment of Heilesheim's historic might.

The sun was not yet up when Valdaimon's litter was borne from the square back down the Royal Road to Ruprecht's palace, the ancient fortress that protected both the harbor and the river approaches to Hamblen.

"A curse on all gods and priests," Valdaimon muttered, still enraged by Sigurt's treachery and the impossible restrictions the god's terms had placed upon him. And the healing hadn't even been completed. True, his face was as whole as it had been before Bagsby's attack, his right arm and hand restored and functional for spell casting, and his other wounds somewhat improved, but his right eye was still missing, the socket merely grown over with more of the same dead flesh that covered the rest of Valdaimon's bones. Wojan had determined, Sigurt had announced airily, that the sight of both eyes was not necessary for Valdaimon's magical powers and for his new role as Wojan's agent in the affairs of men. Someday, Valdaimon thought, someday, perhaps even the gods themselves will tremble at the power of the one who can command the very fires of heaven! But in the meantime, there was work to be done. First and foremost was the task of finding Bagsby and the treasure he had stolen.

"Faster!" the wizard screamed at his litter-bearers. The tired, frightened men broke into a jog, struggling to keep their burden level as they increased their speed toward the palace. For an instant, the silk curtains on the side of the litter parted, and a scrawny arm protruded. Sitting on the arm was a fat, bedraggled crow who cawed once, loudly, and then took flight into the black sky.

3

A Plot Is Hatched

Bagsby STROLLED BRISKLY down the open roadway between flat fields of summer grain that had already grown as tall as his knees. The sun overhead was in a midday position; the next three hours would be the heat of the day, but Bagsby did not even consider pausing. He felt better than he had for several weeks. He was in his own element again: he was alone, he had no ties, he had no other people to slow him down, and he had his own interests and no one else's to care about.

All I need now, he thought, is a bit of cash. A horse would be good, too; the quicker he could get to Laga the better. There was no telling how quickly Shulana might decide to follow him.

Bagsby suppressed the unfamiliar rush of guilt that flooded him when he thought of Shulana. After all, he had gotten them across the river, given George enough tips to get them safely to Hamblen, and even left a note for Shulana, promising to meet up with the group once his current quest was done.

The river crossing had been strenuous—difficult work, but not as dangerous as it first appeared. From the branches of the plentiful trees by the riverbank, the group, at Bagsby's direction, had crafted a crude raft, held together by mud, wood tar, bits of rope, and belts from Marta's battlefield pickings. The swift river current had lapped between the logs, soaking the group, but the raft had floated—and once free from the shore had been carried rapidly by the current downstream to the west. Using more branches as crude paddles, the foursome had managed to guide their makeshift craft across the center

41

of the wide stream, and it was only a matter of time until the coincidence of turns in the river and the vagaries of the current sent it bobbing toward the southern bank. Eventually, the craft had foundered on a mud bar, only ten yards from shore; but the river was only neck-deep there—even on Bagsby. Dripping and cursing, the three humans and Shulana had waded onto the soil of Heilesheim with all their gear in tow.

"Well, George, that's a job well done," Bagsby had said cheerily, as the former soldier dropped his bundle on the bank and sank to his knees, exhausted more by fear of drowning than by any exertion.

"Right, well done," George had gasped. The fighter had watched with continued and growing horror as a rush of high water washed over the mud bar where the raft was stuck, lifting it off and, in the process, tearing away part of one side. "By the gods, Bagsby, that could have been us," George had whispered reproachfully.

"True. But it wasn't," Bagsby had replied lightly. "Now listen to me, George. Here's the plan."

"It 'ad better be a good one," George had said. "You've almost got me drowned. Now I'm in Heilesheim, and you're like to get me caught for a deserter and 'anged."

"Not at all, not at all. Listen to me." Bagsby had leaned over, placing his mouth close to George's ear as if to impart a great confidence. "Everyone knows that Ruprecht and Valdaimon hate elves, right?"

"True enough," George had replied. Even before the war had begun, the officers of the Fifth Legion, George's unit, had been giving lectures to the troops about the menace of elves, how elves were to blame for the troubles of Heilesheim, how the plotting of the elves was probably behind the aggressions of the Holy Alliance that made the "defensive" conquest of their lands a sad necessity. Neither George nor the other Heilesheim infantry had paid much heed to this; their motives for fighting had little to do with politics. They were in it for fun, adventure, and plunder.

"Well, then, if anyone stops you, you're a Heilesheim soldier who got cut off from his unit at the great Battle of Clairton—that much is true and should be easy to stick to—

and after the battle, you caught this female elf spying on the army. Then you enlisted the aid of Marta and myself, poor refugees, in taking this unusual and important prisoner straight to the capital," Bagsby had whispered. "It's your right as a Heilesheim soldier to ransom your own prisoner, and since this one is obviously a spy, she should be brought before the king's own court for disposition."

A light gleamed in George's dark eyes, which widened with glee and surprise. "An' I thought you was in love wit' 'er," he had replied in a low tone.

Bagsby had grimaced. Would George actually turn Shulana over? Of course he would. Still, Shulana had always demonstrated every ability to take care of herself, and she should know how far George could be trusted. . . .

Bagsby had taken the first watch that morning while the group settled down to sleep, a few hundred yards off the great road that ran along the south side of the river, stretching all the way from the desert city of Laga in the far east to Hamblen on the coast of the Great Sea in the west. He had watched as George and Marta, lying in the shade of a spreading oak, had drifted off to soggy sleep. He had watched Shulana as she drifted away from the group, out to an open meadow, there to lie down and disappear in a mass of green grass and beautiful golden flowers whose faces tilted eastward to catch the rays of the rising sun. Then, on a piece of scrap leather plundered from Marta's horde, he had scrawled a note, using the point of a dagger to carve the crude letters into the pliant bit of cowhide.

Shulana,

Leaving to learn value of treasure. You understand. Will meet you and Elrond. Four weeks at most. The gods travel with you.

Bagsby

By now, Bagsby thought, one of them at least will be awake. Soon they'll discover that I'm gone, and then Shulana will find the message I left. She'll know—she'll even know I'm headed east, because I once told her of the holy man out here who is rumored to know the secrets of the past. But she won't come after me, no matter how much George wants to. She'll go to save Elrond. She can't afford to lose the Golden Eggs and have Elrond killed as well. She'll go to save Elrond.

"Bah!" Bagsby shouted out loud, shaking his head savagely, trying to shake out the thoughts the way a dog shakes off water. "Enough! I am the way I was—on my own, on the open road, seeking my own fortune!" Bagsby raised his head and looked resolutely ahead. His old smile spread across his face at the sight that faced him—ten soldiers in standard Heilesheim armor, led by a single officer on a horse. *And here comes a bit of that fortune*, Bagsby thought.

"And then the Argolian center broke. It was like a piece of taut string, suddenly snapping. One minute they were in line fighting, the next a fleeing mass of frightened men— all ranks, even the Argolian nobles, galloping away to save their lives." Bagsby gestured dramatically as he stuffed another handful of the fresh, white fowl meat into his mouth with his free hand. "Then our men were all over them, footmen and knights together, in a glorious pursuit," he continued, his words interspersed with the sounds of chewing as flecks of the white flesh dribbled from his lips.

"And you saw it all?" one incredulous young soldier asked. "You actually saw our footmen attacking their knights and defeating them?" The rest of the small company—ten fresh recruits for the front from among the merchant-class families of Laga—leaned forward, eyes glued to Bagsby. Their officer, a veteran, rolled his eyes as he turned another chicken over their noonday fire.

"May all the gods strike me if I did not see these things with my own eyes," Bagsby declared. He didn't bother to add that he, too, had been among the fleeing Argolians. "I saw it from a hill overlooking the field, where I'd parked my wagon."

"By the gods, men, if this is true," the young recruit exclaimed, "we can all be rich men before this war is over, even if we are but footmen!"

"Aye," the officer called. "By the way, you said your name was . . . ?" He directed his stern glance at Bagsby.

"Oh, sorry, didn't I properly introduce myself?" Bagsby replied. "So much excitement these last few days. First the battle, then losing my wagon to that band of Argolian deserters who were wandering around our rear area—turned into nothing but a bunch of ruffians, you see, and I. . . ."

"Your name?" the officer demanded, rising to his feet.

"Wilhelm Mater of Hamblen, merchant, tinker, and jack of all trades, as they say," Bagsby responded quickly, jumping up himself and extending his hand in formal greeting. "At your service, officer. And you?"

"Hans Frisung, Leader of Ten, Eighth Legion, on rear-area duty," the man replied, ignoring Bagsby's gesture of friendship. "How fared the Eighth in the big fight?"

Bagsby saw the way the man cocked his head as he asked the question, saw his eyes narrow as they studied Bagsby's face. A trick question, no doubt.

"I was nearest the Fifth Legion," Bagsby said, calling up the one unit name of which he could be certain. "There was so much confusion, once the fighting started, I'm not even sure which Legions were engaged, or if all our troops got to take part in the rout."

"Hmm," the officer snorted. If this man was a liar, he was a shrewd liar. Seemed harmless enough. "And now you're headed where?" Frisung asked.

"Laga," Bagsby replied. "Is that other chicken done? Been a long time since I've had real food. Been on the road since the battle."

"Why didn't you stay with the army?" the young soldier asked. "Many of the soldiers must have been loaded with plunder after a fight like that—plenty to barter with."

"True enough, true enough," Bagsby said sadly, sitting down by the fire and hacking a leg off the still roasting chicken with his dagger. "But I had nothing left to sell, once my wagon was ruined by those Argolian scum. Besides, the army is so rich now, you need more than the standard geegaws to coax their money and plunder away. I'm off to Laga, where I figure to get a wagonload of k'alah, the wine of the desert people. It'll be new to most of them—exotic, kind of," Bagsby explained.

"Hmmph," Frisung snorted again. "Well, well, that's enough now." The old veteran grabbed the spit from the fire, raised it to his mouth, and bit into the hot white meat. "Put out this fire and prepare to move out," he called to his tiny corps of recruits.

Bagsby moved back from the fire, strolling casually behind Frisung. He glanced about cautiously as the men, a few grumbling, most laughing, slowly rose and began gathering their gear. One man picked up a shovel and began tossing dry earth over the cooking fire. Bagsby continued to stroll randomly about until he stood very near the officer's horse. As he had hoped, the horse was still saddled; the brutish fellow hadn't even bothered to lighten its load by removing his saddle roll and bags. No doubt there would be a bit of gold left from the recruiter's money. . . .

Bagsby was on the horse in a flash. Before the startled officer could even shout a protest, the little man had ridden beside him, reached down, grabbed him beneath the chin, and yanked him off his feet with one arm. In Bagsby's left hand, a dagger flashed. He pressed the tip against the officer's throat.

"What! Treachery! Thief!" one of the men cried. The youths scrambled up in their inexperienced way, drawing their swords with a great clatter, glancing at one another, uncertain what to do.

"Sorry, lads, but war is dangerous," Bagsby said, grinning. "Now back away, or this officer dies." The helpless Frisung tried to scream an order, but his throat was already nearly crushed in Bagsby's arm; a stifled *gawk* was all he could manage. The youths spread out into a semicircle, slowly retreating.

"That's better," Bagsby said, grinning. "Now, you boys know that the next place you can get any supplies is a two days' march to the west. If you try to come east, you'll hit the desert. True, there is a merchant camp there, but without your money," Bagsby glanced at the bags tied to the saddle, "you'll find little aid there. I suggest you start marching."

"What about him?" the boldest of the young men cried, pointing with his sword to Frisung.

"Him?" Bagsby asked. "Oh, well," he said, plunging the point of the dagger into the man's neck and neatly slitting his throat as he let him fall to the ground, "he won't be joining you." Bagsby grabbed the reins, turned the horse, and headed east, spurring his mount to a canter.

There were shouts of youthful rage behind him, and two of the duller recruits even tried to chase him on foot. In the end, they were reduced to hurling clods of the dry, plains earth at him, their breath having given out and the horse easily outdistancing them. Fools, Bagsby thought. They don't even realize that I could just as easily have killed them all.

Bagsby rode east a few miles before stopping to take account of his booty. As he'd hoped, there was gold in one of the bags, more than enough to provide all he needed for his journey across the Eastern Desert to Laga. As an added bonus, he found a list with the names of the recruits and their families. Good, he thought. It had been many, many years since Bagsby had been in Laga. It was always a good thing to have the names of a few contacts.

The soldier did not mind the flies, the heat, the stink, and the noise of Laga's crowded, winding and incredibly dusty streets. He did not mind because he was dead. There was nothing left of the soul of Harold Otison—whom the man had been in life—in the body that now walked awkwardly down the narrow alley. The corpse was now animated by a fragment of the great wizard Valdaimon's life force. It was Valdaimon's intelligence—or rather, a tiny part of it—that guided the man's movements, moved his lips, and raised his legs. And Valdaimon's intelligence cared nothing for any discomfort the corpse might experience.

The armored figure stalked on down the sandy street, head turning this way and that in a constant searching motion, looking, always looking, for one man, and one man only. Somewhere in Laga, Valdaimon knew, there was a holy man, a man who was said to know the secret of the Golden Eggs of Parona, the secret of the fire from heaven that could consume all things. This zombie's task was to find that man and, in the crudest way possible, persuade him to divulge that secret.

The small part of Valdaimon's mind that inhabited the zombie recoiled in disgust from this city. Laga had never been kind to Valdaimon. He remembered an earlier journey here, many years ago, on this same mission. Maddened by the constant, swirling sand that infested everything in Laga including eyes, shoes, hair, and lungs of anyone so foolish as to be in the city, Valdaimon had killed a passing man who crossed him—only to be attacked by the man's brazen five-year-old child. The little monster had escaped Valdaimon's wrath then, and he had lived to become the thief, Bagsby, who was proving Valdaimon's bane now. That earlier mission had been cut short. Valdaimon had never found the holy man he sought. But this time there would be no Bagsby, and there would be no failure.

It had taken the zombie a long time to journey from Lundlow Keep to Laga—two weeks, for its progress on foot was slow, and its coordination too poor to allow it to ride. The journey on foot had not been kind to the corpse. A few very simple magics disguised the extent of its corruption, but a careful observer would note that the lips hung limply, never tightening except when the man would speak, and the strange, ugly patches of purplish green discoloration about the eyes and beneath the nostrils, neither of which ever widened or contracted. Had anyone save the gods been watching, they would have noticed, too, that this soldier never slept. He simply walked the streets, looking, looking, always looking. But the citizens of Laga paid no heed. Men in armor were a constant sight, what with the war and all. Soldiers came to Laga, raised recruits, and led them out. More soldiers came; other soldiers left. It was all the routine of war; the merchants, harlots, and thieves of Laga prospered, which meant that most everyone in the city prospered, for few of the permanent inhabitants failed to fall into one of those classes.

Bagsby was exuberant when he passed through the gates into the city of his birth. The desert sun poured its yellow gold with special favor on the sandy streets, and the endless parade of people in their colorful garb—each costumed more extravagantly than the one before—lifted his spirits even more. After a long odyssey, Bagsby was home at last.

He did not remember the city well from his childhood days, and it had grown much since. But the basic flavor was the same, that he could tell at a glance. Here was the place where the dark desert nomads came—each tribe once a year—to barter the goods of dwarfs from the eastern mountains and even the unknown lands beyond for the necessities of their roaming desert life. Here, thieves in bulky silk trousers of yellow, blue, or red and short open vests ran barefoot and barechested through the streets, skillfully cutting the purses of those same nomads. Here were the great gambling houses, where the merchants of the caravans could while away their leisure hours losing all the profits of their long journeys from the western coast, while being charmed by the most beautiful, seductive, flattering, and thieving of women.

Bagsby breathed deeply of the aromas of the city before starting down the great, wide street. He led his horse, carrying two daggers conspicuously in his belt, and in one hand held a staff that he had fashioned on his trip from a tree limb. When a horde of laughing, naked children came running toward him from his right, Bagsby quickly stepped to his right and swept low with the staff, sending the leaders of the wave sprawling. His own guffaws blended with theirs, and urchins sped away toward the next mark coming through the gate; this one knew their ways.

"At least I thought I knew their ways," Bagsby said half aloud, lifting his foot to look at the sole of one of the fine leather boots he had bought en route. He had successfully avoided the thievery of the children, but not the steaming piles of dung that littered the main thoroughfare everywhere. When the desert men came into the city, they brought with them everything—their goats, camels, horses, and cattle. It was said that the winds that constantly swept Laga's sandy streets would have long since blown those streets away were it not for the manure constantly worked into the sand by the passage of thousands of feet over the droppings of thousands of animals.

Bagsby's first order of business—aside from protecting his belongings—was to find a room. The main street near the gate was lined with elegant hostelries, competing for space with the richest of the merchant shops, which in turn were half hidden by the carts of countless vendors whose hawking could be heard well into the small hours of the night. But Bagsby was a native; he knew that any such elegant place of repose would soon leave him stripped of everything he owned—either by outright theft, which was common enough, or by the clever means of pandering to his every human desire and adding it to the bill he owed. Escape from such bills was virtually impossible except for the most experienced of scoundrels, for each hostelry employed teams of cutthroats who specialized in collecting.

No, not there, Bagsby thought. To find a safe room, he would need to go deep into the city, into streets where the endless rows of whitewashed buildings were mainly the shops and residences of artisan merchants and tradesmen. Somewhere there, he would find a shop run by a widow or orphaned daughter, who would gladly give him safe room and board in exchange for a few coins and the relative safety of his presence.

Bagsby made his way from the main street down the maze of connecting side streets into such an area. His fine, new boots were covered with dungy grit and the sand stung his eyes, but he felt a warmth that had been lacking in his soul for many years as he surveyed the shop fronts and smiled at the enticements of the women who leaned from the occasional upper balcony. His progress was so pleasant that he hardly noticed the gangly, awkward soldier until he nearly walked into the man.

"Oops," Bagsby said absently.

"Bagsby," the mail-clad form growled. One arm shot forward and grabbed the reins of Bagsby's horse from the little man's grasp; the other put forth a hand that closed with a crushing grip on his windpipe.

"Bagsby," the form muttered again, lifting him off his feet with the one strong arm. "Time to die, Bagsby."

The little man kicked out violently, felt the toes of his boots strike the chain-mail shirt, then the jarring, sickening thud of impact as his toes met the rigid flesh beneath the armor. Bagsby's eyes bugged out wildly; the strangely rotting face of this odd behemoth filled his vision, and the constant scents of animal dung, men's sweat, and cheap perfume were driven from his consciousness by the sickening stench that came from the man's mouth as he spoke.

Then Bagsby heard wild cheers. Even as the vision slowly faded and his lungs filled with pain, he knew at some deep, distant level what was happening. Thieves were coming, swarming from the countless doorways and windows, stripping the horse, knocking aside the soldier's restraining arm, stealing the mount and all that was on it. The native of Laga, however, had no vain illusions that any of these thieves would for an instant do anything to help him.

Bagsby's kicks became more feeble, and he felt the cold, greasy deathgrip on his throat become even strong, if indeed that was possible. Only one thing to do, he thought, his vision starting to swim. He kept his eyes locked as best he could on his foe's face and kicked ever more weakly to distract the strange man. Fumbling with his arms and hands, he finally purchased a grip on one dagger with his right hand, which was already starting to tingle and grow numb. He raised the knife high and struck the strongest blow he could, cutting into the man's arm just above the wrist. The blade bit into the cold flesh and sliced through the meat, but it jarred to a stop against the bone. Again Bagsby raised the dagger, striking a second blow, and then a third. The bone gave way, and the steel cut through the remainder of the stringy flesh. Bagsby fell to the street, the ice-cold hand still locked about his throat.

The soldier stood motionless. Bagsby rolled onto his back, clutched the hand that continued to choke him, and pried back the thumb. He hurled the severed member into the crowd that had gathered to laugh, jeer, cheer, and strip the soldier's body of anything that could be cut loose from it. The man seemed not to even notice their presence. He stood, Bagsby assumed, stunned, looking blankly at the empty space that a moment before had contained his hand and Bagsby's head. Very, very slowly, a few droplets of black blood began to drip from the severed end of his wrist.

No time to waste. Bagsby rolled his head in the sandy muck of the street, and saw his staff which he had dropped when the man grabbed him. He rolled, grasped the weapon, hopped to his feet, and then doubled over as his lungs vomited up the fluid that had begun to fill them. Bagsby hacked and gagged, coughing violently, trying to suck in great gasps the air that his burning lungs rejected.

"Go on," voices from the crowd shouted. "Kill him!"

"Somebody get that horse," another called.

"Can't make him let go of it," answered another man, who was prying at the zombie's grip on the reins. "Have to cut bridle and reins, I guess. . . ."

The zombie whirled, rocking unsteadily on its feet, and landed a crushing blow with the bloody stump of its right arm against the side of the man's head. The thief went sprawling.

Bagsby managed to stand erect, and he saw the would-be owner of his horse go flying into the crowd. He hefted his staff, lowered his head, and swung—aiming for his assailant's unprotected shins, which protruded from below the midcalf length of the chain mail. The blow landed solidly; Bagsby felt pain in his hands as the staff shattered from the impact.

Unnoticed by the jeering crowd and the stunned Bagsby, a decrepit, fat, old crow circled lazily down from the sky far overhead to land on a nearby rooftop.

Bagsby stared at his opponent, not believing what he saw. The man had not even flinched from the blow that should have filled his mind with overwhelming pain. Bagsby thought he might even have broken the shinbone, or at least cracked it. But the soldier showed no reaction. He turned his head slowly to face the shorter man, and his dull eyes seemed to gleam for an instant.

"Bagsby," he growled, spitting the word into the air.

"Nice to see you again," Bagsby taunted back. "But I really have no time for a chat just now. Maybe later!" Bagsby dropped the worthless staff, swept up his dagger, and took a running leap into the crowd that circled the two combatants. A well-placed boot here and a fist there soon cleared him a path. The little man ran down the narrow street, came to the first intersecting alleyway, turned, and ran some more. He kept running, taking widening circles through the backstreets for several minutes, until he was well away from the scene of the fight, and the crowds no longer recognized him as the little man who had just been half-killed by the strange, one-handed soldier.

Finally he stopped running, drawing up to rest against the whitewashed wall of a two-story building. He leaned back and drew quick, deep breaths. What in the name of all the gods, he wondered, had that been about? He was sure he didn't recognize the man, and most of the victims of the more elaborate swindles he had pulled he would certainly know on sight. Other victims of his vocation either did not know him or seldom lived to describe him, and the young soldiers he'd robbed on the road were still days away from Laga by foot— even if they had come east instead of west. Bagsby shook his head. It didn't make sense. He tried again to picture the soldier in his mind. Was there something about the livery markings that was familiar? But Bagsby had never really had a good look at anything except the man's face and legs.

He stood up straight and began threading his way down the street, sidestepping to avoid three goats driven by a nomad in his black desert clothes, jumping aside again to avoid a nobleman on horseback who rode straight down the middle of the street, little caring whom or what his horse stepped upon. Overhead, the fat crow cawed once, gleefully, but the sound was drowned by the perpetual noise of Laga—to all sets of ears save one.

Bagsby continued walking, only half-noticing where he was going. Now he had no money; he'd have to revert to stealing in a town full of thieves, and wary of thieves' tricks. He heard the voice behind him just an instant before the cold, clammy hand tried to clutch the back of his neck.

"Bagsby," the low voice grumbled.

With reflexes trained by a lifetime, Bagsby dove forward into the muck of the street, somersaulting. The dead hand scraped harmlessly down the back of his tunic as he spun in the air. He came to his feet, whirled around, and saw the man drawing back a great broadsword with his one remaining hand. Bagsby ducked the blow, heard the blade swish just above his hair, and felt the wind of its passing. He jumped back, spun, and ran.

"Bagsby!" the figure shouted, lumbering awkwardly after him, the sword arm raised to strike if the soldier could only close the range. Bagsby called on his aching calves for another burst of speed. He turned at the first junction he came to, bounced off a fat woman trundling a cart of baubles down the middle of the narrow lane, stumbled over the ragged children who tugged at the hem of her dress, and blundered on ahead through the milling crowd—most of them moving in the opposite direction and laden with piles of sweet fruits. He ducked past a fruit vendor's small white shack, then stopped cold in front of the three-foot wall that sealed any exit from the alley. Dead end! A large crow landed on the edge of the wall, looking down at Bagsby, cocking its head and cawing.

Bagsby turned again. The thing was already coming toward him, hurling people and their goods aside as though they were dolls. The thing possessed the strength of a giant, Bagsby thought. No good way out—there was a second-story window, but nothing to serve as a platform to leap up to it, and the wall was too high and smooth to scale without a running start.

Bagsby drew both his daggers. If he couldn't run, then he would fight. People were screaming now as the one-handed soldier advanced and swung his sword in great, broad strokes to clear bystanders from his front and sides. He slashed at men and women alike but never took his eyes from his intended prey.

Bagsby braced himself in a wide-legged stance—knees bent, weight on the balls of his feet, and arms partly extended to his sides—ready to spring in any direction.

The last of the crowd cleared the space between Bagsby and his foe. He stared now at the man, who seemed no different than a hundred other soldiers, guards, watchmen, and cutthroats that he had fought successfully before. And yet, and yet. . . . His eyes lighted on the livery on the man's tunic, half hidden beneath the links of his chain armor. Bagsby had seen that insignia before, he had fought men with that insignia before, but where? His mind raced as his opponent moved slowly forward, his gait ragged, like a man wading in thick water against a heavy current. Lundlow Keep! The guards at Lundlow Keep had worn that insignia, Bagsby suddenly knew. Could this man—this incredibly strong man—have followed him all the way from there?

No time to wonder now, Bagsby realized. The shorter man began to circle as the larger foe approached. If he could get the man turned around, if he could get an opening to run back down the alleyway. . . .

But Bagsby saw that plan would never work. The crowd, its alarm passing, was already formed across the width of the street, packed densely in a concave semicircle, ready to watch the sport. Bagsby doubted now if even his opponent could hack a path through that bloodthirsty throng. He was sure that he couldn't. Therefore, Bagsby thought, he himself would seize the initiative.

Bagsby darted forward suddenly, shouting a loud "Heeee-yaah!" as he attacked. His opponent, as Bagsby had expected, drew back the great sword. Bagsby leapt up and forward, landing on the man's chest with his legs wrapped around the man's waist. He stabbed with his dagger as the man lunged ahead and swung. The momentum of the soldier's own empty blow, suddenly added to by the weight of Bagsby's body, toppled him forward. Bagsby's dagger bit deep into his neck as the two of them hit the earth, Bagsby on his back with the mysterious figure on top of him. Even with his elbow driven into the ground, Bagsby could still control his dagger, and with a jerky motion, he sliced away at the neck of the thing. The monstrous man tried to pin Bagsby down by shoving his stump into the little man's stomach, but Bagsby kept hacking at the neck. Strange, Bagsby thought, as the head finally severed and rolled off to the side; no spurts of bright red blood.

The crowd cheered as the soldier's head plopped off and rolled in the street. Bagsby turned his own head in the dirt to acknowledge the cheers, then he noticed that the body atop him had not collapsed. It remained rigid, the knees and the bloody stump still pinning him to the ground! Bagsby drew up his arms, hands in the dirt, pushed upward with all his strength and rolled to the right at the same time. The headless corpse tumbled over on its side. Another cheer went up the crowd, and Bagsby jumped to his feet, smiled, and bowed to his audience.

"All idiots who desire death will be pleasantly served," Bagsby crowed. There was laughter from the colorful crowd, laughter that suddenly died out. Then a moment of silence, then muttering, and the front ranks of the crowd began pressing backward, seeking escape from the narrow alleyway.

"No, friends, I mean you no harm," Bagsby called. "I am a Lagan myself, born here, returned here. . . ." Why were they so afraid of him?

Bagsby spun around in time to see the decapitated body, now standing, bend over and fumble with its one hand to grasp its severed head by the hair, lift the half-rotted trophy up, and set it back atop its neck.

"Bagsby," the thing wheezed, "you will die."

The crowd screamed and panicked. It was like the rout on a battlefield—larger men running over smaller men, trampling them; everyone was screaming, the stench of fear in the air.

"That's it," Bagsby said aloud. "That's it for me." He ran headlong toward the crowd and jumped upward. One foot struck a back; he pushed down, hard. The other foot found purchase on a head; he looked, stepped up lightly, and sprang upward with the force of that one leg. This sent the hapless woman whose head served as his platform sprawling to the ground. His upstretched hands grabbed the bottom section of a balcony rail. Bagsby drew himself upward swiftly, folded his legs up between his arms, lapped them over the balcony top, and landed on his feet. Without pause he dove into the open window.

"Ouch!"

He landed bellydown on the backside of a scrawny merchant, who was himself lying atop a buxom harlot.

"Sorry," Bagsby said.

The large four-poster bed collapsed with a crash.

"Love to stay, but got to go," Bagsby explained, grinning, and slapped the startled woman on her exposed bare thigh before crawling over the couple. He sprang to his feet, and bolted out of the chamber into the narrow hallway beyond.

"Who was that?" he heard a female voice ask behind him.

No time to stay and play, Bagsby thought. Suddenly, an image of Shulana flashed in his mind's eye. No time to feel guilty either, he thought, charging down the dimly lit hall past narrow, wooden doors. There were the stairs!

Bagsby pounded down them and barged into a tawdry sitting room. Startled shrieks came from the bevy of ladies, some with gentleman callers, who occupied it. A red velvet curtain barred the way to the front door. There should be a vestibule, then the door to the street, Bagsby thought. Don't want the street. He, it, whatever, is out there. He turned left, bumped into a chair, did a double take to admire the exposed beauty of the young woman in the chair, then ran down the hallway to the rear of the building.

He crashed through a door and found himself in the kitchen where two older women tended the pots. A round of beef sat steaming on a platter. He stopped, cut off a chunk of meat and popped it in his mouth.

"Delicious," he called to the old hags, who grinned their thanks.

"This way out?" Bagsby asked, pointing to a back door-way.

The crones nodded.

Bagsby ran, threw open the door, and stepped outside into the brilliant midday light. He was in another alley, but this time with no dead end. He turned right, away from the alley where he'd fought the—whatever it was—and ran. The crowds were thinner here. He made good progress but soon became winded. He slowed then stopped. He rested his hands on the fronts of his thighs and sucked in the air as he looked about.

The alley emptied into a kind of tiny square formed by the backs of many buildings and the front of a one-story hovel. The square was almost deserted; Bagsby hurried into it, cast about for any sign of his nemesis, saw none, then stopped again.

Overhead, a lone crow cawed once, but Bagsby did not notice.

"Are you not hearing?" a voice called to him. Bagsby looked again at the only human figure remaining in the tiny square. He was an old man, very thin, naked to the waist, barefoot, and clad only in a pair of short, dirty, white linen trousers. He sat in the doorway of the one building that fronted the square, his arms resting atop his bent knees. A few fine wisps of white hair shot out randomly from his tiny, brown, bald scalp. The old man's eyes were also small, but they burned blue with an intensity Bagsby had seldom, if ever, seen before. In his weathered hands, the man held a small, white, cloth bag.

"Didn't I hear what?" Bagsby asked.

"The call of the bird," the man said.

"What bird?" Bagsby asked, growing slightly exasperated. If that thing was anywhere nearby, he didn't have time for this.

"Ah, it is nearby. In fact, it will be here very soon," the old man croaked.

"What? How do you know. . . . How did you know what I was . . . ?"

"Look," the old man said, nodding and pointing to the narrow alley.

Bagsby whirled. The figure stood in the alleyway, sword in hand, a broad, light green silk sash tied around its neck.

"No," Bagsby breathed.

"You will be needing this," the old man said softly, extending the hand with the small white bag.

"What? What's that?" Bagsby asked, drawing his daggers, bracing again for the renewed struggle.

"Oh, no, no, no. It wouldn't do to be saying," the old man said, not moving. "He might be hearing."

"I've no time for riddles," Bagsby snapped. "That gentleman over there is looking for me, and his intentions are not kind."

"Oh my goodness, yes, that I know," the old man said. "But he is looking as well for me. Let us be seeing which will the most interest him." The old man slowly unfolded himself and stood. "Hello there, friend," he called to the hideous corpse. Without the slightest show of fear, he walked calmly across the small square, his tiny brown feet padding softly on the sand. He stopped directly in front of the soldier. "I think I am someone you are wanting to talk with, is it not so?" he asked.

"You!" the zombie gasped. "You are . . ."

"Yes, yes, I am the one you are much seeking," the old man said, smiling pleasantly. "Please, now, I have not much time. Bend down here and in my ear whisper what is it you wish to know."

"But Bagsby . . . ," the thing wheezed.

"Without what I know, of what use to you is this little thief?" the old man asked, his eyes twinkling brilliantly blue, his voice high-pitched and singsongy, fascinating to Bagsby.

The soldier looked slowly at Bagsby, then back at the old man. The old man was short, shorter even than Bagsby. The thing leaned forward, lowering its head and bringing its foul mouth near the old man's ears.

In a flash the old man grabbed the top of the soldier's head by the hair and gave a mighty pull. The head popped off again. The little man scurried across the square to where Bagsby stood. The headless corpse trembled, extending an arm for balance.

"Please, now, you will force open the mouth. Please do it very quickly," the old man said.

Bagsby didn't know what to think. The headless corpse was lumbering slowly forward now, feeling in front of itself with its one good arm like a man in a very dark room. Bagsby looked at the smiling, mischievous face of the old man. Could he trust him? Why not? The thief grabbed the jaw of the head and pulled it open.

"Oh, I am very much thanking you," the old man singsonged. He pulled the string that opened his bag, lifted the bag above the open mouth, and poured in the contents. There was a sudden, loud gust of foul air from the mouth—the best the thing could manage for a scream. The headless corpse toppled over into the dust. From a nearby roof the fat crow cawed in anger and took flight.

"There, you see?" the old man said to the stunned Bagsby. "All done. All dead."

"I see," Bagsby said slowly.

"Now, you will please be showing to me the fabulous Golden Eggs of Parona, will you not?" the old man asked, smiling and nodding. "For all of my life I have for this moment been preparing, don't you know, and now, I must confess it, I am some eagerness experiencing."

"This much I was knowing," the old man explained, sitting back against a tree on the side of the mountain, "that two men would be seeking me. One would be being alive, and the other would be, oh my goodness, so much an undead, not being alive."

"Animated corpse," Bagsby said knowingly, shielding his eyes with his hand and gazing out over Laga. The vastness of the white city gleamed in the last rays of the day's sunlight below. "Cut off the head, stuff salt in the mouth. I knew that."

"Yes, you are knowing that, but you are not thinking," the old man replied in his innocuous singsong voice that was never insulting, even when telling painful truths. "What good is it to be knowing if you are not using the knowing?"

"Good point," Bagsby admitted. "But now, tell me . . ."

"Soon, soon. But first we must be going a little farther up this mountain—there, behind that ridge, you see? There we can be having a fire and not be being seen from the city below," the old man interrupted. "You will please be building the fire." Without another word, and despite Bagsby's muttered protests, the old fellow stood and walked placidly upward. Bagsby cursed, scowled, and fretted with impatience, but in the end he gathered wood and made a fire.

"Now, if you don't mind . . . ," Bagsby began, as the old man warmed his hands by the flames and stared delightedly at the dancing colors of the burning kindling.

"I am not minding at all. I told you, I am myself experiencing some eagerness. But all must first be ready. Please be looking in that small cleft of rock behind you."

Bagsby turned, saw the small hole the old man indicated, and reached his arm down inside. He felt the open end of a coarse sack and pulled on it. The opening must have been larger than it seemed, for the sack turned out to be huge. It contained large chunks of raw meat, cut-up and salted for preservation.

"Thank you," Bagsby said, "but I really don't want to eat now. I want to find out. . . ."

"That is not for our eating," the old man said. "That is for . . . later."

Bagsby jumped to his feet, enraged. His hand drifted toward a dagger hilt, but he thought better of it. "Old man, I have no more time for your games and riddles. I have come. . . ."

"You are coming from Lundlow Keep," the little man interjected, "where you are stealing the Golden Eggs from the great

Valdaimon. You are seeking the desert shaman that as a youth you heard of, he who is knowing many strange secrets from the past, for you would be learning the secret of the Golden Eggs. Well, sit down, learn patience, for I am that shaman, and you will be learning everything soon." ·

Bagsby sat. His tired rump thudded against the sandy rock of the mountain. He stared at the old man, waiting, but the old man merely gazed up into the darkening sky. Bagsby, too, turned his gaze upward, and the two men sat quietly, watching the deepness of night overtake the heavens and the broad banner of the stars gradually come into being across the roof of the earth. The fire grew lower, and the din of Laga grew softer in the distance. Bagsby felt a strange solace coming over him. For once, at least, he didn't need a plan, didn't need an angle, didn't have to fear or hurry or scurry or steal or fight. Not this night.

"It is being much better that your soul is composed," the old man said softly. "You will need this feeling many times in the future, and you have not been having much practice of it."

Bagsby nodded, drawing a deep breath. "Peace is not something I am used to," he admitted.

"You must come to be at peace with yourself, Bagsby, oh my goodness yes, for you have much else with which to be being at war. And the time of trial is coming, so you must be being prepared."

"Time of trial?" Bagsby asked, laughing. "If you knew what the past few months had been like for me. . . ."

"Oh, I am knowing much of this," the old man chuckled. "These times have been like the scurrying of clouds in the sky before the coming of the great storm."

"Great storm?" Bagsby asked. "What great storm?"

"A time of testing for the world. And you are being in a major role placed," the old man said, his gaze intent now on Bagsby.

Bagsby shook his head back and forth. "No major roles in the great testing of the world for me!" he said. "I'm just a little guy, a thief. I've pulled off some good jobs, from time to time, I'll grant you that. And this last, well, that should earn me a reputation, certainly. But I'm not much of one for major roles in the testing of the world." Bagsby cast about, found a stick, whittled a quick point on it with his dagger. "I'll tell you what I am for," he said, plunging the sharp point into one of the chunks of beef. "I'm for something to eat."

"You will soon be regretting doing that," the old man said.

"Why? This meat poisoned?"

"Oh, goodness, no. But you will be needing it much more in just a little while. Be trusting the words of Ramashoon."

"So," Bagsby said, watching the salted meat begin to sweat grease into the fire, "your name is Ramashoon. Tell me, Ramashoon, how do you know so much about me and the future and the testing of the world?"

"I am spending my entire life in these mountains," Ramashoon replied. "I am spending much time in meditation and communion with the spirits that be residing here, and even with the gods of the world, you know. There is much that I am not knowing, but what I am telling you, I am knowing."

"Then tell me about the Golden Eggs," Bagsby said suddenly, leaning forward and thrusting his face close to Ramashoon's. "That's what I've come for. What is the secret of the Golden Eggs that even an elf woman who loves me refuses to divulge?"

"Be producing them, please," Ramashoon said quietly.

Bagsby reached beneath his tunic. From there he produced a small cloth sack. Without further comment, he opened it and shook out into his hand the two Golden Eggs of Parona.

"Full size, please," Ramashoon said.

Bagsby looked quizzically at the old man. "I won't be able to shrink them down again," he said.

"It is not mattering if they are shrunk for carrying after tonight," Ramashoon said simply.

Bagsby was perturbed. If he only had his wits about him, he thought, he'd find a way to make this strange old holy man talk, and then take his treasure and be on his way. But the old wits were failing him. If he wanted to know the secret, he would have to play along. Carefully, he set the eggs side by side on a flat spot of ground.

Bagsby inhaled deeply. Speaking slowly, forming each syllable with great care, he spoke the magic word of command that released Shulana's spell. In less time than the blink of an eye, the eggs were full size—three feet from base to crown, gold gleaming with inset gems in the reflected firelight.

"There," Bagsby said. "Now, tell me. What is the great secret of this treasure?"

"Be watching," Ramashoon said. "You will be that bag of meat much needing."

Bagsby flopped back, completely exasperated. This old holy man would tell him nothing. He had come all this way for nothing. Better to have taken the eggs straight to the elves and. . . .

Ramashoon softly muttered a few words of magic. Bagsby felt the earth tremble ever so slightly beneath his body. He sat upright and stared at the eggs.

The two eggs were moving, vibrating, shaking. This was the same movement he had detected from them many times in the past, but never with such force. Now the eggs were quaking, and the vibrations were being carried right into the ground, running along it.

"What's happening?" Bagsby demanded.

"Be watching," Ramashoon said. "For this, you and I were both being born."

Bagsby watched. The violent shaking of the eggs grew more and more pronounced until suddenly the quiet night was shattered by a loud popping sound. The crown of one egg flew up into the air, borne aloft by a stream of golden-yellow flame that rose to a height of thirty feet or more. The crown of the egg melted in the fire, falling molten to the earth.

Bagsby heard a low growl, and lowered his gaze from the top of the gush of flame to the earth. The broken egg had tipped over on its side, and out of the hole protruded a red, scaly, lizardlike head, with an enormous mouth rather like a crocodile's. The ruby-colored lizard head extended farther and farther out of the egg, until its body emerged—long, sinuous, and covered with deep red scales. There were two tiny legs in the front, ending in appendages almost like lizard hands, but in the rear were two large, powerful haunches, and then a tail that snaked around in coils. The sides were covered with great, wet flaps of flesh that the creature extended, slowly at first, then forcefully. Wings—they were wings, Bagsby realized. The creature slowly moved the wings back and forth in the still night air, drying them.

Then, without seeming to notice anything else in its surroundings, the red monster turned its attention to the other egg, still quaking and shaking violently. The creature drew in its breath, opened the huge mouth, and shot forth another gout of multihued flame, bathing the remaining egg until Bagsby could no longer see it for the flames. As suddenly as it had appeared, the breath of fire disappeared, and where the egg had stood another creature, seemingly identical to the first, slowly flexed its wings.

This second creature raised its head, breathed once, and shot its own column of fire into the black sky. Then it lowered its head, fixed Bagsby with a stare from one huge, black eye, and opened its mouth again.

"Feed us," the creature said.

His arm trembling, Bagsby reached for the bag of meat. Ramashoon rocked back and forth in the dim firelight, giggling with delight.

"Oh my goodness, yes, my friend Bagsby," Ramashoon's voice lilted. "Now there are being upon the earth dragons again, and you are responsible for them!"

4

A Rescue

"WHERE IS VALDAIMON?" demanded Baron Manfred Culdus, his angry voice echoing down the corridors of the east section of the king's palace in Hamblen. Anger flashed from his dark eyes as he clanked along the hallway, throwing open one door, then another, in his personal search for the author of his discontents. Nor was Culdus's anger a thing to be taken lightly. It was not the evil, chaotic rage of a creature like Valdaimon, nor the impotent, decadent rage of a besotted youth like King Ruprecht, but the cold, efficient anger of a professional soldier. All the court of Heilesheim knew that when Culdus was angry, there would be efficient, ruthless corrective action.

Unlike most of the court, Culdus, general in chief of the army of Heilesheim, designer of the military system that had borne such great fruits in the conquest of Dunsford, Argolia, and now the Duchies in the Land between the Rivers, knew full well that he could take efficient action only at the pleasure of the king. And the king's pleasure, more often than not, was guided by that stinking pustule Valdaimon, with his foul black arts, his zombies and ghouls, and now his damnable League of the Black Wing, which was supposed to be providing political consolidation of all the recent conquests.

"Where is Valdaimon?" Culdus bellowed again, into the empty halls. In the various rooms that occupied this section of the palace, the servants cringed at the sound of Culdus's voice. No one knew where Valdaimon was.

Culdus knew that no one knew, and that only made him angrier still. His massive form strode back down the hallway the way he had come, his impressive six feet and three inches of height so great that he had to duck his head when passing through the lower archways.

Ten thousand devils drag that wizard in pieces to their separate hells, Culdus thought, as he stomped back to the central section of the palace where the king awaited him. This kind of thing was just like him. In midcampaign, when the army was winning victory after victory, Valdaimon had disappeared. Normally, Culdus would have been grateful to him for taking his perpetual stench out of the way. But not now, when he was needed. So needed, in fact, by the dissipated king that Ruprecht demanded to be brought back to the capital, to the comforts and safety of his own palace, until the wizard was found. Culdus had no choice but to follow, leaving the army in the capable hands of the Legion commanders, but leaving undone much of the work needed for planning the next stages in the conquest of the Holy Alliance.

Culdus stormed into the royal presence. With Valdaimon absent, he could be much bolder with the king than he would ever dare when his archrival was on hand. The tall, thin, pale youth lounged on his high throne, his white blouse open rakishly in front to tempt the household serving girls. The king's gangly legs were propped over the sides of the throne. But fear showed in the king's eyes, and Culdus decided to make good use of that fear.

"Valdaimon is not here, Your Majesty," he reported. "His conduct is nothing short of treason. He has disappeared at a vital moment in Your Majesty's campaign. His League of the Black Wing, which was supposed to provide temporary governance for the conquered territories, is doing nothing. No decrees are posted, no instructions given for the cultivation of crops, no plans made for the harvests. The roads are unpatrolled except by the army; cutthroats, deserters, vagabonds, ruffians of every sort prowl everywhere at will. The common people, so far from productively pursuing their trades, are either taking to the open fields in fear for their lives and their few remaining goods, or else gathering in sullen mobs demanding action from the officers of the occupying forces. The drain on our manpower is staggering. In a campaign of a few months, Your Majesty has more than doubled the size of the territories ruled by Heilesheim, but thanks to the failure of the League, more than half Your Majesty's troops are now tied down with occupation duties. At that, they are barely able to keep the vital lines of supply open. There are no troops to spare for civil matters."

The king pulled himself around to a sitting position and gazed out into the emptiness of the great wood-paneled throne room. "I do not care about the pursuits of the common people in the occupied lands," he said acidly. "I want Valdaimon, and it is your job to find him for me. Can your army truly not find one man, a man who is rather . . . distinctive, at that?"

"Nothing would give me more pleasure, Your Majesty, than to find Valdaimon and so fulfill Your Majesty's desire," Culdus said carefully. By the gods, was the wizard's hold on the king so great that even this behavior would work to Valdaimon's advantage and Culdus's disadvantage? "Has it occurred to Your Majesty that Valdaimon has not been found because he does not want to be found? That his disappearance is simultaneous with the expected arrival of the great treasure, the Golden Eggs of Parona—and that no sign has been seen of that treasure? Your Majesty will recall that a high price was paid by Your Majesty to obtain that treasure from Parona. . . ."

"You don't understand!" the king said, suddenly rising. "I do not trust Valdaimon; but I do need him. I need him, do you understand?"

Culdus stood silent—he could think of no reply.

"Then Your Majesty's need is fulfilled," a familiar voice called from the entrance to the great hall. "I beg Your Majesty's forgiveness for my unexpected and unavoidable absence from the royal presence."

Culdus turned on his heel, his great face contorting in anger. "Traitor!" he shouted at the form of the withered wizard. "I arrest you for high treason against the king and the army of Heilesheim!"

"Silence, Culdus," the king ordered, relief visibly flooding through his thin form. Then the royal face betrayed alarm again. "Valdaimon, you are wounded . . . your eye. . . ."

"Lost in Your Majesty's service," the wizard replied, wrinkling his face with pain as his stooped form bowed slowly and deeply.

"It is our pleasure to hear our wizard's story," the king said, glancing sternly at Culdus, "before judging of his actions. Valdaimon, come, sit, and tell us where you have been."

Valdaimon slowly hobbled into the royal presence, smiling all the while at Culdus, his old enemy and rival for the king's favor. "It is good that our young king has a greater sense of justice than the general of our armies," Valdaimon said slowly. "But Your Majesty knows the military mind—it is all one way or the other for them, there is no room for the subtleties of thought enjoyed by men like Your Majesty."

Culdus saw how this game would be played, and he knew he could not win. If the old buzzard had lost an eye, more power to whomever had wounded him, Culdus thought.

"As Your Majesty has located Valdaimon," the general said dryly, "I beg to take leave of Your Majesty. There are pressing matters pertaining to the administration of the army—and the occupied lands—that demand my attention on Your Majesty's behalf."

"No, Culdus," the king said merrily. "Stay. After we hear old Valdaimon's tale, I have a surprise for you. A new campaign—that should excite you!"

Valdaimon and Culdus stared at one another, both shocked. Neither had anticipated any such development. Both knew that if the idea was genuinely Ruprecht's own, it could only mean grave danger for Heilesheim, and for both their ambitions.

"I will gladly stay to hear Your Majesty's intentions," Culdus managed to choke out.

"And I will gladly defer my boring story," Valdaimon said, nodding to Culdus, seeing that the general understood that for once they should act in concert, "so that Your Majesty may thrill us with the plan that has come to his mind."

George was surprised to find himself the leader of a group that consisted of two females and himself, and more surprised to realize they were on a fool's errand while Bagsby slipped farther and farther away with the treasure.

Shulana was the first to notice him missing. She arose from her time of communion, a time when her spirit touched the spirits of all things green and living and she immediatly knew. She had actually known while he was leaving, for the grass sprouts that bore his footsteps carried the burden of their passing to the flowers nearby, and the flowers in turn transmitted it to a small, sapling oak, which passed the impression on to a larger oak with roots extended deep into the meadow where Shulana lay entranced. From the shoots of grass beneath her head she felt his step as he slinked away— felt the lightness of his step, his gladness to be free, and the heaviness of his step, the guilt and confusion he carried with him. When Shulana emerged from her communion, these impressions were formed into conscious thoughts in her mind. *He's gone,* she thought, a rare elven tear forming in one eye, *and he's taken the treasure with him. He's taken my affection as well,* she thought—then quickly drove self-pity from her heart.

She pondered before waking George and Marta with the news. She, traveling alone, could easily overtake him—but to what end? She knew full well that her own feelings for the little thief would prevent her from killing him and reclaiming the treasure, and she knew his burning curiosity and stubbornness would prevent him from coming with her to the rescue of Elrond. Thus, there was no point in going after him. It would be better, she reasoned, to go at once to Elrond. If she could free Elrond from the clutches of Ruprecht, the older elf would know what to do next.

Bagsby's note confirmed her decision. He knew as well as she that freeing Elrond would now be her first priority.

But for that mission she would need George and Marta. She woke Marta first, calling the woman's name softly from a distance. She knew from experience that it was unwise to be too near when Marta first awakened.

"Hunh—what?" Marta startled awake, leaping to her feet, casting about on the ground for her weapons, a look of terror on her face.

"Marta, all is well, Marta. It is safe," Shulana called in a soft, gentle voice. "I only awakened you so we could talk."

Marta's furrowed brows slowly uncreased, and her eyes gradually lost their squinted appearance. The huge woman took a short, deep breath, snorted, and began rolling up her bed gear. "Then talk," she said shortly, her face slightly pink with embarrassment.

"Before we wake George, I wanted you to know that Bagsby is gone," Shulana said. The elf cocked her head slightly and studied the big woman's reaction.

Marta didn't even break stride. Stooped over, tramping around the campsite and gathering the multiple pieces of discarded junk that constituted her gear, she replied, "Gone, huh? Can't say I'm surprised. He's a thief and a knight, you know. Those types can't resist gold."

Shulana walked closer to Marta, put out one thin, pale hand, and touched the older woman on the shoulder. Marta lifted her head, the trace of disappointment and anger visible on her face, but fading already.

"You aren't . . . emotional about this?" Shulana asked. The elf was genuinely puzzled. She had expected anger from Marta, although not as much as she expected from George. But the woman looked more as though she had been betrayed than robbed; what traces of emotion showed in her face were more grief than anger.

"What good would it do?" Marta replied. "I joined on with Bagsby to strike against the murderers of my husband, not to get rich. There'll be time enough for that after Heilesheim is beat down into the dust."

Shulana nodded. She understood. "Would you be willing to work with me and continue to strike blows against Heilesheim?" she asked.

Marta stood to her full height, then bent backward, pushing with her hands against the small of her aching back. "Yes," she said, through a deep yawn. "I can do more damage with you than I can without you. What do you have in mind?" Marta shook her head once, to clear it. "Still wanting to go free that old elf in Ruprecht's dungeon, like Sir John suggested?"

"Yes," Shulana responded.

"Well," Marta said, picking up her sword and scabbard and attaching them to the wide sash of cloth she used as a belt, "I'm with you."

"What about George?" Shulana asked.

"Don't you worry," Marta said, looking up to judge the position of the sun. Midmorning. Time to get the lazy deserter up anyway. "I'll take care of George," she declared firmly.

"What?" George shrieked as Marta's kick bit into his back between two ribs. "What? Who?" The soldier rolled onto his back, reflexively grabbing for the aching place in his back, his dark eyes glinting their anger. He suddenly squinted as his turn brought his face directly under the midmorning sun.

"Get up!" Marta demanded. "We've got to march all the way to Hamblen, and we might as well get going. It's bad enough that that no-good thief snuck off while we slept, and now you think you have to sleep away the day and leave the women to protect your sorry ass," she barked, ignoring George's stammering attempts to reply. "Now get up and let's get going, before you take a notion to desert us like you did your blackhearted army."

"Marta!" George finaly managed. "Wot's got into you?" The man rose to his knees, kneading the bruise that was forming on his back. "Just because Bagsby's run off, there's no reason to . . . Bagsby's run off? Wit' the treasure?"

"That he has," Marta affirmed. She tossed George's meager roll of weapons and clothes onto the ground in front of him. "And if you ever want to see that treasure again, you'll help us get to Hamblen in a hurry."

Shulana stood silently, awed by this performance. She had seen bluff and bluster used by humans before—Bagsby was a master of it—but she had never seen a female utilize such a presumptive attitude. Any decent elf would have sat down and calmly discussed the facts of the situation, allowing George to form his own opinions and choose his own course of action. Or they would have threatened him—although under the circumstances, Shulana could not think of any credible threat she could use against George. But this Marta, she was . . . remarkable.

" 'Ere now," George said, " 'Ow long 'as Bagsby been gone? Can't be that long. The elf there could trail 'im. 'E can't just take my—our—treasure like that and disappear," the soldier protested, slipping into his pants and pausing, puzzled, to notice they were clean.

"Pounded them out on a rock for you," Marta declared. "Couldn't stand to see you wearing them stinking things day after day after day, smelling and drawing flies. . . ."

"But our treasure!" George protested.

"Sir John's gone with the treasure and that's that. He can travel twice as fast as we can, maybe faster, and we could spend the rest of our lives trailing after him and never see one gold coin in our pockets," Marta said firmly. "Now get dressed. We're going to go get that old elf. And when we do, he can set the entire elven race out to find Bagsby, which I'm sure he will, bad as he wants them eggs." Marta started trudging across the field toward the high road to Hamblen. "And if we don't get the price of the treasure, we'll at least get a reward for helping the old elf find it," she called over her shoulder.

"Bless my 'arse, Marta, but if you ain't the smartest thing wot ever was, I don't know wot is!" George said, stumbling forward through the grass, drawing his tunic over his head with one hand as he tried to keep up with the behemoth who had captured his desire.

Shulana silently trotted forward to take her usual position at the head of the party. She would never understand humans, she decided.

" 'Ere now, elf girlie," George called. " 'Ere now, not so fast. 'Ey Marta, stop there a minute, stop I say," George growled, stomping the earth with his foot. "This ain't like it was on the other side of the river. We're in Heilesheim now, and any elf is goin' to be taken for a spy and any woman refugee is goin' to be . . . ," George paused, uncertain of what words to use, ". . . badly used," he finally said. "Now, 'ere's the plan. You, Shulana, you're my prisoner see, and I'm takin' to 'Amblen for the bounty on spies and elves and such like." George smoothed his tunic over the top of his breeches, and began the slow process of putting on his chain mail. "And Marta, 'ere," he continued as the mail shirt slid over his face, "she's a wench wot I picked up along the way, and she's like my woman, understand? And I got legitimate orders, I do, from Sir Harold von Dorningberg, commander of the Fifth Legion, to take this elf traitor to the king's court at 'Amblen for questionin'." George secured his sword and scabbard, then picked up his huge pike and slung it over his left shoulder, leaving his right arm free. "And the reason she ain't tied or nothin' is, well, I didn't want 'er to 'ave no excuse for slowin' me down, see?" he concluded.

Marta turned her back to George and caught Shulana's eye. She gave Shulana a huge wink, as if to say, girl to girl, "That's how to handle them." But to George she said, "Well, George, now you're doing a man's job. See why we need you to help us?"

George was surprised at how easy their progress was, and how slow. The first day they made good time, until they passed the intersection with the great road running north–south of Shallowford. There, the great highway was choked with soldiers, prisoners, and the endless streams of slow supply wagons which, by military order, took precedence over everything else. There were also camp followers, occasional dignitaries with their own armed guards and lengthy trains, merchants with their trains of goods, and companies of retained guards—heavier guards, it seemed to George, than usual. This stream of humanity moved in both directions on the road, with many, many stops to allow the priority supply trains to pass.

George learned to spot the signs that a supply train was coming. First, he'd see cavalry in the distance, a small troop of ten or so, moving at a slow trot, calling out a warning or whacking in the head with the flat of their swords any pedestrian or rider who was slow to get out of their way. Behind them would come the plodding wagons, some drawn by oxen, some by mules, and some by horses—it seemed to George as though half the beasts of Heilesheim must have been pressed into service. Each train contained at least thirty wagons, and some were much longer; George and Shulana counted one train that contained no fewer than sixty-three heavily laden, large wagons. Other trains contained other vehicles as well: small carts, pushcarts propelled by the strength of impressed peasants, and even some large carriages—too weathered and worn to be of use to the appearance conscious nobles, but with enough room to contain barrels and boxes and casks of the various impedimentia demanded by the mass of troops now located in the Duchies and Argolia to the north.

Marta was impressed. "Never saw so many things— never dreamed there were so many things in the whole world, George," she said to the soldier as the odd threesome stood by the roadside, awaiting the passage eastward of one of the long trains.

"The army is requiring an enormous amount of supplies," Shulana observed. "I thought it was the way of Heilesheim troops to live off the land as they traveled through it."

"It is," George acknowledeged. "That is, when they're movin'. Ever been in a village where one of our legions has camped for a bit?"

"I have," Marta said, her voice flat. "What they can't eat, rape, or carry off at once, they burn," she said. "Senseless."

"Supposed to strike terror into the 'eart of the enemy," Geroge said, by way of explanation.

"How much terror do you see in the heart of this enemy of Heilesheim, George?" Marta retorted.

George looked at her, puzzled; it had never occurred to him that his former officers might be wrong about such a basic matter of policy. He tried to think about it for a moment, tired of the effort, and shrugged.

"Look, there," he said, pointing to the cloud of dust on the horizon. "There's the last of them. We can move out soon."

And so the group progressed with painful slowness toward Hamblen. Most days they spent more time sitting by the roadside, letting higher-priority traffic pass, than they actually did moving.

"Why don't we move away from the road and travel west over the open fields," Shulana suggested during one of their countless stops.

"Traffic off the road will draw attention," George explained. "Besides, nobles don't like it. Tears up their fields. If we go off the road, them camp followers will take up the idea. Then a few merchants will try, and next thing you know, m'lord's good grain field is a trodden mess, and no hot bread for his lordship's breakfast come winter."

But George was suprised at the ease with which they moved among the crowds and the armymen. Whenever any officer was in sight, George took pains to stand stiffly erect while marching along, a scowl on his face and his eyes, looking as mean as he could make them, glued on Shulana whom he would occasionally push and curse. Not once was he stopped and questioned concerning his orders or intentions.

There were occasional incidents, but not of the type George had expected. The first occurred when they encountered a troop of one hundred recruits on march to the front. The men were spread out by the roadside, apparently having decided that it was futile to take to the highway. George noticed at once that these were green troops, poorly led, and city boys at that. Most had discarded their armor, preferring to let the packhorses carry that weight—something no regular officer would ever have allowed a troop on the march to do. The men looked lean and hungry. No veteran would ever be hungry in the midst of such abundance on the road. And their hands, George noticed, passing close by them, were smooth—they didn't have the calluses that wielding a soldier's pike or a farmer's scythe quickly built up—though several seemed to have a fine set of blisters on both hands and feet.

They were in the midst of passing the group when the first catcalls began.

"Ah, lookee there!" one fresh imp called. "What we got there? Is that an elf—the little pointy-eared devil—is that an elf there?"

"I think it is an elf—and a female elf at that," a second youth bellowed. He was a large, burly man; George quickly guessed him to be about sixteen years old. The stocky fellow got to his feet and planted himself in the road, squarely in front of Shulana, who abruptly stopped.

"By all the gods, it is a female elf," the young brute called to his comrades. "Look at it—scrawny thing, ain't it? No wonder them elves are already a dying race, if this is what they have for breeding stock."

Guffaws greeted this remark, encouraging the lad.

"Wonder what would happen if we was to . . . invigorate their race a bit?" he taunted, reaching out to run a thick finger down Shulana's cheek.

" 'Ere now, laddie, don't be 'armin' me goods," George sang out. "This one 'ere is me prisoner. Going to collect the bounty for 'er, after the king's own court questions 'er."

"Can't damage an elf," the youth replied, looking back to his comrades for support. "They're either dead or they ain't dead. And if they ain't dead, they're no good, so how could you damage one?"

More hoots of laughter. George joined in. "That's a truth," he chuckled. "Still, I'll be gettin' this one to 'Amblen, if you don't mind."

"We don't mind," the boy persisted. "We just want to make a quick detour, don't we lads?"

A cheer rang out from the roadside. Many of the men were on their feet now, expecting a bit of sport. By the gods, George thought, don't these rabble have an officer?

"Is it a bit of sport you're wanting?" George asked.

"That it is," the stocky blond answered, running his hands down Shulana's sides as George stepped up beside him.

"Then I suggest," George said, swinging his pike down and to the side in one smooth gesture, catching the ruffian squarely in the shins and sending him sprawling on his backside, "that you practice your manual of arms. That's sport enough for the likes of you." George spat in the young man's face. "And learn to show some respect for veterans," he said, shoving Shulana in the back and propelling her rapidly on down the road, "who've been killing enemies of Heilesheim while you were still growing fat and soft at your mother's breast!" George raised the pike and turned with his front squarely to the gathered crowd of men. "The rest of you, as you were. If you ain't got no officer to keep some discipline about you, take your orders from one that could kill the lot of you before 'avin' breakfast in the mornin'."

The recruits drifted back from the roadside. George snorted in disgust and backed away, while Marta marched ahead, keeping a keen eye to both sides of the road as she came up behind the trembling Shulana. The threesome walked on for about a mile before any of them spoke.

Shulana broke the silence. "I am not used to such treatment from humans," she said. "I did not know there was such hatred of elves in Heilesheim."

"Not all of Heilesheim, and not all humans, dearie," Marta said, soothingly. "Me and George here, we thinks the world of you. And elves was always treated with courtesy in Shallowford, before these army beasts showed up."

"Don't recall as there ever was so much problem about elves in Heilesheim before," George remarked, genuinely puzzled. "Just before the war there was a lot of talk about elves doin' this and that, but I never took it serious."

"It would seem that attitudes have changed," Shulana said. "I doubt the Covenant is respected in this hostile land."

"Well," George admitted, "there was some talk among the officers about how the Covenant was just an elvish trick to keep us from getting justice on elves who came into Heilesheim and made lots of money on the trade." He shrugged. "I never paid it no mind."

"I am grateful to you," Shulana said. "Those men would have harmed me."

"Ain't nobody goin' to 'arm you or Marta while George is about," the soldier said proudly.

"Let's hope not," Marta rejoined.

How much better it would be, Shulana thought, if Bagsby were about.

George's story about his elven prisoner was enough to get the threesome through the great gate of Hamblen, through which they passed well after midnight with a stream of other weary travelers. So great was the traffic that the guards were halfhearted in their duties, eager to pass through one group so they could get to the next and keep the bottleneck at the gate from becoming even more chaotic than it was.

Inside the gate was a modest plaza, normally quiet at night but crowded now with vendors, hawking their wares to the incoming throngs even in the darkness, and hundreds of plump, well-dressed children who competed with one another for the attention of the most wealthy travelers, to whom they would extol the virtues of one of the city's numerous places of lodging.

But dominating all was the great marble archway at the far end of the square. It was covered with friezes of battle scenes from Heilesheim's past and crowned with a row of golden battle flags from which the black dragon-wing insignia of Ruprecht's house looked down on every visitor to the city. The great arch led to the Royal Road, which connected the Temple of Wojan in the heart of the city with the royal palace and great fortress on the River Rigel on the city's eastern side.

Marta stopped, stock-still, when she saw the arch; her large mouth hung open, momentarily giving her the appearance of someone rather stupid. Shulana, too, gazed about in some wonder, but not awe. Rather, she wondered how humans could live in such mobs and surround themselves with such unnatural things as the arch—which with its massive size and solidity seemed to her the antithesis of all things living.

"C'mon," George said. "Through 'ere." George had been in Hamblen countless times; he thought no more of its wonders than Marta would think of a sack of flour. "Pull that cloak on against the chill," George said to Shulana.

The elf understood George's subtle hint. From the small bag in which she carried her few belongings she took her magic cloak and quickly donned it. The result was remarkable. Even George, who stood directly beside her, could hardly see her— so completely did the cloak blend in with the dark background. It was just as well, George thought. If the troops were so worked up about elves, there was no telling what the stupid people of Hamblen might be like on the subject.

"Follow me," George said, striking off boldly through the crowded, dark street and heading toward the massive arch to the Royal Road. There he paused, wondering at the masses of humanity who were flowing westward on the road, deeper into the city. Many times had he been to the capital, but never had he seen it this crowded, and never had he seen the Royal Road so thronged at night. Somewhere in the inarticulate recesses of his mind, George sensed that something was amiss. But such questions would have to wait. His own route, and that of the two women, led east.

The crowd thinned dramatically as it made its way toward the palace grounds; only an occasional mounted soldier sped from east to west down the broad boulevard. Along its sides, the kings of Heilesheim—immortalized in marble—glared dumbly at the passersby, frozen in postures of war. George stared back at them, a mindless fury slowly rising in his breast.

"These are the kings of Heilesheim?" Shulana asked.

"Who else would these barbarians glorify but their war kings?" Marta curtly rejoined.

"Aye, these are our kings," George muttered savagely. "Look at 'em. Every one of 'em dreamin' of killin' and conquest and lands and booty—an' never a thought for once about them wot 'ad to do the killin' and the conquerin' for 'em."

"To have raised this city, and to have created the sheer abundance of things we have seen on the roads from this place, some of these kings must have had some skill or merit," Shulana said. She had thought George would be proud of the accomplishments of his people. She had noticed many times that George had no love for the nobility, but the intensity of the anger she sensed building in him was incomprehensible. How could he hate his own race? How could he hate the people who bore him?

"Lots of folk 'ave built cities," George said, "an' made themselves rich while doing it. It takes a special sort to delight in the destruction of it all, and an even more special sort to think that men like me got nothin' better to do than slave away to make men like them more mighty and rich." George stopped walking; his eyes squinted into the dark distance. "Speakin' of kings, there's where the one we got now lives," he said, pointing with his pike into the dark distance.

Marta strained her eyes as the threesome moved forward again, this time more slowly. Ahead of them, the Royal Road ended in a massive iron gate, about which a group of slouching guards were clustered. The great iron structure, fully eighteen feet high, seemed strangely incongruous, for its mighty stone supports were flanked by a small fence of iron spikes that even a mischievous child could cross in a matter of seconds.

Beyond the fence, the gardens stretched out, gently rolling, with a small stream meandering through them. There were mazes of hedges off to each side, and small paths through carefully sculpted beds of flowers. In the center of the great gardens, the stream fell over a small hilltop and down into a clear pool, forming the backdrop to another small rise on which the great dragon insignia of Heilesheim was sculpted in flowers that, with the aid of Valdaimon's magic, blossomed black.

Though she could barely see the colors in the darkness of the night, Marta shuddered involuntarily at the sight of the spread dragon-wings design; it was the same design that Ruprecht himself had burned into the flesh of her back that dreadful night that seemed so long ago.

" 'Ere now," George said, leading the party to small bench at the roadside between two of the sanguine royal statues. "We'd best bind your arms, Shulana. You're supposed to be a prisoner, you know."

"What is your plan?" Marta demanded, in a hoarse whisper.

"Walk in the front door," George said. "Them gardens is just the beginning, and they let almost anybody in there. Beyond is the fortified wall, where the real gate is." George casually reached out and took Shulana's hands. He quickly wrapped a long, narrow leather thong around her wrists, making more than a dozen loops before tying the thong off. "I learned a few things from ol' Bagsby," he said, grinning at Shulana. "The best way to get in anywhere is to act like you belong there." His skillful fingers had woven a tight knot. Only two very short pieces, the ends of the thong, protruded from the knot. "Lookee 'ere, girlie. If we get in a bad way and you needs your 'ands, just put one of these ends in your mouth, grab it with your teeth, and pull hard. This whole knot'll fall apart in a flash."

"Her you can march in as a prisoner," Marta said. "What about me?"

"You're the witness wot saw 'er spyin' on the army 'afor the battle at Clairton," George said, smiling broadly. "Come to tell 'is Majesty wot you saw."

Marta nodded. Anticipating the new environment of the city, she had already toned down her customary costume; she no longer wore armor or carried a visible weapon. Instead, she dressed like a common peasant woman in a coarse, brown, full-length tunic, tied around the waist with a bit of rope. She still wore good boots, though, and had a dagger secreted in the right one. The remainder of her belongings were tied in a large bundle strapped to her back.

"Awright, let's go," George said.

The threesome again made their way onto the roadway. George led them at a smart pace straight up to the gate, pushing Shulana in the back from time to time, causing her to stumble forward. It was the effect he desired.

"Who goes there?" one of the slothful guards challenged as the group came into clear sight, heading directly for the gate. The man stepped forward to meet the party, his arm extended in the gesture meaning "halt." George noticed he didn't bother to draw his sword, and the rest of the men continued their conversation, not even reaching for their pikes.

"George, miller's son, of the Fifth Legion, with a prisoner for the royal dungeon and the royal court," George answered smartly.

"Prisoner?" the guard said, stepping up to George and looking curiously at Shulana, who averted her eyes from the man's gaze.

"Elf. Caught spying on the main army at the battle of Clairton. I've got orders to deliver her personal to main dungeons 'ere, and see she's questioned proper," George explained.

The guard nodded. An elf prisoner. Well, the officers ought to like that, he thought. The man turned his gaze briefly to Marta. "No camp followers, though," he said. "Orders is orders."

"Ain't no camp follower," George protested. "She's a witness. She's the one wot caught this 'ere elf in the act. Come to tell about it, she 'as."

"Well . . . ," the guard mused.

"And," George added, leaning forward to convey a confidence, "she's a great one for sportin' wit', if you know wot I mean. Help an old soldier wot's earned 'imself a reward stay a bit more comfortable on a warm summer night." George poked the man gently in the ribs.

"Alright, alright," he relented. "Pass."

By similar means, the threesome continued through the inner gate at the fortress wall. There, the captain of the guard, more smartly alert than the fellows at the outer gate, detailed one of his men to escort the group directly to the dungeons so the elf could be put safely under lock and key. "Take them to the lower dungeon in the east wing, where they keep that other old elf," he instructed. Watching the group depart into the bowels of the palace, the captain had a second thought. "Go inform His Majesty," he told another man, "that an elf spy has been captured at the front and is now being placed in the lower dungeon near the other elf prisoner."

George, Marta, and Shulana were afforded only the briefest glimpse of the entry hall to the great central section of the palace, the official quarters of the king. What little George saw rekindled his smoldering anger. The hall was paneled with dark hardwoods; the amount of the wood used to make the walls would cost a whole village's annual earnings. Over these wooden walls were hung tapestries whose threads of crimson, azure, gold, and silver gleamed in the light of great crystal chandeliers, ablaze with countless candles. There were rare furnishings—small tables, chairs, and settees, any one of which would be worth a thief's life for six months. Everywhere there was an air of opulent decadence such as George had never before encountered.

"King lives well," George commented to their guard and guide.

"Hunh," the stout, slightly flabby man snorted. "Ain't nothin'. You should see the rest of the place." The man turned immediately to the right outside the entrance to the hall and led them down a narrow corridor of stone lighted by torches in wall sconces. "But," he added, "them parts of this place ain't for the likes of you and me." The man stopped before an iron-banded, wooden door, fumbled with a jingling ring of black, iron keys, and finally got the door open. "Down 'ere's where we belong, and down 'ere's where we go," he joked.

The group made its way down a narrow, winding, stone staircase. Shulana noticed that the stone steps were well worn, with smooth depressions in their centers. They descended for five full revolutions before coming to another locked door. Again the guard fumbled with his keys, before ushering the group into a narrow corridor, the walls of which were made of cut stone. The sconces were less frequent here, and there was a slight chill of damp in the air. There were more corridors, more doors, more stairs.

"A fellow could get 'imself lost down 'ere," George commented to the guard.

"Aye, if he don't know it well," the man answered. "Part of the plan, I reckon. Once in a great while someone gets loose down here. But I ain't never heard of no one makin' it out."

"Only a fool would test the strength of the garrison in this maze," Shulana said, the first time she had spoken since entering the palace grounds.

"Shut up, you scum!" the guard barked, shoving Shulana's head savagely against the stone wall. "Prisoners don't speak."

"Careful!" George interjected, wrapping an arm around the elf as she began to sag to the floor, stunned by the force of the double blow to her head. "If you damage me goods, I may not get me full reward." The elf had courage, George thought to himself. He realized she was telling him not to worry about memorizing the maze—she had some other plan in mind for getting them out. That was good, George thought. He certainly hadn't seen any way for them to get away from this place.

"Hunh!" the guard was saying. "Awful protective of that little thing, ain't you? Is she good for a bit of sport, too?" he grunted.

"Not after your lot gets done wit' 'er," George jested back.

"Hunh," came the reply. The man stopped in front of yet another narrow, locked door, selected the key, then opened it. "Through here." he said, throwing the door open.

The smell hit all three of them at once—a damp, fetid smell, mixed with the pungent, sharp-but-sweet odor of rotting flesh and slowly decaying dried blood. Only Shulana detected an underlying odor of something green and living, even in that environment of death—the smell of damp moss growing in the cracks between the stones in the floor.

"This here is where we keep the instruments," the guard explained. He grabbed a torch from the nearest sconce and bounced into the room, lighting the wall tapers as he chattered merrily. "There's the rack," he said, pointing to a large wooden table equipped with iron cuffs for the feet and hands and surrounded by a complex series of iron chains and wooden cogs. The man lit another taper. "This here is the prisoner's wife," he said, pointing to an upright chest that was rather like a sarcophagus, with a vaguely feminine shape. It stood open, and from the interior of both the top and bottom iron spikes protruded in abundance. The guard went on to illuminate the rest of the large room. There was a large fireplace, with rows of knives, spears, pokers, and brands neatly arrayed nearby. A wooden chair sat off in an open space, equipped with thumbscrew. Large iron buckets were scattered about the floor, some filled with water, some with foul waste.

"We hear many a fine song in here, you might imagine!" the guard said. "There's a wheel, too—right through that door," he added, gesturing to one of the three exits from the room.

"Impressive," George played along.

"Yes, but where do they keep the elf prisoners?" Marta whined. "I'm tired," she clamped a firm hand on George's shoulder, "and I need something to eat and some sleep. And you promised me I could see any other elf prisoners." The fat woman contorted her face into a pathetic pout.

"Alright, alright," the guard said, answering George's unspoken plea. "We keep that other elf right through this door," he said, fumbling again with his key ring. "The old wizard, Valdaimon, is mostly in charge of him. He keeps him here so we don't have to take him very far when we want to hear him sing," the man said, chuckling.

George glanced at Shulana, who nodded in the affirmative.

"No you don't," Marta said aloud. "This one is mine."

"What?" the guard said, turning from the door where he had just inserted the proper key.

Marta rushed up to the man, grabbing him around the waist from behind. "You're so cute and funny," she said, "I want to give you a little hug!"

Marta lifted the man off his feet and, against his laughing protests, carried him back across the room.

"Hey, now, I thought you was with him," the man said. "C'mon, put me down, and we can work something out."

"First, you're going to get your hug," Marta protested, releasing the man, spinning him around, and slamming him backside first into the bottom of the prisoner's wife.

"Aaawwk!" was the only sound the stunned man could manage as the iron spikes dug into his flesh. Blood spurted from a dozen wounds, and the man flapped his still free arms, trying to grasp the edges of the device to gain leverage to pull himself off the points.

"No, no, stay still," Marta scolded, deadly fire in her eyes. "Here comes your hug."

Marta slammed shut the lid, then threw the full weight of her body against it, pressing hard. Stifled wet sounds came from within, then silence. A pool of blood slowly formed as the red fluid trickled through the crack in the bottom of the device.

"Let's go," Marta said.

Shulana had already unbound her wrists and sprung to the doorway. She flipped the key in the lock and pulled open the door. There, in the darkness, cruciform in manacles and hanging against the far wall, was the frail, horribly thin, white-haired form of Elrond, leader of the Elven Council and the oldest member of his race. His face was pressed flat against the cold, wet stone, and his pale eyes were rolled upward so that only the whites were showing.

George peered into the chamber over the stooped Shulana. He could see little in the darkness and motioned for Marta to bring a torch. As his eyes adjusted, aided by the sputtering light Marta held above the threesome, George shook his head.

"We're too late," he said. " 'E's dead."

"No," Shulana said very softly. "He is listening to something—something very far away."

* * *

Culdus stifled a groan as the servants lugged into the throne room a table that the general immediately recognized as his own large worktable, for it was covered with his campaign maps and blocks of wood he used to mark the positions of his legions on the maps. If these idiots had disturbed his papers. . . .

"I wanted to show you this on your own maps, Culdus," Ruprecht enthused. "I've figured it all out completely. You will be amazed."

Culdus again exchanged glances with Valdaimon as the servants arranged the table and brought heavy wooden chairs for the king and his two highest servants.

"Sit, sit!" Ruprecht commanded, his dark eyes ablaze with the excitement that he usually reserved for moments of lust or torture. There was a different lust burning in that decadent brain now, Culdus thought. What was it?

"Go!" the king ordered the servants. What he had to say was for the ears of Valdaimon and Culdus alone.

The youth crawled up with his knees in the seat of the chair, his body perched forward on the table. "Look," he said. "Here is a map of the entire area of our current campaign."

Culdus hardly needed to look—that map was emblazoned in his memory. The long, east-to-west expanse of Heilesheim in the south, its border, the River Rigel, separating it from the patchwork of states called the Duchies and from Dunsford to the immediate north. Farther north was Argolia, and beyond that, the southern border of Parona, the great power of the north. In the far east, beyond Heilesheim's own eastern desert where the city of Laga marked the farthest extent of civilization, the great Eastern Mountains rose, running northward the length of the known world. Those same mountains formed the eastern border of Parona and then turned to the west, forming its northern border as well.

Another great river, the Pregel, ran southwest from the northern mountains. Tucked against the south side of that river was the Elven Preserve, a long, narrow stretch of woodlands where the remaining elves of the world lived, protected by the Covenant that had ended the horrid wars between them and humankind. On its western and southern sides, the Elven Preserve bordered the occupied lands of Argolia and the Duchies.

Wooden blocks, carefully arranged by the king, showed the current positions of the Heilesheim army's ten legions. Six were in Argolia, all within two days' march of the northern border of that land, ready for rapid concentration against Parona, the next target in the plan of conquest. Two of the other four were currently involved in sieges against fortifications along the Rigel, strongpoints of the already doomed resistance. Two more were now scattered to the winds, occupied in garrison duties. These the king had indicated as being present in Dunsford—as good a representation as any, since the land route through Dunsford was the vital supply and communications artery of the entire army.

"Here," Ruprecht said proudly, "are the present locations of our troops. Is this accurate, Culdus?" The eager young face turned up from the table.

Culdus stared at the narrow head, the sharp, aquiline nose, the thin chin, the greasy, tangled locks of curly, black hair that spilled down the king's neck. Why, he wondered, was he giving his genius, perhaps the greatest military genius in a millennium, to this whelp who was in the thrall of Valdaimon?

"Accurate enough, Your Majesty," the general replied.

"And as any fool can see, we are poised like a dagger near the southern border of Parona. Yet we are dispersed just enough to keep the enemy wondering where the blow will fall," the king lectured.

"We are not yet at war with Parona," Valdaimon reminded the king. "The schedule prepared by Baron Culdus—"

"Is not being met," the king said shortly. "The invasion of Parona should have begun a week ago, and we are behind, behind, behind!"

"As I have earlier tonight attempted to explain to Your Majesty," Culdus began, seeing an opening, "the failure of the League of the Black Wing to. . . ."

"No matter," the king snapped, cutting him off. "We are not going to invade Parona."

"But Majesty!" thundered Culdus, "never has there been such an opportunity for Heilesheim's arms! We have swept the center of the world—only the northlands remain! With time to organize our rear areas, we can yet. . . ."

"Truly, Culdus is correct, Majesty," Valdaimon cut in. "War with Parona is inevitable, and it could never come at a better time than. . . ."

"Than after the conquest of the Elves!" the king shouted, leaping to his feet on the tabletop, sending the carefully arranged wooden blocks flying.

Valdaimon and Culdus stared dumbly at the king.

"It is our will," the wastrel monarch began. "No. It is our order, Lord Culdus, that you prepare the army for a movement against the Elven Preserve. We will attack first from the southwest, the narrow end of the Preserve nearest us. We will march north and east, clearing their forest world as we go, and then larger forces, now deployed in Argolia, will invade from the flank, crushing the remaining elven resistance. In the meantime, those troops will play the great role of guarding our invasion against any interference from Parona, or the few bands of rebels still roaming about in Argolia."

Valdaimon was the first to break the awkward silence that followed the king's outburst. The old wizard spread his thin, long, yellowing fingers flat against the smooth surface of the map, stroking it gently. "Your Majesty has obviously given this great thought," he said. "But not even I had an idea that Your Majesty intended to renew the wars against the elves, which proved so . . . difficult to our ancestors."

"See, see!" the king jubilated. "Even Valdaimon is surprised! Isn't that grand, Culdus! Even the very father of cunning and intrigue is surprised. The whole world will be stunned by our boldness!"

"I confess that I, too, am quite surprised," Culdus said. "Pray confide to me Your Majesty's reasons for wishing to delay war with Parona while fighting the elves—who are not part of the Holy Alliance and have thus far maintained their neutrality in all human struggles."

Ruprecht leapt from the tabletop to the floor. He spun around to face Culdus, a smirk on his face. "Because," he said, "I don't like elves." The young ruler's face was alight with a broad smile. His voice lowered to a hoarse whisper. "What greater proof of our absolute power could there be," the king demanded, placing a hand on Culdus's mighty forearm and stooping to gaze earnestly into the old general's eyes, "than the extermination of an entire race merely to satisfy our royal whim? We shall be thought of as a god!"

You shall be thought of as a demon, and a damnably stupid one at that, Culdus thought.

"Your Majesty's point is well taken, well taken," Valdaimon said thoughtfully. "However, there are certain practical . . . obstacles to the immediate execution of this . . . inspired plan," the old man oozed.

"What obstacles?" Ruprecht demanded, standing erect, a slight pout showing on his pale face. "Have not both of you informed me that I now command the greatest military force in the history of mankind?"

"That is true, Your Majesty," Valdaimon soothed. "Very true. However, the magic of the elves is very. . . ."

"We know all about the fabled magic of the elves," Ruprecht retorted. "We are not impressed. At this moment is there not an elf, a very old and powerful one at that, in our dungeon in clear violation of the Covenant? What magic has he used against us? What protest has been forwarded from the Elven Council? What reprisals have the elves taken? Their magic cannot be of such great power, or they would not allow themselves to be so treated," the king concluded.

"Their magic could destroy the entire world if it were unleashed all at once," Valdaimon said plainly, struggling to rise. "Your Majesty is very young, and does not understand the nature of magical power. That is why Your Majesty has always relied on my judgment in such matters, and why I must implore Your Majesty to do so now. Strike Parona! Rule the human world! But do not break the Covenant at this moment. What would your own subjects say?"

"His own subjects," Culdus interjected coldly, "would applaud such a move. At His Majesty's orders, the entire army and much of the population has been subjected to endless tirades against the elves. I did not before see the purpose of these. Now I do," the general said, his voice tinged with sadness.

"Precisely!" The king ran through the great empty room and leapt onto his throne. "Precisely! You see, I have politically prepared the kingdom for this step, and you did not even notice. As for the elven magic you fear, Valdaimon," Ruprecht said, glaring at the old man from his seat of power, "if you cannot find some way to deal with it, then perhaps it is time we sought counsel from another mage, someone more youthful, more vigorous."

Valdaimon sensed great danger. He had played for years on the boy's ego, never dreaming that he would produce the full-blown megalomaniac that now confronted him. For his own aims to be achieved, Valdaimon still needed this king. But war with the elves was a risk beyond all calculation. How could magic of that most magical of all races—save dragons—be negated? And how could that be done now, when all Valdaimon's energies were urgently needed to find the Golden Eggs and obtain their secret?

"I am ever Your Majesty's servant," Valdaimon said smoothly, forcing his stiff, withered form into a painful bow. "I shall, of course, obey Your Majesty's will." The old wizard turned his eyes to catch those of Culdus. *Help me, my old enemy,* he thought, *help me.* "If my services are no longer desired by. . . ."

"Enough!" Ruprecht snapped. "As long as you obey, you may maintain you position in our court."

"It cannot be done," Culdus said flatly, slamming his great right hand flat on the table. "It is madness and suicide. It will destroy the army for no gain."

"Explain yourself," Ruprecht said coldly.

"Our entire military system is based upon fighting in open ground. We have won victory after victory that way. To fight in those tangled, infernal, enchanted woods, where our mass formations cannot be used—where the tactical finesse we have perfected over the years will be meaningless—to risk the entire army in such a campaign with untamed Parona lurking to the north, it is. . . ."

"It is our will," Ruprecht said, rising slowly. "Do you mean to tell me that the greatest army in history cannot root a few thousand elves out of a wood? I will not hear such nonsense. Speak it again, and you will no longer be our chief general!"

Culdus rose and bowed deeply from the waist. From the bottom of his heart he wanted nothing more than to draw his great sword, step forward, and cleave that arrogant runt from crown to crotch, ending once and for all the charade of Ruprecht's rule. The army was the soul of Heilesheim. It had ever been the soul of the country, and it ever would be. Kings were but ornaments, like banners at the head of the marching columns. But, Culdus thought, for the army to rule, it must dip itself in the stench of politics. It must truck with the likes of merchants and peasants, and mire itself down in the trivia of politics. For the army to rule, it must corrupt itself, and thereby corrupt the soul of the nation. More honorable, Culdus thought, to die in battle than to rot from within.

"I and the army are ever Your Majesty's loyal servants," Culdus said slowly. "The army will obey Your Majesty."

"Your Majesty," a voice called from the entrance to the hall. "An urgent communication from the captain of the palace guard."

"Enter," Ruprecht said lightly, waving a hand toward the groveling soldier in the doorway. "Up, up, you two," he added, waving merrily to Culdus and Valdaimon. "We are disappointed you do not embrace our plan with enthusiasm, but we are gratified by your loyalty. Now," he continued, turning to the messenger, "what urgent report awaits our pleasure?"

"Your Majesty," the soldier said, kneeling with his face downcast while he spoke, "the captain of the palace guard bids me report to you that a prisoner has been brought to the palace for questioning, a spy taken at the battle of Clairton. The prisoner is an elf, Your Majesty."

"Another elf?" Ruprecht cried, his eyes wide with delight. "You see, you see?" he called to Valdaimon and Culdus. "They were spying on us? They have broken Covenant—they have broken the Covenant, and openly!"

"Your Majesty," the soldier continued, "I am instructed to report that the prisoner is a female elf. She is being lodged in a cell near to the other elf prisoner in Your Majesty's most secure dungeon."

"A female elf? What luck! What luck!" Ruprecht exclaimed. "You see? These creatures have no shame—they even use their women as spies!"

Valdaimon began to tremble with a strange mixture of rage and joy.

"I must be about Your Majesty's business," he interjected bluntly. "I beg your leave to prepare the magical elements for the attack on the Elven Preserve."

"Yes, yes, that must be done, but first, let's all go see our new elven toy! You will join me for the interrogation of this prisoner. You, too, Culdus. It would be well for you to know what the elves have learned about our arms." The king strode jauntily out of the great hall, leading the way gleefully toward his chamber of tortures.

"What do you mean, he's listening?" George asked Shulana as his dagger pried at the bolts that held the old elf's manacles to the cold, slippery wall. "Ten thousand hells!" the man added, as the blade slipped off the wet rock and jabbed him in the webbed flesh between thumb and forefinger.

Shulana thought for a moment. How could she explain to humans the matter of elven communion? How could she explain that one's life force could seem to leave the body, flowing through the endless chain of green life that humans called plants, becoming one with that life, spreading, ever spreading, where plant was in reach of plant, observing, hearing, absorbing on a level beneath that of consciousness? Of course, only the most powerful elves could use this communion for practical purposes; for most it was a spiritual exercise and spiritual nourishment. But just as Shulana had known that Bagsby had left their camp, so Elrond now knew . . . what?

"Heilesheim will attack the Elven Preserve," Elrond whispered, his eyes rolling back to gaze upon the face of Shulana.

Shulana looked startled at the news.

"Wot?" George exclaimed, prying again at the iron bolts. "Not even that sap Ruprecht is that daft," he declared.

One of Elrond's arms fell from the manacle that had held it for what seemed like countless years.

"Just another minute, guv," George said respectfully. "Get the other one in just another minute."

"We came to rescue you," Shulana began. "How strong are you?"

"My body is very, very weak," Elrond confessed. "But my mind is as strong as the body will allow it to be. The eggs— you could not . . ."

"No," Shulana said, hanging her head.

Elrond nodded wearily. The bolt holding the other manacle flew out of the wall, and Elrond's other arm flopped weakly down. Gently, George and Marta lowered the old elf to the wet floor of his cell.

" 'E needs rest, and food," George said. "Get 'im some bread, Marta—you elves eat bread?" he asked, suddenly startled to realize he had never actually seen Shulana eat.

"Bread will do, and a bit of wine," Shulana said. "Elven fare will have to wait."

Elrond moistened his lips from the wineskin Marta produced from her great pack, and then licked a few crumbs of the bread she placed on his lips.

"No time. The king comes," he muttered. "And Valdaimon."

Shulana whirled in alarm, then steadied herself, closed her eyes, and listened intently. In the distance she could hear the sounds of footfalls on the corridor paving stones.

"He's right. We must leave here at once," she told George.

"How are we going to do that?" Marta asked. "I can carry the elf, George can fight, but which way do we go?"

Shulana turned back and gazed into Elrond's eyes. "I do not know the spell, but you do," she said.

Wearily, with great pain, the old elf sat upright and crossed his legs. He raised his skeletal arms, drawing George and then Marta into an embrace, forcing them to sit. Shulana quickly sat opposite Elrond and threw her arms around the two humans, thus completing the circle. Elrond, braced against George and Marta, leaned far forward, head down. Shulana did the same, until the crowns of their heads leaned against each other.

George caught Marta's eyes and rolled his own. Were these elves mad? Marta shrugged.

Shulana relaxed, growing more and more limp. She opened her mind, as for communion, fighting the fear of the force she knew she would feel. Elrond knew the spell, but his body was weak. She would have to cast the spell, using his knowledge and his mind. But that mind was so powerful! Once before she had felt it, for only an instant—a mind so forceful that her own could be drowned . . . .

Peace! The thought exploded in her consciousness, washed over her body, quieting the invisible trembling that had begun in her muscles. *Peace. Shulana. Elrond. Elfkind*, the voice intoned in her blank mind. *Elfkind. Greenlife. One, one, one.* . . .

George and Marta sat still as stone, seeing the two elves become silent, almost paralyzed. By the gods, George thought, they'd better hurry whatever it is they're doing. He could hear the steps outside now, hear the clatter of footsteps in the torture chamber.

Shulana's arms floated upward. Her delicate hands began weaving a strange pattern in the air. George watched, fascinated, unable to tear his eyes from those floating, weaving hands, even though his ears heard the invaders just in the next room. . . .

"It's Ruprecht!" Marta shouted. "Ruprecht, you murdering bastard!" Marta's leg muscles tensed, and she started to spring up to hurl herself through the door, dagger in hand, and on the man who had branded her flesh and her spirit. But her muscles could not move her bulk, for a force came from Elrond's feeble arm, laying across her back, a force pushing her downward, downward—a force like the weight of the whole universe, holding her still. . . .

"It's her!" Valdaimon screamed, unable to contain his excitement at the sight of Shulana, seated in the cell in the strange circle. "Where are they? Where is Bagsby!" the old man screeched. He stood in the doorway, his face contorted with unbearable anger.

Control, Valdaimon told himself. *Control. Hold them.* He drew back both arms, focused his mind, recalled the word of command. . . .

Shulana's voice spoke a single word, and the four creatures vanished into thin air. At the same moment, Valdaimon spoke a word of command, and magical chains appeared where the foursome had been sitting. For an instant, ever so brief, the chains seemed to outline the figures who should have been beneath them. Then they clattered to the floor.

Valdaimon screamed his frustration. The sound reverberated off the walls of the empty cell.

Fireflies twinkled over the leaves of the tall oaks, their glitter not unlike the twinkling of the great band of stars that crossed the forest sky, casting pale illumination on the countless enchantments below. This forest was ancient, deep, and thick. Green, leafy creepers wound their way up the trunks of the aged trees, which towered so tall many humans could not see their tops. Vines dangled from the countless branches that formed the overhead canopy, which was still strangely transparent to the sky—as though one could see either sky or darkness at will. The forest floor was covered with a rich spread of grasses, bushes, and fungi, which was broken in places by great, huge tree trunks that lay on the forest floor like fallen soldiers. The trees, the elves knew, did not bury their dead; they left them to become one with that from which they had come, and from which they would come again in the endless turn of seasons and years, ages and eons.

George had heard a faint popping sound, and opened his eyes to this strange sight. Now, less than half an hour later, he sat as part of a greater circle, Marta by his side, while the strange, angular faces of a dozen elves gazed speechlessly into the center of the ring. Softly, Elrond's voice lilted across the still air, which seemed strangely tangible, laden as it was with the sweet fragrances of the thousands of wildflowers that blossomed in the surrounding wood.

"Our quest for the treasure of Parona has failed," Elrond announced. "Despite our futuresight, this Bagsby has not brought us the treasure, but rather has taken it himself in an attempt to discover its nature," the old elf said, a trace of weary sadness in his voice. "By now, I fear, he may have solved the mystery."

"Do you mean . . . ?" Shulana asked softly.

"I do not know. If not yet, soon. But now a more immediate danger faces us. What comes from the Golden Eggs may in time come to destroy us, but what comes from Heilesheim now does, and it comes swiftly."

"Heilesheim will break the Covenant, openly, with an open attack on us?" a stern-looking, vigorous member of the Elven Council declared. "So be it. If they want war, we can give them war."

"But will it be war with all mankind?" Elrond asked.

"Those are the terms of the Covenant," the younger male replied. "If any elf attacks mankind, all mankind is attacked and all elfkind are responsible. And if any man attacks elfkind, all elfkind are attacked and all mankind is responsible. Heilesheim dooms the human race."

"Heilesheim dooms us all," Elrond replied. "For if we loose the magic at our disposal, the effects could well destroy the whole earth. Is that what we desire? To kill the world to avenge ourselves on Heilesheim?"

"That was the only way we could find to end the wars before," the younger elf reminded Elrond. "Even then, in those years, you were Head of the Council. It was you who drafted the Covenant. Would you now renounce it?"

"Renounce it? No," Elrond said. "But I would realize that all things change, as the river of time flows through the wood of the world. The Covenant was made to prevent war with man. It has done so, until now. But now it is not man who makes war on us. It is Heilesheim."

"Beggin' your pardon, gents," George said, his voice sounding strangely loud and coarse in the still night. "I'm a man; I'm even a man from Heilesheim, and I ain't at war with you. If you're going to fight Heilesheim's nobles, I'll be proud to stand beside ye," he said cheerfully.

A murmur arose among the council members—they had invited George and Marta to sit with them out of gratitude—but for humans to speak in the Council was unthinkable!

"I have learned something," Shulana called out, standing up. The murmurs at once fell silent. For when any member of the Council announced a learning, a truth on which he or she would stake their life, all members were bound to listen with the utmost attention and respect, no matter how heated the discussions had become.

"You wish to state a learning?" Elrond asked the ceremonial question.

"I do," Shulana said.

"State the learning, that all elves may know new truth," Elrond said, using the ancient formula.

"All men are not the same. They are different from one another, more different from one another than elves. I am different from Elrond, but we are still the same, we are elfkind. But George here is different from Ruprecht, and different so much so that he is not the same kind."

"Has this learning application to the topic at hand?" Elrond asked, as the ceremony demanded.

"It does," Shulana answered.

"State the application."

"When the Covenant was made, our understanding of men was poor. We thought of them as one kind. They are not. Now that we understand this, we should negotiate a new Covenant with those among men who will embrace it. With those who will not be our enemies." Shulana spoke forcefully, then sat down.

The young elf spoke again, rising and walking to the center of the circle, an indication of the deep passion that motivated his words. "Do you mean," he asked, "that we elves, after centuries of keeping ourselves apart from the affairs of men, are about to become involved in their endless squabbles? For the practical outcome of this course would be to ally ourselves with some men against other men. And men are shiftless allies. Even now, the Holy Alliance dithers while Heilesheim devours its member states! What security will there be for elves under such a Covenant?" The speaker eyed the circle, glared hard at George and Marta, and retook his seat.

The Council sat for a long time in silence. Overhead, the silent stars moved in their courses toward the dawn. Still the silence prevailed. The calls of daybirds began to sound from the wood when Elrond at last arose.

"The Council has before it," he announced "the old way, honored by tradition, that will surely lead to destruction for all; and a new way, untested, full of perils, that may or may not mean salvation for our kind. I, Elrond, oldest of living elves, slayer of the Ancient One, Head of the Council, shall set my feet on this new path, save the Council dissent. Let silence be approval." Elrond then extended his right hand, palm up, and walked to the first council member seated on his right. He touched the elf's chin, lifting his face, and said, "Speak." The elf said nothing. This Elrond repeated around the full circle. When it was his time, the youthful elf gazed deeply into Elrond's face. His pain was clear, but he said nothing.

"It is decided," Elrond announced as the first rays of dawn began to peek through the forest canopy. "I shall go to Parona to begin negotiating the New Covenant. I will take with me Shulana and the two humans who have served this Council so well."

Hunh, George thought. *Leaders are the same, elves or humans. Always deciding what someone else is going to do.*

5

Reunions

Bagsby TOSSED A chunk of preserved beef that weighed at least twenty pounds onto a flat rock. The enormous red mouth seemed to inhale the flesh; the rows of sharp, pointed teeth snapped shut once, and the dragon swallowed. Quickly, Bagsby tossed out another chunk. The dragon's seeming twin gulped it down. Two pairs of black lizard eyes turned to stare at Bagsby.

"More," the dragons demanded in unison.

Bagsby jumped to his feet, hefted the sack of meat, and dumped the entire contents on the ground.

"All I've got," he said, dropping the bag and spreading his arms wide. "See? All gone."

The entire contents of the bag were devoured quickly; the only immediate response to Bagsby's explanation being occasional soft slurping sounds.

"What do I do with them?" Bagsby gasped, watching the feeding spectacle with growing alarm.

"Well, my goodness, I am thinking that is for you to be deciding," Ramashoon said, still chuckling.

"Why do you think this is so funny?" Bagsby demanded. The little brown man sat there in the glow of the firelight on the side of the desert mountain laughing! "These things may decide you're a tasty morsel in about three more minutes!"

"Oh, my, I am thinking they will not be eating me. I am being very thin, and not very good of taste," Ramashoon said, as though he were stating the obvious. "Look at them. Are they not being beautiful? Their like has not been seen on

99

the earth for five thousands of years, and now here they are."

Bagsby flopped down on the ground, disgusted. Shulana had been right—they should have destroyed these things before they hatched. Dragons! Fire-breathing dragons! Talking dragons! What would keep them from overrunning the whole earth once their race was replenished? Bagsby buried his head in his arms. What was to keep them from eating Bagsby, who, being a bit plump, probably looked more like a dragon's dinner than dried-up old Ramashoon? And what difference would if make if they did? Bagsby had no treasure now, and he certainly had no future with Shulana, who would be furious with him for crossing her, abandoning her, and then allowing these eggs to hatch. Even Bagsby had heard tales of the great war between elves and dragons, when men were hardly known upon the earth. Now Bagsby, doing a commission job for the elves, had managed somehow to bring back their worst enemies.

Something heavy, warm, and prickly nuzzled Bagsby's thigh. The thief raised his head, saw the cold black eye of the one of the dragons gazing up at him, the great snout tucked under his knee.

"She likes you," the other dragon uttered, lifting its neck to let the last of the beef slide down its throat. With its tiny forepaws, the creature began digging in the hard, sandy earth.

"She?" Bagsby responded, looking on with despair as the female dragon wrapped her tail around his body.

"She is Lifefire," the female's counterpart said, continuing to scrape out a deep, shallow, bowl-shaped hole. "I am called Scratch, after my father." The dragon's voice was raspy, and the words were sometimes mangled, but overall Bagsby could understand the creature clearly enough.

"I am Bagsby," the thief said, his voice hollow.

"We know," Lifefire murmured. "We have awaited you for a very long time."

"Awaited me?"

"You will be our friend in these early days of our race's rebirth," Lifefire said.

"Wait a minute!" Bagsby howled, shaking the curling dragon off himself and standing up. "Wait a minute. How can you talk? How do you know my language? What makes you think I'll be your friend?"

"A dragon counts as friend any who does him no harm," Scratch said, beginning to dig a small, shallow ditch leading into the hole.

"Yeah, well, I've heard of dragons eating a lot of things that hadn't done them any harm," Bagsby retorted.

"What greater measure of friendship than to become one in the flesh?" Scratch said. He finished the shallow ditch, which ended by the cooling fragments of what remained of the dragons' eggs. The creature climbed up to a rock overlooking both the ditch and the hole. "Stand back," it said to Bagsby.

Bagsby took a few steps backward. Scratch inhaled, and breathed a roar of fire down the ditch into the hole. The flames scorched the ground for ninety feet. When they died, and smoke cleared, the sides of the ditch and the entire surface formed by the hole were glazed, like a clay pot.

"Ready," Scratch said to Lifefire. Lifefire rose on her rear haunches and opened her wings to the night sky. Back and forth she began to beat them, at first slowly, then more quickly, until the wind began to howl in the space around her. Then the creature gave a great shove against the ground with her powerful rear legs and, wings attaining a new speed, rose into the air. She hurtled skyward at an amazing pace, disappearing into the darkness. Seconds later, she was visible again, her form blotting out a tiny portion of the band of stars that stretched across the desert mountain sky. She hovered above the remains of the eggs, then breathed her own breath of fire upon them.

Bagsby flinched as the flames poured from her mouth. Even though he was more than thirty feet away from the stream of fire, the heat was intense. The short man backed farther away.

The dragon poured her firebreath on the remains of the eggs until the gold coatings, already partly melted during the hatching, became molten. Gradually, the molten metal began to flow down Scratch's ditch into the fire-hardened hole he had created. Bagsby could see the gemstones that had once adorned the great Eggs flowing into the hole along with the molten gold.

When the entirety was melted, Lifefire stopped her flaming breath and lowered herself gently to the ground near Bagsby. The molten mass had filled the hole, where it took on the shape of a sphere cut in half.

"It will harden as it cools," Lifefire said. "Then you can carry it for us."

"Carry it for us?" Bagsby asked.

"For Scratch and myself. It is the beginning of our treasure hoard."

Ramashoon, who had been content to observe all this silently, laughed aloud. "Well, Bagsby, it would be seeming that your own time of testing is at hand. I am thinking you believed that the gold was yours!"

"Everyone's entitled to a mistake," Scratch responded. He and Lifefire burst into laughter, deep, growly, rumbling, dragon laughter, such as the earth had not heard for five thousand years. Ramashoon's giggles tinkled high above the dragon sounds, and eventually, in the midrange, Bagsby's laughter joined in, too.

Bagsby awoke in midmorning. He rose, strode out of the depressed area in the side of the mountain where he, Ramashoon, and the dragons had spent the remainder of the night, and looked out over the bustling city of Laga below. Shielding his eyes with hand against the glare, he watched the puffs of dust that marked the steady stream of traffic into and out of the great city. What would the people of Laga think, he wondered, if they knew there were two fire-breathing red dragons encamped on the mountain above?

He knew what they would think. They would think: kill the dragons, kill them while there's still time, before they can breed, before they become a family or, worse yet, a race. Dragons had struck terror into the elves, and those two races had come close to exterminating each other in their death struggle. Then men had fought the elves and, for all intents, the men had won. Elves beat dragons, men beat elves. Men could beat dragons—maybe—if the dragons weren't too strong before the struggle began.

That was one option, Bagsby thought. He lifted a dagger, studied its short, gleaming blade in the morning light. It would be simple: The dragons were still young, and although they seemed to know a fearful amount for newborns, they were still vulnerable physically. A man of Bagsby's cunning could trick them, get them to lower their guard, then ram the blade up into the space between a couple of scales, or drive it through an eye straight into the brain. Dead dragons. End of problem.

Bagsby wondered why he wasn't going to do that. He honestly did not know—it wasn't that he was squeamish about killing. He'd slit many a human throat in his day, and for much less reason than he had for ridding himself and his race of this potential threat. And killing the dragons would stand him in good stead with Shulana—after all, she'd wanted to destroy the eggs before they hatched.

But he wasn't going to kill them. Maybe that was because Ramashoon simply assumed he wouldn't. Maybe it was because there was something about them—something strange, mysterious, powerful and beautiful—that appealed to him on some level that he could not talk or even think about. And maybe that was just the way it was supposed to be.

Bagsby shrugged. He was not going to kill them. Then what? He'd have to feed them. Given that he didn't want to kill them himself, he certainly didn't want an armed mob coming out from Laga to hunt them down with sword, spear, and bow. And that would happen, certainly, as soon as the beasts were hungry enough to go hunting on their own. Dragons needed meat, and lots of it. Laga had lots of meat—all the livestock brought in by the nomads, not to mention the populace themselves. All the same to a dragon, Bagsby imagined. Couldn't let them hunt—not here.

That left only one alternative.

"Ramashoon," Bagsby called back up the mountain. "Ramashoon, wake up."

"Oh my goodness, the sun is already being high in the sky," Ramashoon called back. "I am much thanking you for waking me."

"I'm going to Laga," Bagsby announced. "Will you stay here and watch . . . Scratch and Lifefire?"

"We are watching each other right now," the holy man's voice lilted back.

"You mean they're awake? We were up almost all night. Don't dragons sleep?" Bagsby shouted, exasperated.

"Not when we're hungry." The raspy reply came from Scratch, whose head popped up from behind the dip in the mountainside.

"Get back down," Bagsby called, turning and running back up to where Scratch lay. "Don't let the townspeople see you."

"They would come for us?" Scratch asked.

"Almost certainly."

"Then we must stay hidden," Lifefire said, slithering over by Scratch, "until we are larger, stronger, and have many eggs awaiting the hatching time."

"We must go north," Scratch declared. "The northern mountains are full of food and hiding places. We will grow and breed there."

"Ah, well, that would be very good for your friend, as well," Ramashoon volunteered.

"What? Why is that?" Bagsby asked. "I'm getting pretty tired of you making these little surprise announcements about the course of my life."

Ramashoon stood, smiling, and bowed. "I am not meaning to offend. But my spirits spoke to me last night, in the visions in my mind," the holy man began.

"Yes, yes, you had a dream," Bagsby said, impatient. "What did you dream?"

"Your friends are headed north. They seek the great court of Parona, and will try to bring Parona to the aid of the elves in the war against Heilesheim."

"What war against Heilesheim?" Bagsby demanded, ready to strangle this bizarre little man.

"Oh, that you must be learning for yourself. My time to spend with you is almost being ended."

"No!" Bagsby exclaimed. "You can't leave me now, not with all . . . this . . . to take care of!"

"Oh, you will be doing very well. If you are not doing very well, you will be dying—either way, it will soon bring you rest, is this not so?"

"Let me get this straight," Bagsby said. "The dragons want to go north. If I go north with them, I can meet up with my friends at the court of Parona. You, Ramashoon, are going to do a disappearing act and leave me with some inscrutable statement that's supposed to encapsulate ancient mystical wisdom."

"Ah, how wonderful!" Ramashoon replied, smiling, bowing and chuckling. "I marvel at your understanding! Oh yes, but first, I must be giving this to the little dragons."

Ramashoon reached into a hidden pocket in his white breeches and produced another small, cloth bag. This he handed to Bagsby. "Please to be mixing this with their next feeding," Ramashoon said.

"Will it do me any good to ask why?" Bagsby said cynically.

"Well, it is not for me to be saying what will be doing good for you, is it?"

"That's what I thought," Bagsby replied.

By midafternoon Bagsby was in the streets of Laga, fully dressed in the armor of a Heilesheim minor officer, a leader of a hundred. The former owner of that particular armor and livery had no further need for it, nor did the brothel owner who would be stuck with the soldier's burial expense.

A few well-placed inquiries among officers of the same rank had soon led Bagsby to his goal, the home of one of the young recruits whom he had encountered on his journey to Laga. The house was typical for those of its class, the outer walls whitewashed to reflect the heat of the sun. The structure was two-storied, with balconies extending out over the street from the upper-story windows. The house looked to be reasonably large; there was probably an interior courtyard inside.

Bagsby approached with a bold stride and pounded loudly on the door with his mailed fist.

"A messenger from Hans Frisung with news of the son of this house, who is now engaged against the enemies of Heilesheim in far Argolia," Bagsby said to the startled house servant who threw open the door.

The fine home did have an interior courtyard with a small garden, and even a tiny fountain. Bagsby was shown to a bench by the fountain to await the master of the house.

"Well, well," the plump man called as he came bustling into the courtyard. "You are a messenger from the army? You have news of my son?"

Bagsby took in the man's entire appearance at a glance. He wore colorful breeches of red silk, a large gold sash about his waist, and a patterned blouse of rich, soft material imported all the way from the Five Ports of the Rhanguilds in the far northwest. The man was unarmed. His home was tastefully yet sparsely furnished. His hands were soft and fat, and his face did not yet show the severe lines that would be normal for a man of his fifty-some years. The man was obviously wealthy, but not as rich as a minor noble. Bagsby all but calculated the man's cash value before he replied.

"Sir, I have the honor to bear news of your son. He is in Argolia with his unit, where there is some fighting against scattered resistance," Bagsby began.

"Is he well?" the man cut in. "Why are you here?"

"Your son is well," Bagsby said, reassuring the troubled soul. "The fighting goes well. It is said your son distinguishes himself," Bagsby reported.

"It is?" the man said, surprised. "I am amazed. My son did not even want to go into the army. But I told him it was his duty. . . ."

"Then you have done well, as he does now," Bagsby said.

"Ah, ah, my manners. You would care for some refreshment?" the man said, clapping his hands for his servants.

"No time, I fear. My business in Laga must be completed quickly. I have come to tell you how you can help your son."

"What? He needs money?"

Bagsby paused. It was too easy. But he decided to stick to his original plan. "No," he replied. "Not exactly. As you may know, the supply lines for the army are overburdened. The lands of Argolia proved less wealthy than we had thought. The army there often wants for food."

"I have heard, I have heard. And I see the huge orders that leave Laga every day for the Argolian lands. Wagon after wagon of. . . ."

"Yes," Bagsby interrupted. "Now, I have been sent by your son's Hundred to raise funds for the purchase of livestock to be driven to Argolia for the benefit of the troop."

"Well then, you shall have my cooperation. How much have the other families contributed?"

"Sad to say," Bagsby responded, "my time is very short, and I have not yet been able to contact the other families. I need assistance. . . ."

Shortly after sunset Bagsby, with the help of ten soldiers he'd dragooned from the local grog houses, set out from Laga at the head of a flock of livestock that included twenty sheep, a dozen cattle, and a small horse-drawn cart loaded with crates of chickens. He waited until the sun was fully down and the first stars were visible in the sky before ordering his column to turn widely to the left, leaving the road, and eventually heading eastward to the mountains. Once they were in the open plain at the foot of the steeply rising desert mountains, Bagsby released the men under his command, sending them back to the pleasures of the city. Then, tying the horse to some scrub brush, Bagsby climbed upward.

He did not have to wait long for the sinuous form of Scratch to appear, slithering down the mountainside toward him. Lifefire followed behind.

"You have brought food, as we agreed?" Scratch demanded.

"See for yourself," Bagsby replied proudly.

"We shall feed," the dragon said. "Give us the holy man's powder."

Bagsby produced the small cloth bag, opened it, and asked, "How do you take this?"

Lifebreath reached out one of her tiny forearms and grasped the bag. She snaked her long wet tongue down into the small opening, coating it with the white powder. She held the pouch for Scratch, who did the same. Without another word, the dragons began beating their wings, building up speed with them, until they launched themselves into the night sky.

Bagsby was relieved to see that they stayed low, soaring over the plain below. Soon, he saw several short bursts of flame drop from the darkness of the night onto the ground below. There were a few bellows and bleats, then more short bursts of flame. In all, though, their performance was very restrained. If any watchman along the city walls spotted the brief gouts of flame, he would be unlikely to send anyone to investigate. Bagsby trooped on back up the mountainside to the spot where they had camped the night before. No sounds came from the plain below.

Bagsby shed his armor, checked his packed gear to make sure all was in readiness for the morning, and lay down, a flat rock serving him as a pillow. The dragons had explained to him that they would feed for some time, eating an immense amount of flesh, but that they would then be sated for a week or longer. So long as they were not seen, all would be well. Bagsby gazed up at the stars above, and his eyes drifted shut. Somewhere from the back of his memory, the face of Shulana drifted into his consciousness, and he felt a pang of loneliness as he sank into unconsciousness.

The wind hit him suddenly with its full force. He awoke to the stinging of sand and dust in his nose and eyes and saw his heavy pack go flying off the mountainside, driven by the gale. He clutched the flat rock and tried to dig his toes into the earth; otherwise the force of the wind would blow his body along the depression in the mountainside like a dead weed across the desert. The roar of the rushing air was deafening, a hollow, deep, bass, roaring that pummeled his ears. It was as terrifying as the winds of the gods, which he had once seen called down upon Valdaimon's wyvern-riding troops.

Then the fear struck him—sheer, dumb terror, unlike any he had ever felt before. It was blind, unreasoning fear; Bagsby didn't even know why he was afraid, only that he was, that he would do anything to get away from that place and that

time—anything except let go of the flat rock that anchored
him. He did the only thing that animal instinct allowed him to
do. He screamed. He screamed loudly, a high-pitched, terrified
wail that was blown away by the winds as soon as it left his
lungs and mouth, a scream of pure terror dissolved into the
nothingness of the night. He screamed until his raw throat was
swollen and he could scream no more.

The wind ceased as suddenly as it had begun. There was
silence, and then . . . then . . . as sober consciousness slowly
returned to the little thief and the terror receded into the deep
recesses of his mind from whence it had come, he heard it. He
heard the deep sounds of breathing, of huge quantities of air
being sucked into living lungs and snorted out again through
wet nostrils. Bagsby waited, still clutching his rock, his eyes
still shut against the terror, waited to see if the horrid breathing
would go away, or if. . . .

"Bagsby."

The voice was deeper than the deepest bass he had ever
heard, deeper even than the bass tones of the priests who
chanted the praises of Wojan in the temples of Heilesheim,
deeper than the sound of thunder, deeper than the rolling sound
of an exploding fireball. And underneath that incredibly deep
sound was a gravelly rattle, as though a million small stones
were being shaken inside an earthenware jar.

"Bagsby," the voice called again.

Slowly, Bagsby forced himself to open one eye, then the
other. He kept both eyes glued to the earth, not ready, just
yet, to see the source of that sound.

"Bagsby. Wake up," the voice boomed again.

Bagsby raised his head and looked out at the depression in
which he lay. In front of him it was swept clean, as if a broom
wielded by a god had swept away every large rock, every bit
of scrub brush, every loose grain of sand. The voice had come
from behind him. Bagsby thought about looking around but
decided not to, not just yet.

"Aaahhh," Bagsby gasped. He tried to say, "I'm awake,"
but his raw throat could not form the sounds.

"Bagsby, what is wrong? It is time for us to travel," the
voice called.

It couldn't be, Bagsby thought. It was not possible. The exhausted, trembling man drew on all his courage, all his physical strength and, with a great effort of will, flipped himself over onto his back, his eyes open, ready to confront whatever it was that addressed him so.

The first thing he noticed was that the dragon's head alone was bigger than he was. In fact, the dragon's snout alone was bigger than Bagsby. *It could swallow me whole without ever having to chew*, he thought. Nor would Bagsby ever allow a dragon to nuzzle him again. The nostrils at the end of the long snout were protected by two huge crescents, covered with red scales, their edges sharp as razors. The same type of ridges protruded outward over the creature's eyes, which were set wide to the sides of its enormous head. The teeth were truly a marvel, visible as it sat with its mouth only slightly open, double rows top and bottom of gleaming white, sword-sharp, pointed teeth, flecked now with blood and bits of flesh after the dragon's feeding.

Bagsby gathered the courage to sit up. He made no effort to speak. His fear was ebbing now, being replaced by sheer awe. He wanted to see the beast in its entirety, to be able to say he had once seen such a sight. He looked down the length of the sinuous body on its right side. The back, of course, was covered with sharp ridges that jutted outward, protecting the spine. The sides bulged, bloated by the just finished feeding frenzy. Even in the pale light of the cold night, Bagsby could make out the ruddy hue of the countless thousands of scales that armored the beast. Its underbelly, barely visible as the creature lay on the sandy, rocky ground, was a lighter shade, perhaps even a yellow—Bagsby couldn't tell in the dark.

Then there were the wings, which Bagsby slowly realized were the cause of the gale-force winds he had experienced. They were folded now, two great spikes of black blotting out the stars. Extended, how far would they reach? Bagsby couldn't tell. He stood, mouth agape, and walked slowly to the side of the creature, gazing upward at the peaks of the wings. He tried to gain some perspective, but could not; the dragon's spine was higher off the ground than his head, and Bagsby could not measure how much farther the wing fold truly was.

The little thief walked the length of the giant's body. Almost forty paces he counted before he came to the end of the tail, with its magnificent, deadly barb. Bagsby circled behind the beast and came up along the opposite side. He saw the bulging muscles of the great rear haunches. Protruding from beneath the body were the long, armored toes, culminating in claws so large and sharp that a scrape from one of them could split open an armored man.

His tour completed, Bagsby stopped in front of the dragon. The creature raised its head, and an expression something like a smile seemed to form on its snout. The huge eyes were wide and gleaming, not listless as they had seemed before.

"You admire me," the beast said.

Bagsby tried to speak, felt a stab in his throat like a knife blade, and gave up the effort. He mutely nodded his assent.

The ground trembled slightly. Bagsby shook, extended his arms, and fought for his balance.

"That is Lifefire," the dragon boomed.

Again Bagsby nodded.

"We grew," Scratch told Bagsby—for it was he.

"Aah, aah, how?" Bagsby croaked.

"The magic powder that Ramashoon gave us. An ancient potion of dragon growth. Prepared by a race that was old even before the elves came upon the earth, a race that once lived in the lands beyond the mountains. I am an adult now," Scratch boomed. "I am the equal of any mighty one of my race. I am in my prime. I am ready for any battle, any challenge. . . ."

"Enough, Scratch," Lifefire called, her voice not noticeably higher in pitch than his, but somehow less threatening in its rumblings. "We have terrified Bagsby."

"All creatures are terrified at our appearance," Scratch bellowed, elated. "Behold us! Are we not the true terror of the world?"

Uh oh, Bagsby thought.

"Remember," Lifefire said. "Remember the fate of our father and mother, and temper your pride with humility."

"Ummmhhhh," Scratch rumbled. "The elves killed them."

Bagsby saw the black eyes light up again when the dragon mentioned the elves. And this time, it was not the fire of pride he saw.

"Yes," Lifefire said. "And they still have the cunning to kill us. Do not terrify one of our few friends."

"Unnhh," Scratch growled. "Will you ride now, Bagsby?" Scratch asked.

Bagsby shook his head "No."

"Then we will sleep. When the sun comes up, you will learn to ride on my back as we agreed, and I shall carry you to the lands of the north."

The horse saddle fit Bagsby's seat perfectly, but it didn't fit on Scratch's back at all. First, Bagsby climbed up on the dragon, lugging the saddle with him, and tried to place it on the dragon's back, near the point where the long neck joined the torso. The saddle spread almost flat, and the protective ridges on Scratch's spine, which Bagsby took great care to avoid scraping against, bit into the bottom of the leather. Besides, Bagsby quickly saw, there was no way to secure the seat to the dragon's back. Scratch's girth was much too great to cover with any type of strap, rope, or tie.

The solution Bagsby eventually found took most of the day to implement. First he gathered wood, cutting some of the small scrub trees that dotted the mountainside. From this he constructed a chairlike seat, with a back support, and with great piles of sheepskin beneath it for protection from the dragon's spinal ridges. This structure he mounted on the dragon's back, securing it with metal nails and hooks bent from the chain-mail links in the suit of armor he had stolen in Laga. Finally, Bagsby constructed three straps, two of which crossed his chest and passed over his shoulders, the third of which went around his lap, and affixed these to the seat so that the occupant would remain in the seat, even if the dragon flipped upside down in flight.

"Which," Bagsby said hoarsely, showing the arrangement to Scratch, "I sincerely hope you will not do."

"I shall try," Scratch boomed, "to restrain my exuberance. Is it not remarkable that even to ride such a creature as myself you must go to such efforts, while I can take to the skies with the speed of thought, spreading terror at my approach. . . ."

"Scratch, enough," Lifefire said. "Let him mount this device and let us be gone to the north."

"Just a few more details to check," Bagsby said cheerily.

But first, Bagsby busied himself with more of his gear— little items of no interest to the dragons. These moments were important to the little thief, who had quickly realized that he was in the dangerous situation of being a pawn to these dragonspawn. No matter how friendly or reasonable they might be, there could certainly come a time when Scratch, in a grumpy mood, might decide to end the annoyance caused by Bagsby's presence with one snap of those huge jaws. Bagsby intended to provide himself some insurance against that moment. The dragons largely ignored him as he laid out items in rows on the ground, counted them, dug some holes, buried a few items, counted things again, then bundled his gear back together, a contented feeling in his breast. The great beasts had not noticed that one of the items he had buried was their hemisphere of gold and gems, which they had entrusted to him.

Bagsby spent a good hour checking and double-checking the improvised wire hooks and nails to feel certain that the seat was secured firmly to Scratch's back. At last, the seat as steady as Bagsby could make it and his gear loaded aboard, Bagsby climbed once more up Scratch's huge side. Then using the ripples of muscle as footing, he grabbed onto the undersides of scales to gain handholds. Gradually he made his way onto the creature's back, checked his seat one last time, and then stepped inside, extending his legs slightly forward and downward, and leaning his back against the backrest of the seat. He tied off the three straps, and only then did Bagsby allow himself to look down. The height was not that great— Bagsby had been higher many times, climbing the wall of an inviting building to reach a second-story window.

"Ready, Scratch," the small thief bellowed. "Let's try it."

Bagsby felt the subtle motion of the dragon's back beneath him, then the gentle rocking motion as the great dragon began to move forward. To each side, the huge, folded, reddish brown wings began to open and lower. The rocking of the seat became more violent as Scratch gained speed, hurling himself down the mountainside. The wings flapped once, twice, a third time— and suddenly, as the dragon took a great leap with the power of its rear haunches, Bagsby saw that he was airborne!

The dragon soared off the mountainside, gliding downward at first, while the great wings slowly pumped up and down, up and down, until the downward motion stopped and the huge creature, its head extended upward toward the sun, began to climb in the clear summer sky.

Bagsby gripped the sides of his seat in fear; his breath came in short, dry gasps; he tried to lick his lips, and found he had no spit in his mouth. But it was working! The great dragon's wings beat faster and faster, and the heavy creature miraculously rose higher and higher in the air. Bagsby worked up the courage to look out to one side and then the other, but he could barely see over Scratch's huge flanks. Then the dragon turned—for it had been heading west toward Laga and, as they had agreed, did not yet want to be seen by the townspeople. The great body banked hard to the right, and Bagsby gazed out over the vast desert and the city that was already thousands of feet below.

At first he was shocked; he called out in alarm, only to feel a rumble beneath as Scratch chuckled at his exclamation of fear. Then he watched silently, in amazement, as the city passed slowly by below him, the people already so tiny they could barely be seen, the buildings looking like tiny architect's models, the streams of traffic on the great highway no more than mere trails of ants, already receding out of sight. Bagsby marveled; he knew the dragon was traveling at great speed, yet the ground below seemed to pass beneath them at a leisurely pace, much more slowly than it would from the back of a trotting horse.

Scratch leveled off as he approached the mountain from which he had taken off—high above its top now—and then rose suddenly and swiftly, catching an updraft of warm air from the base of the mountain. Bagsby grappled the sides of his seat again, and fought the rise of his stomach toward his mouth. How long, he wondered, could he bear this?

Then Bagsby spotted Lifefire flying alongside. He saw her incredible grace as she rose on the air, wings fully extended, occasionally beating, occasionally tilting to change direction. The remarkable creature seemed to fly effortlessly, as if she had done it all her life. Which, Bagsby thought, in a sense she had. Somehow, the sight of Lifefire reassured Bagsby. He settled back, and began to enjoy the ride.

Higher and higher Scratch soared, riding the gusts at the edge of the Eastern Mountains, working his way northward. Soon the mountains receded below him, until Bagsby could no longer judge their height above the plains over which they rose. Gradually, the desert yellows of the ground gave way to yellow-greens and then greens as the great beast ploughed toward the north at speeds beyond the imaginings of mortal men. Bagsby saw streams and rivers, and then the great, broad Rigel looking like a ribbon laid out across the ground, shimmering in the sun.

Bagsby's spirit began to rise with the great dragon. This was wonderful! This was . . . freedom! Bagsby began to feel a heady elation. No wonder Scratch was so vain! To soar above the earth with the powers of a god—how could one resist this? Then one more thought occurred to Bagsby: Shulana. Shulana had to experience this. As his great mount sliced through the cold air northward, Bagsby lost himself in fantasies of himself and Shulana, soaring up beyond the clouds on the backs of their invincible warrior mounts.

The journey was, for Bagsby, disappointingly brief. It took the great dragons only four days to cover the vast distance from Laga, in the far south, to the icy mountains that formed the northern and northeastern boundaries of the northern kingdom of Parona. Each day, Bagsby became more comfortable in the improvised dragon saddle, more innured to the cold of the high air, more accustomed to the motions of flight. By the fourth day, he felt himself an old veteran of such travel, though he still longed to share its joys with Shulana.

It was just past midday on the fourth day of the journey that Scratch began spiraling downward in broad circles, coming ever closer to the icy surface of the high, frozen, northern mountains. Bagsby sat comfortably in his seat, well wrapped in the furs and skins he had thoughtfully brought with him. He had taken them from the remains of the dragons' first feast. At length, Scratch thundered to rest on a snow-covered ridge on the side of one of the mountains. Stretched out below were the fertile plains of Parona, separated from the mountains by a land of rolling, tall hills.

"Why have we stopped?" Bagsby called from his perch, surveying the ice and snow-covered granite. The occasional sturdy evergreen struggled for life in the bitter cold. Bagsby saw the steam of his breath, felt the chill start to bite into his hands, and dreaded the contact of his breeches and boots with the cold drifts of snow. "We can't stop here—this is no place to camp," he shouted.

"This is where we are going," Scratch said.

Lifefire glided in just then, landing beside her brother/mate. "Lifefire!" Bagsby called, having quickly learned that the female dragon was more amenable to both communication and reason than Scratch, whose main concern seemed to be his own magnificence. "Scratch says we are stopping here."

"We are," Lifefire said.

"I can't stop here—I can't survive in these mountains," Bagsby complained. "I need to go to Parona, a great city on that plain down there," Bagsby said, pointing vaguely to the southwest.

"This is where Scratch and I are going. Where you go now is your own affair," Lifefire said, stating simple facts. "We agreed to give you transportation north in exchange for food. You provided the food. We provided the transportation. The deal is done."

"The deal is not done," Bagsby countered. "There is one thing you've forgotten."

"What have we forgotten?" Scratch roared. "Get off of me."

Bagsby didn't budge from his seat. He had hoped to save this card to play at a later date, but left alone in the mountains he would starve or freeze before ever making it to Parona.

"You have forgotten," Bagsby said, an impish grin crossing his face, "your treasure."

"What?" both the dragons roared in unison.

"Yes, Scratch. You were so impressed with yourself you forgot all about your gold. And Lifefire, you were so busy telling Scratch what to do that you forgot about it, too."

"Where is it?" Scratch roared, smoke starting to pour from his snout as he craned his huge neck around in a vain effort to see Bagsby. "Where is it?"

"It is safe," Bagsby said.

"You were told to carry it for us!" Scratch roared.

"That was not part of our agreement," Bagsby said, folding his arms contentedly.

Scratch howled in anger. A geyser of flame shot from his mouth, devouring the ice and snow in a swath more than thirty feet wide down the ridge. "Eat him!" he bellowed to Lifefire.

"No," Lifefire said. "He's right. That was not a stated part of our agreement."

Scratch howled again.

"Hey, Scratch, breathe some more fire," Bagsby called merrily. "It helps me keep warm."

"What do you want in return for revealing the location of our treasure?" Lifefire said flatly.

"I want a ride to the capital of Parona," Bagsby said.

"Out of the question," Lifefire said. "The city folk would see us. Soon these mountains would be swarming with. . . ."

"Not if we went at night," Bagsby said, his grin intact. Dealing with dragons wasn't as hard as he'd thought at first. They had incredibly literal, legalistic minds. You just had to negotiate very, very carefully.

Elrond sat cross-legged on the cool marble floor, gazing out beyond the elegant columns at the courtyard gardens, enjoying the abundance of green life that was fed by the bubbling springs there. It was true, he thought. Parona was the fairest and most elegant of the human kingdoms. The land was broad, rich, and fertile—well watered and graced with a moderate climate that still provided the full variety of seasons so dear to elves. The people were generally prosperous, and the mercantile and noble classes had developed refined tastes in dress, manners, rhetoric, and the arts. Parona was still distinctly human—possessed of the strange combination of energy and sloth, purpose and purposelessness, tenderness and savagery that seemed to Elrond to characterize all the kingdoms of man.

Here, listening to the bubbling of the springs and lounging in the graceful cool of the palace courtyard, Elrond could almost forget that his mission was to negotiate a new alliance for the purpose of bloody warfare, warfare brought about by the same creatures who had built this beautiful palace! Elrond shook his head. He must remember Shulana's learning: all men were not the same; human cultures and human individuals could be radically different from one another.

Parona, for example, was quite different from Heilesheim. Heilesheim was all bluster and force; a violent tide flowing across the world. Parona thus far had refused to become so; despite the pleadings of the invaded lands, Parona's partners in the so-called Holy Alliance, Parona had refused to take up arms, preferring instead to maintain a posture of guarded neutrality—no doubt in the hope that bloodshed would not be needed to satisfy the demands of the voracious Heilesheim leadership.

Now Elrond would meet with the king of Parona, and the other surviving leaders of the Alliance in an attempt to drag Parona not only into war with Heilesheim, but also into a new understanding of the relations between elves and men that would allow elves to participate in those wars! Strange indeed, Elrond thought. Strange indeed.

Elrond looked again into the courtyard garden. There George and Marta sat peacefully, pleasant flights of their merry conversation borne to Elrond's ears on the cool breeze that broke the heat of the summer day. Shulana sat by the edge of the bubbling springs, gazing into the blue clearness of the summer sky. Did she long, Elrond wondered, for the human who had duped her? The old elf lowered his head. Even if he were successful in his mission to Parona, there was still the matter of the Golden Eggs. If dragons, and the power to master them, were to fall into the hands of Valdaimon. . . .

"Elrond of the Elven Preserve," a servant's formal voice called out from the large doorway that framed the entrance to the king of Parona's main council chamber. The elf stood slowly and waved an arm to his companions in the garden, then smoothed his flowing tunic. The sheeny, patternless fabric seemed to cause rivers of color to flow down and around its length. George and Marta ceased their chattering and walked, as stately as possible, to Elrond's side. Shulana joined them.

"The High Council of the Holy Alliance, the lords of the lands in conference assembled, will receive the special delegation from the Elven Preserve to discuss an urgent matter pertaining to the great issue of war and peace between elves and men," the servant droned.

The foursome stepped through the high, double wooden doors, Elrond in the lead, the other three clustered behind. The wide, light council room was dominated by four sets of broad, double, stained-glass windows in the rear, thrown open to the breezy air, and a very large, round, hardwood table in the center. Arrayed around the table were the surviving lords of the conquered lands of the Holy Alliance. Most resplendent of these was King Harold of Argolia who, despite the loss of a kingdom, had lost neither his royal dignity nor his taste in clothes. Though his ermine-trimmed, heavy azure robe was much too warm for the day, causing beads of perspiration to form on his brow, Harold endured the discomfort to maintain the dignity of his kingdom.

The host of the gathering, King Alexis Aliapoulios, felt secure enough on his throne that he had no need of ostentatious display to reinforce his position. The king wore a simple ankle-length tunic of shimmering purple, accented with a plain band of gold trim about its neck, short sleeves, and hem. A thin, gold coronet graced his thick, black, curly hair. The king's features—graceful and thin without being angular—were pleasing, but Elrond noticed a certain lack of passion on that face, a quiet contentment that defied the impulse to violent action. Elrond immediately sensed that his task would not be easy.

Elrond's train of thought was interrupted by a sudden, short gasp from Shulana, a growl of anger from George, and a sudden exclamation from Marta.

"Sir John!" the large woman shouted, abandoning the sense of decorum she had carefully cultivated in anticipation of this meeting. "You little rascal, where have you been?" she bellowed, bounding past Elrond into the council room and half-trotting in excitement to the seat where Bagsby sat, at the right of King Harold.

"My dear Marta," Bagsby said, rising and making a great bow with a flourish. "A pleasure to be reunited with a comrade in arms in the struggle against Heilesheim."

Marta cooed with awe, for Bagsby's splendor was second only to that of his patron, King Harold. Though that sovereign had long known Bagsby for what he truly was—a commoner and a thief—he was grateful to the little man for his heroic efforts against Heilesheim at battles before the debacle of Clairton, and at that great conflict as well. Enough of the Argolian treasury had escaped with the king to provide Bagsby, now legally Sir John, with a wardrobe appropriate to the royal esteem in which he stood. He wore a brown velvet doublet with gold brocade over a brilliant scarlet tunic that was barely visible beneath a tasteful, yellow, silk ascot. Tight, full-length breeches of brilliant green stretched down inside his fine, ankle-high, brown boots adorned with gold buckles. On the table beside him was a long cap of green, tapered at the front, with peacock feathers flashing in a spray from the left side.

"Reunited?" George shouted, his eyes grown wide at Bagsby's seemingly obvious wealth. "Reunited? Caught is more like it!" The soldier stomped across the room in Marta's wake, his eyes glowering. "Wot's you done wit' it?" George demanded. "Where is it, and where's me cut?"

Astonished at such conduct, anger flashed on the faces of the assembled lords; only King Harold, knowing many details of Bagsby's past, realized something of the implication of George's words, and flinched. The King of Parona rose, motioning to the company of guards kept within eye and earshot of the council room.

"My lords, my lords," Bagsby quickly interposed. "Do not be alarmed if this gentleman shows neither manners nor knowledge of our more civilized customs, for this poor wretch who stands before you has personally engaged in battle the entire company of the guard of the demon Valdaimon, and was successful in penetrating the very palace of Ruprecht himself in order to free the head of the Elven Council—held there in torments in direct violation of the Covenant—though he was once nothing more than a common soldier in that same army of Heilesheim, which now threatens us all."

George stared dumbly at Bagsby, his angered mind trying to sort through the little man's syntax. George wasn't sure, but he thought he'd just been complimented—something that had never happened to him before in the presence of nobles.

Bagsby, however, kept his attention focused on his audience for this speech, carefully gauging the reaction caused by the double shock he just thrown on the table: one, that Heilesheim had violated the Covenant, inviting war with the elves; and second, that a Heilesheim commoner had succeeded at feats of arms that had so far defied the abilities of the greatest knights of the Holy Alliance. The murmurs of disapproval at George's conduct quickly died as the implications of Bagsby's speech sank into the somewhat thick skulls of the assembled lords.

"Yes," Bagsby said slowly, beginning to stride in a grand circle around the table, stopping from time to time to gesture for emphasis or to look in the face of one of the highborn who was slow to grasp the point, "this common Heilesheim soldier, no longer content to fight dumbly for the evil represented by Ruprecht and Valdaimon, has twice been able to overcome forces many times his number. If but one Heilesheim soldier can do that, what do you think an army of them will do to Parona, once they are allowed to cross its border?" Bagsby stared at the king of Parona who, for the first time, looked interested in the proceedings. "And if the elves—who have every right under the Covenant to unleash all the magic at their command against all of mankind—have refrained from our certain destruction to seek rather our assistance in punishing those few humans who are guilty of this infraction, should we not gratefully embrace the proposals now brought before us not by just any elf, but by the head of the Elven Council who was himself the single most injured party by this violation of the most sacred pact ever entered into by mankind?" Bagsby bowed gracefully with a gesture of invitation toward Elrond, who had watched this performance in mute amazement.

Slowly the old elf advanced into the room. He had never laid eyes on Bagsby, but he knew that the strutting Sir John must be he. And amazed as he was at the eccentric but effective performance of the little thief, he had no intention of allowing this moment of advantage to slip away.

"Noble lords of the Holy Alliance," Elrond began, "I bring you greetings of peace from the Elven Council. Peace," he added gravely, "despite the clear violation of the Covenant which would entitle my race to launch a war of extermination against man." Elrond paused, allowing that simple thought to hold the attention of his human audience. Then, smiling ever so slightly, he added, "That, however, is not what I have come to propose."

"Another draught, barman, and keep the ale flowing," Bagsby called cheerfully across the crowded tavern room. He sat with George at a small wooden table near one of the tiny establishment's two windows. The crowd was already roaring drunk—laborers, their women, and a handful of thieves, Bagsby noted. It was as well. This was the type of place where George would feel comfortable.

"You still ain't tol' me nothin' about me cut," George said, his words only slightly slurred. "So you 'ad to go find out about the treasure—I unnerstan' that." He was genuinely sympathetic with the empathy provided by ale. "But you 'adn't no cause to go run off like that an' take our treasure wit' you. That wasn't very nice," he added, wagging his finger at Bagsby.

"I'm sorry. I wish I could have told you what was up, but it was something I had to do by myself," Bagsby said, wondering whether this stab at an explanation would suffice.

"Sometimes a man's gotta do things by hisself," George slurred back. "I unnderstan'. Now, w'ere is it?"

"George, that treasure is as safe as if it were in the hands of a whole family of dragons," Bagsby began.

"Yeah? Where?"

"Far to the north. That's where I'm going soon, when the Council is finished with its business." Bagsby leaned forward and whispered confidentially into George's ear, "I'm heading for the north country. Be back in about a week or so."

"An' then I'll get me cut?"

"Of course," Bagsby reassured. "You'll get riches beyond anything you've imagined."

" 'Ow can I trust you? You ran out on us once," George remonstrated loudly.

"Well," a new voice responded from behind George's shoulder, "if he's going to the north country he can't get into too much mischief."

Bagsby's head popped up at the intrusion, and George whirled about unsteadily on his bench. The stranger was a tall man, over six feet in height, with broad shoulders and a well-muscled frame showing beneath his simple white, linen blouse and brown breeches. He wore his dark brown hair long, far past his shoulders, and his broad face was of slightly pale complexion, setting off his large, dark brown eyes.

"You have keen hearing, friend," Bagsby said, sitting back on his bench across from George and slowly working his hand down toward the top of his boot where his dagger was concealed.

"No need for that weapon," the tall man replied, smiling at Bagsby. "I couldn't help overhearing—We northerners are known for our keen ears," he explained. "And eyes," he added. "Just looking for an empty bench, and you've got the only one in the place."

The stranger sat down next to George without awaiting an invitation.

"So you're traveling north?" he asked Bagsby.

"My business," Bagsby snapped back.

"As you say. But that's my country, up there, and I could tell you many things that might be useful—if it's your first visit, which it clearly is," the stranger replied.

"Who are you?" Bagsby demanded. "And how do you know where I've been and where I haven't been?"

"Arnulf of the Northwest Canton," the man replied. "You've never been north or you'd know about the hearing and eyesight of my race."

"Wot else would he know," George challenged, a surly look crossing his face. This intrusion was most unwelcome to the little soldier.

"He'd know we're a clean, honest, hard-working and free people who bend the knee to no lord, not even to Sir John Wolfe," Arnulf replied merrily.

"You know me?" Bagsby gasped.

"Who in Parona does not know of Sir John Wolfe, whose place is the most honored in the Council of the Holy Alliance, next to the place of kings themselves?" Arnulf replied.

"Wot's that you said about no lords?" George asked, his interest peaked.

"The Cantons are the northernmost provinces of Parona," Arnulf explained. "We're tucked right under those icy mountains, in foothills rich with spring flood soil and forests rich with game. We are free provinces; we acknowledge no landed lord, save the king—may the gods bless him!—who agrees to honor our rights as free men."

"We'd better be going," Bagsby interjected. "Another time," he said, nodding to Arnulf as he slammed his mug firmly on the wooden table.

"No, no," George protested, "wait a minute. I want to 'ear more about this land wit' no lords. Don't seem possible to me. Them bastards always takes wot they wants."

"Are you including Sir John in that assessment?" Arnulf asked, laughing. "You seem a strange companion for a noble knight, and this seems a strange place to find a knight so distinguished," he added, draining his mug in one huge gulp between phrases. "Barman!" he roared. "More drink!"

"Oh, well, Sir John 'ere," George said, warming to the stranger, " 'e's alright. 'E ain't like them others. But 'ow do you keep 'em out?" George inquired, staring in wonder at Arnulf's broad, smiling face. "More ale!" he bellowed, adding emphasis to the previous orders.

"We keep them out with our bows," Arnulf said firmly. "We northerners are the best archers in the world—better than the elves, they say, though I've never seen an elf—and one of our men can knock down an armored knight on horseback at over a hundred yards. After a while," he continued, winking knowingly, "they learned better than to mess with us."

"Who rules your lands, then?" Bagsby asked, intrigued by a possibility that had flashed through his brain with the speed and heat of summer rain.

"We govern ourselves. Don't need much government, really," Arnulf said. "We're hunters and farmers and fighters. Who needs much governing for that?"

George sat back in amazement. "Well," he commented, "if that don't beat all."

"Yes," Bagsby said thoughtfully, resuming his seat. "That could very well beat all. Tell me more, Arnulf, about these bowmen of your people. . . ."

Bagsby wiggled his chubby toes in the warm, bubbling pool fed by the hot springs. He leaned back, resting his weight on arms thrust out behind him, and gazed back through the courtyard toward the council chamber where the deliberations dragged on.

"They're debating now who will lead the combined forces," he said wryly. "That should take them another week or two to decide."

Shulana ran her hand over the surface of the closely trimmed grass. "The thing of importance is already decided," she said. "Parona will fight with the Alliance, and both will fight with the elves."

"Yes, thanks in part to some brilliant diplomacy by a certain knight whom I won't name," Bagsby said, attempting merriment.

Shulana, her eyes downcast, did not reply. It was the first time the two of them had been alone in the week of the meetings of the Council. Bagsby had sought her out often, but she had always avoided him. Today, she had decided it was foolish not to confront him—she would have to sooner or later—but now, alone with him, she did not know what to say. How could she express her feelings? They were so much more complex than any feelings she had ever had before. Elves had simple emotions. They were usually guided either by reason or by their inherent sense of the cosmic flow of the life force throughout the confusing welter of events. Elves loved their friends, hated their enemies, respected those of honor or prowess, reveled in the flow of life, and reverently manipulated the powers of magic. But Shulana today felt love and hate, respect and scorn. The flow of the life force clearly impelled her toward Bagsby, yet he represented too much danger, too much risk, such a history of betrayal, that she could hardly trust what, under normal circumstances, would have been her surest instincts.

Bagsby studied the lithe, female form that had graced his fantasies so often over the past few weeks. He, too, was puzzled. How had this woman obtained such a hold over his mind and heart? For he now was forced to admit that he loved her—or at least, that life without her was not a life that he would willingly choose. It was for this reason that he had come to Parona, had taken up his guise as Sir John Wolfe, had ingratiated himself once again to King Harold of Argolia, and had even set up the Council of the Holy Alliance so that it could not ignore whatever proposals Elrond was bringing. All the skills of guile, deception, and the con that he had, all his life, used for his own private advantage, he had sacrificed to her cause—and still she could not respond to him.

"I had to know," Bagsby said softly, shaking his feet dry in the warm summer air. He stood and walked over to her, looming above her, looking down with all the softness his life-hardened face could manage. "I thought you would understand."

"I do," Shulana said. "I do not understand your refusal to tell Elrond what has become of the Eggs. You do not understand that they could yet be the vital key to this entire war. They could decide whether my people live or die, and whether yours live in base slavery or maintain what is good in their civilization."

Bagsby sat on the grass beside her, running his hand through the green blades very close to hers. He had not wanted to reveal that he, too, now knew the secret of the treasure. He had not wanted to reveal that the Eggs had hatched, and that even now, in the mountains of the north, Scratch and Lifefire were beginning the process of reestablishing the dragon race. He had wanted to wait until the need of the elves and men for the dragons was so great that news of the existence would be welcomed rather than feared. He had wanted to wait until he could find a way to bind the dragons to the cause of the Alliance. But now he could wait no longer.

"I do know," he said, grasping Shulana's hand.

The elf raised her face in shock, her small mouth forming a simple *O* of surprise. "Then they have . . . ," she breathed.

"Hatched," Bagsby said, nodding. "Hatched and grown to full adulthood, with a little help from some magic powder."

Shulana sat straight up, alarm, even fear, showing on her face. Her hand became cold and trembled; her lower lip quivered. "Grown?" she asked. "Grown to adulthood? Capable of breeding? They must already be . . ."

"They are," Bagsby confirmed. "At least, I assume they are. I learned not to ask many questions about the personal lives of dragons. I don't think they would take it kindly."

"I must tell Elrond!" Shulana cried, leaping to her feet, wresting her hand free from Bagsby's. "They will strike; they will strike in league with Valdaimon to destroy us!" The slim figure began to run, but Bagsby shot out a hand and grabbed her by the ankle. She sprawled forward, facedown, onto the grass.

"No!" he said forcefully. "They will not strike the elves."

"Why not? Dragons have racial memory," Shulana explained. "Every detail of the old wars lies somewhere in the backs of their minds. They will want revenge. . . ."

"They may want peace," Bagsby said. "They remember that they were defeated in that war."

Shulana looked at Bagsby in full amazement. "You have spoken with them of these things?"

"Well," Bagsby hedged, "we've had a few conversations."

"And?" Shulana asked, anxiety mixed with hopeful eagerness on her face.

"And," Bagsby said, "there are a few details yet to be worked out, but I plan to have the dragons with us when the elves and the Holy Alliance stand together against Heilesheim."

Shulana stood and, resisting her instincts no longer, threw her arms around this strange human to whom her heart had become attached. Bagsby felt her slim form against his thick body, wrapped his arms around her back, and buried his face in her long, straight brown hair. It seemed to him as though his very soul heaved a sigh of relief and joy.

So entranced were the two that both failed to hear the clink of armor as the soldier-messenger came running up to them.

"Uh, humm!" the man said, making gentle coughing sounds.

Bagsby opened his eyes, cocked his head, and looked at the man askance.

"What is it?" he growled. "I'm busy at the moment."

"Sorry to interrupt your leisure, Sir John," the man said, head lowered in a curt bow. "But the Council of the Holy Alliance requests your presence to assume the office of Commanding General of the Holy Army of Men and Elves for the prosecution of the war against Ruprecht of Heilesheim."

Uh oh, Bagsby thought.

6

Preparations

CULDUS SAT ALONE in his study in the royal palace at Hamblen, his eyes pointed dully at the maps on which he had once planned the conquest of the Holy Alliance. But his eyes were not focused on the maps; instead, they were focused on the visions of disaster being manufactured by his imagination—an imagination that could draw upon a lifetime's experience of war to foresee the thousands of things, large and small, that could go wrong in the best-planned campaign.

Culdus saw his well-trained legions marching in their stunning pike columns up to the very edge of a towering wood. Up to that point they were invincible; only magical fireballs or other spells could harm them, and the rows of mages that always accompanied Heilesheim's armies were more than a match for any wizards in the world. But as the formations began to inch their way into the forest, it would be the beginning of the end of Heilesheim's greatness. The leading ranks, composed of the bravest and best troops, would maintain some cohesion as they moved at a snail's pace into the dense undergrowth of the forest floor. But their cohesion would do them no good: They would be mowed down by arrow fire from elves perched in the high trees all around them, out of reach of humans' deadly pikes. The rear ranks of the columns, of course, would lose their cohesion; individual men becoming separated, wandering in the undergrowth, getting confused, becoming turned around. More arrows would now come down from the trees—a downpour, a deluge of arrows. And then the spells would begin to pop, each elf enemy in his own right a minor mage. More men would drop, and still more would wander, stunned, dazed, and panicked. Then the elves would drop from their high perches to the forest floor, where they, long accustomed to the wood, could move with the speed of lightning, slitting throats, running men through, destroying in fifteen minutes the formations it had been the work of Culdus's entire lifetime to create.

The general shuddered. He knew his imaginings were not far from accurate. To attack the elves in that vast woods they called the Elven Preserve was suicidal. Ruprecht thought that the elves could be defeated by sheer weight of numbers. What foolishness, Culdus mused. The more men that were thrown into that endless tangle—where not even the light of sun could penetrate save at the elves' desire—the more men would be killed. And as for the king's idea of a flanking attack—sheer nonsense! Bad enough to penetrate into the wood; even worse to attempt to coordinate two separate attacking forces when communications between the two forces were not secured.

And yet, Culdus knew he had no choice but to obey. It had taken Culdus his entire life to devise the tactical system that had so far destroyed every human force opposed to it in battle on an open field. Now he would have only a few weeks to devise a system that would defeat elves—magic-using elves—in their own enchanted forest where they knew every tree, bush, and stick, and where every living thing of green could be a spy, a scout, and a trigger for a preset magic spell. And he had to do it.

Culdus beat his fist against the table in frustrated rage. It could not be done! Even a mad fool like Ruprecht should be able to see that it could not be done!

"The problem," said the scratchy voice of Valdaimon, "is, of course, the forest."

Culdus looked up and saw the old wizard, who had appeared out of thin air as was his wont, walking slowly across the spacious room toward the table. Normally he would have greeted the sorcerer with curses. Today, for some reason he could not fully understand himself, he was actually glad for the intrusion.

"Certainly the problem is the forest," Culdus barked. "Aside, of course, from the elves themselves," he added, dripping sarcasm.

Valdaimon inched closer to Culdus, his eyes riveted on the general's face. "The problem," he repeated, "is the forest. Your mass formations cannot be brought to bear there. The elves can murder them from the trees. Our own wizards cannot be sure of the effects of their spells there, for the plant life itself is said to be enchanted. Your men will become separated, panicked, slaughtered in detail."

Culdus returned the wizard's stare. Instinctively, he sensed that, despite their deep and abiding hatred for one another, each needed the other now.

"Yes," Culdus responded simply.

"Yet, if the elves could be driven into the open—a field, a valley, or even a plain—the outcome would be very different." Valdaimon came to stand next to Culdus, his leering face pressed close to the general's. Culdus stifled his impulse to retch at the stench that always accompanied Valdaimon; despite years of interaction with the wizard, he had never grown accustomed to that smell.

"It would," Culdus acknowledged. "In melee, the elves fight as light troops with bows and swords. Our cavalry could circle them, then charge, driving them headlong into our massed pike formations," Culdus said, visualizing the scene clearly. "Your wizards could do what was necessary to negate their spells," he added, giving the greatest acknowledgement he had ever given to Valdaimon's contribution to Heilesheim's previous victories. "The result would be a slaughter." Culdus stepped up to his maps, pointed to the broad expanse of Argolia, where the bulk of his army lay to the immediate east of the Elven Preserve. "Especially if it were well planned, in advance," he muttered, showing with a few brisk motions of his broad, brown fingers the potential movement of his corps. "The elves cannot field more than a few thousand fighters, even including their women. On three days' notice I could mass thirty, forty, even fifty thousand men against them."

"Then I have a solution," Valdaimon announced, smiling, his few yellow, scraggly teeth peering obscenely from between his narrow, dry lips.

"And what is that?" Culdus demanded, skeptical. He had heard promises from Valdaimon before—countless promises—

and he was hard pressed to remember when one of them had been fulfilled.

"Burn the forest," the old wizard said with a shrug. "Burn it root and branch. The elves can either die screaming in the flames or march out to face you in the field."

Culdus stood stock-still for a moment, the simplicity and brilliance of the idea seeping into his soul. "It would have to be magical fire," he answered slowly. "The elves would use their magic to try to stop it."

"Of course," Valdaimon said, surprised that a point so obvious would even have to be mentioned. "It would be a small contribution from my league to the victories of the army."

"And so say you all?" Sir John Wolfe asked the assembled nobles of the Holy Alliance.

The lords of the lands stood behind the chairs they had occupied for many weeks of council sessions. These were men of power, Bagsby realized—men born to power, raised with power, used to the everyday exercise of power. They were men of great pride, who found it difficult to submit to any outside authority. If he were to lead them in battle against Heilesheim, which he had no wish to do, he would have to be sure of their loyalty.

One by one, the noble heads dropped ever so slightly in courteous bows, acknowledging their assent to Bagsby's selection. He had been a compromise candidate—any one of these men was better qualified in terms of pure military background or skill in traditional, personal combat. But being proud men, they could not submit to one another. Besides, Bagsby—or Sir John as he was known in this company—was the only knight known to have defeated any force of Heilesheim regulars. Bagsby watched intently until every head save one was bowed in submission.

"And the elves, Elrond?" Bagsby asked. "What says the head of the Elven Council?"

"Sir John is well aware that there are unresolved issues between himself and the Elven Council, issues that could be considered . . . divisive," Elrond responded, speaking slowly. "Still, as no other leader could be agreed upon—and as we elves suspect that our forces will fight as a . . . separate contingent—I will consent to the choice."

"In giving this consent," Bagsby pressed, "do you or do you not pledge your obedience?" Bagsby did not demand absolute power, but if his plan were to succeed he must be given it, voluntarily, by men and elves.

Elrond was slow to respond. He studied Bagsby's face with a look of distaste on his own. And in the back of his mind, he remembered an ancient prophecy concerning the end of his race at the hands of a lesser race. Dare he put the fate of his race in the hands of this unreliable human who had already betrayed his trust? And yet, under the circumstances, what choice had he?

"So far as military authority extends," Elrond said carefully, "I will pledge the obedience of the elves. But in return I demand a pledge that the defense of the elves will be given equal weight with the defense of any human kingdom in the struggle to come. If this pledge is not kept, then I shall consider myself and my people released from our pledge to you," the old elf finally responded.

"So be it," Bagsby replied solemnly. "My lords, Your Majesties, I pray you be seated."

Bagsby alone remained standing as the nobility resumed their seats around the conference table. Bagsby smiled broadly as he surveyed the group. Not bad, he thought, for a little thief from Laga to be the acknowledged leader of the civilized forces of the earth. Not bad. And not enviable. There was much to be done.

"Good men and women, humans and elves," Bagsby declaimed, "I shall endeavor to my utmost to keep the trust you have placed in me. It is my determination to destroy the enemy in one, large battle."

Shouts of "Hurrah!" and "Hear! Hear!" rose around the table.

Bagsby held up a hand for silence. "This battle will be fought, I strongly suspect, in the plains and valleys of Argolia, in the lands not many miles east of the Elven Preserve and south of the border of Parona." Bagsby studied the reactions of Elrond and King Harold to this announcement. He was not certain how Harold would respond to the presence of a large army from Parona in Argolia, and he was uncertain as to how Elrond would react to learning that the great showdown would not be in the Elven Preserve, where the old elf surely expected it. Harold kept his face stony still, betraying no emotion. Elrond looked at Bagsby with frank curiosity.

"To prepare for this engagement, I will demand of each of you obedience to a set of commands that may seem . . . unusual," Bagsby continued, "to those skilled in the traditional arts of war." He paused again for effect. "We have learned from bitter experience that traditional methods are less than effective against the powerful arms of Heilesheim."

There were general nods of agreement around the table, mixed with looks of frank apprehension on the faces of the more powerful nobles.

"Nothing that will be asked of you will compromise your honor," Bagsby said, assuring them, "so long as you remember that your true honor lies in victory."

The assembly banged its assent with mailed fists on the top of the great table.

"I am glad of your response," Bagsby said. "Over the next week, I want all forces for the battle to be assembled here, in a great camp outside the capital of Parona."

King Alexis Aliapoulios visibly blanched at this announcement. The destruction that could be caused by even a friendly army could cost hundreds of thousands of crowns.

"King Alexis," Bagsby said, "as the member of the Holy Alliance which will be supplying the greatest number of troops, Parona will also have the honor of feeding and housing those troops."

"That is an honor," the king responded quickly, "that our treasury is ill equipped to receive. Perhaps if the elves, whose treasure is legendary, were to assist in defraying the expenses . . . ," the king began.

"Then we would be asking much too much of them," Bagsby dared to interrupt. "They will be required to abandon their forest in order to lure the enemy to the chosen battle site. They will supply most of the magic our forces will use, and they will almost certainly bear the brunt of the enemy's first attack.

Surely, that is contribution enough when Parona has been and will remain unscathed by the presence of the enemy."

"I fear our new commander has little experience in the financing and equipping of armies," Alexis said, rising. "The other members of the council. . . ."

"Are well aware that Parona recently sold to the enemy, Heilesheim, for purposes undisclosed, the most fabulous treasure owned by humankind—and that the treasury of Parona is filled to overflowing with the gold Heilesheim used to make payment for that treasure," Bagsby snapped. "Your Majesty has pledged his obedience to *me* in these matters," he added.

King Alexis resumed his seat, silenced and embarrassed. It was a bitter draught Sir John had made him drink—and publicly—one the king silently vowed not to forget.

Bagsby continued, noting to himself with satisfaction that with sufficient presumption and a bit of hard facts, one could silence even a king.

"It will be necessary for me to be gone for the next week or two, to arrange for certain matters pertinent to the coming conflict that are best not discussed publicly," Bagsby declared. "In my absence, the footmen who gather will be trained by my trusted lieutenant, George of Heilesheim." Bagsby silenced the murmurs of rising outrage that rippled through the noble audience by quickly adding, "What better way to defeat a Heilesheim force than by understanding its tactics? Mounted knights are to work out their own order of battle during my absence." That, Bagsby thought, should keep the nobles occupied for the better part of much more than the time he required.

"And now, my friends," Bagsby said, reaching to the table and pouring a golden goblet full of Parona's best rich red wine, "let us drink to The Holy Alliance, and to victory!"

Bagsby took Shulana with him, and only Shulana. For what he was preparing, he wanted no witnesses, save for the one person he knew would never willingly harm him. He had pondered the risk to her when he formulated his plan, and he knew it was considerable. But if she died, he would die with her. And what more pleasant fate could a man have than to die with the woman he loved?

Bagsby stole a glance at Shulana. As always, she was very lovely, in her simple green tunic, with her magic cloak folded and tucked neatly beneath her small saddle. She wore a small bag on a strap around her shoulders, and it rocked gently with her horse's motion. A quiver of arrows bobbed on her back, and by her right leg her bow and sword were carefully secured, ready for instant action.

She really is beautiful, Bagsby thought. And so unlike other women—so cunning in battle, so skillful at reading the plots of others, and yet so naive in her love and trust. He wanted to reach out to her, to draw her to him, to envelop her in his protecting, loving embrace and float away to oblivion with her in his arms.

Bagsby's horse made a small jump over a large, fungus-eaten tree trunk that had fallen across the narrow forest path. The jolt to his backside brought the knight errant back to the present reality. It had taken three days' ride to bring them to these mountain foothills, and now they had at least three more days—hard days—ahead as they ascended the great mountains whose icy fingers could be seen in the far northeast, reaching for the sky above the tops of the trees.

Shulana laughed as the surprise of the horse's movement registered on Bagsby's face. Her rare elven laughter carried in the thin summer air, and to Bagsby it sounded like the tones of wind chimes, a music at once strange, beautiful, and soothing.

"You must pay attention, Sir John," Shulana chided, "to where you are riding. We can ill afford to lose you now to a spill from a horse."

"That would be an inglorious end for the commanding general of the Holy Alliance," Bagsby bantered back. "But I'll wager you the secret of our destination that I can still outride a mere slip of an elven girl." Still gloriously attired in his role as Sir John for purposes of this journey, Bagsby spurred his much larger mount. "To the top of this rise," he called, as the large horse—laden with gear, armor, arms, and clothing—broke into a heavy, thunderous gallop.

Shulana laughed again, leaned forward, and whispered in the ear of her mount, which at once broke into a swift stride. The two raced forward down the narrow path, Bagsby slightly in the lead, his eyes glued to the top of the rise at the edge of the woods ahead, with its promise of a dropoff into a sunnier, rockier landscape. Shulana, too, taken up with the excitement of the race, did not notice the two fluidlike patches of cold darkness that glided from the wooded shadows to ripple and flow down the dark path behind the pair.

The race was short, less than half a mile, but Shulana's lighter mount and superior riding skills proved more than a match for Bagsby. The little man maneuvered skillfully, using the bulk of his larger horse to block the pathway, but eventually a break occurred in the trees and Shulana and her steed were through it in a flash. Bagsby's view of the pleasant ridgetop was thereafter blocked by the bobbing tail of Shulana's mount, though his ears were still rewarded with the beautiful tinkling of her continued laughter.

Shulana reached the crest of the rise a good hundred yards ahead of Bagsby. She raised a hand to her forehead to shield her eyes against the sudden brilliance of the sun and gazed out with serene pleasure at the jagged, brilliant landscape that stretched below her. The path meandered downhill through a grassy field lush with wildflowers of a hundred hues which peeked out from around the rugged, gray granite boulders that were strewn everywhere like corpses after a battle. On the far side of the downhill slope, a similar rise led upward along the face of the first true mountain of this northern land. The snowline inched down the face of that rise; they would be traveling in snow and cold by tomorrow, Shulana thought.

The victory hers, Shulana turned to greet Bagsby's arrival with her laughing face. Bagsby, his eyes glued on hers, had already reined in his mount—which was nearly winded—and was now merely trotting toward the same panoramic view enjoyed by the elf. His eyes were locked on the beauty of Shulana, her hair, her form, her laughing face—which suddenly became sharp and alert, with deadly intent in the eyes.

"Bagsby!" she cried. "Run! Gallop for the sunlight!"

Bagsby instead drew his steed to a halt, puzzled. As he watched, the elf's keen-edged sword flashed from its resting place on her horse's flank, and the lithe figure slid down the side of her horse and raced forward, the deadly blade raised high above her head.

"Ride! Ride on!" she called as she raced on foot past the stupefied man. He watched, still unresponding, as she swung the blade downward, striking at the very earth at her feet. Instead of sinking in the ground, as Bagsby would have expected, the blow glanced off, the sword seeming to bounce back upward. Only then did Bagsby's human eyes spot the round, black shadow on the ground in the place where Shulana had aimed her strike. Then the round shadow flitted forward, and another was rippling forward along the path fast behind it. The two forms could barely be seen in the thick shade provided by the forest canopy.

"No!" Bagsby cried, the sight stinging him into action. He had heard, of course, of such undead things as these shadow creatures—beings neither living nor dead, whose very touch could drain the soul from a human or the life force from an elf. He had heard, but never seen. But he also had heard that only a blessed weapon would avail against them.

Bagsby turned in his saddle and fumbled with the bundles strapped to his horse. That sword—it was here somewhere—was the one that the high priests of the Holy Alliance had blessed at his ceremonial investiture as leader of the Alliance forces. His fingers fumbled over knots and the outsides of knapsacks. Where . . . ?

His hand found the hilt of the sword. Bagsby turned forward, spurred the horse, and jerked the reins around in one motion. A second later the great sword was free. Designed more for appearances than for function, the blessed blade felt like a weight of lead in his hand, and his arm strained to raise it as he guided the horse forward, his eyes searching the dark ground for a place that was slightly darker.

Shulana, her attack foiled by the natural resistance of the creatures, was fleeing back up the path toward the safety of the sunlight—these creatures could not bear exposure to the light of day. Even as his steed gained momentum, pounding forward, Bagsby thought for an instant about fleeing to that sanctuary of light. No good, his instincts told him. *If we don't get them now, they'll come for us at night, and I'll never be able to see them then.*

Bagsby detected the slightest ripple in the darkness on the path ahead. He threw himself to the right of his horse and let his arm drop. The striking point of the huge sword plunged downward and slid without resistance into the ground. Bagsby heard a high-pitched wail as the forward momentum of his horse's movement tore the sword from its hold on the earth. He lifted the weapon to find a quivering, writhing plane of circular blackness impaled on the point, shrinking rapidly, wailing with the cry of the damned, until it vanished into nothingness.

"By all the gods!" Bagsby exclaimed, reining the horse to a jolting stop. He whirled. Shulana was just bouncing out of sight, over the crest of the ridge. She was safe. Now where was the other one?

The plaintive cry of Bagsby's own horse answered his question. The little man felt the animal's legs go suddenly limp, and the beast began to plunge toward the ground, all four knees buckling at once. Bagsby leapt to his feet in the saddle and pushed off backward, throwing himself into a back somersault high in the air and landing on his feet behind the horse. The ripple of darkness was flowing over its back when, with a scream of rage, Bagsby slashed down at it with the blessed blade.

The horrid wail of the creature joined the whinnying screams of Bagsby's dying horse as the blade sliced the shadow in two, brilliant rays of white light leaping from the sides of the sword as it sliced through the damned being. Bagsby staggered backward, breathing hard as much from anger as from exertion, and watched the shadow shrink, like its companion, down into a vanishing nothingness. Then, with a scream of rage and disgust, Bagsby drew back the great sword and again plunged it downward, giving his dying horse peace.

The forest was alive now with the sounds of countless birds, roused from their uncaring peace by the din of battle from the pathway far below their perches. Amid their whoops and whistles and warbling calls, Bagsby could hear the loud, shrieking caw of a crow. Then he saw it: the tattered, large black bird swept past his face, its talons digging into the flesh of his cheeks as it raced past. Bagsby howled.

"Down!" he heard Shulana cry, behind him. Bagsby immediately dropped to one knee, his left hand clutching his bleeding, wounded cheek.

Shulana, too, had heard the cry of the crow, and guessed at its meaning. The attack on Bagsby as the bird fled the scene confirmed her guess. As the black thing flapped its bedraggled wings as hard as it could, slowly mounting the sky, Shulana raced to the side of her horse, grabbed her bow, and strung an arrow. The bird was already high in the sky, hard to see against the canopy of green above, when she let the arrow fly.

Bagsby heard the shaft cleave the air not two feet above his head; had he not dropped on Shulana's command the iron point would have bit into the back of his neck. Instead the arrow sang past him, mounting into the air with a speed so great that Bagsby's eye could not see the deadly missile until it stopped, having neatly pierced the body of its fat, ugly target.

The crow screamed a death cry far louder than any bird Bagsby had ever heard before. Its wings struggled onward for a few futile beats before collapsing. Then, the black, bleeding mass of flesh plummeted to the ground, trailing dirty black feathers in the air.

Bagsby felt Shulana's hand upon his shoulder. His right hand released its tight grip on the hilt of the huge sword, and he moved it up to pat the back of hers.

"Valdaimon," Shulana said flatly.

"What?" Bagsby said, still breathing in deep gasps as the anger and excitement drained from his body. The fingers of his left hand gently stroked his burning, bloodied cheek, seeking to determine the nature of the wound.

"Valdaimon," Shulana repeated. "It had to be. He is known to be a black wizard who commands the lesser undead—those lesser than himself. That bird was what human wizards would call his familiar."

"What?" Bagsby repeated, not comprehending.

"It is like the communion elves have with all green living things," Shulana explained. "Human wizards can have that, too, but only with one animal, and only by means of a very powerful spell. Once the spell is cast, the wizard can see through the animal's eyes, hear through its ears, feel, taste, and smell through its senses."

"Can he taste its death?" Bagsby asked bitterly, moving Shulana's hand aside and rising to his feet. His fine boots were stained now with the puddling blood of his horse.

"Yes," Shulana said. "He used that animal to follow us. He saw this fight. He knows where we are."

Bagsby tramped up to the fallen body of the crow, and spat on the corpse. "I hope he can feel that, too," the little man said.

"No," Shulana said, not grasping the ironic intent in Bagsby's remark. "Once the familiar is dead, the wizard cannot use it, not even an undead thing like Valdaimon. But he will know where we are."

"That was inevitable," Bagsby said, shrugging, removing his fine silk ascot to make a bandage for his face. "Once Sir John made his reappearance in Parona, it was only a matter of time until Valdaimon's agents found him. Better that they found us now rather than later. There will be few men or creatures in these parts that he can call upon to do his bidding. And Valdaimon himself must be far away, in Heilesheim or Argolia."

Shulana nodded. "We've lost a horse," she pointed out.

"We'll walk," Bagsby said grimly. "And I think there is a way to cut two days off our journey. Since I cannot go to the mountain, I must make what is in the mountain come to me."

"Yes," Shulana said, her face suddenly brightening. "I did win our race. You owe me the prize!"

Bagsby tied the ascot around the top of his head, and grimaced with pain as he tried to grin. "Right, right," he agreed. "And you shall have it, though I fear you won't like it," he said.

"Well, then, tell me. What is—or was—our destination?" Shulana asked.

"We're going to meet two friends of mine, who I hope will help us in the war," Bagsby said simply, striding up to Shulana and taking her in his aching arms. He pressed her tiny head against his chest and caressed her hair. "There is one thing you should probably know before we meet them," he added in a soft voice, gently kissing the top of her hair.

"Umm," Shulana said, nuzzling into the warmth of Bagsby's embrace. "What's that?" Her mind refused the obvious.

"They are . . . not humans," Bagsby said.

"Elves?" Shulana asked, pulling her head back in surprise. A sudden doubt clutched her heart. *He wouldn't* . . .

Bagsby shook his head. "No."

"Dwarves, then? I've never seen dwarves, though I've heard much about them. . . ."

Again, Bagsby shook his head.

"Not men, not elves, not dwarves, what could they be if not . . . ," Shulana said, a look of shocked understanding dawning on her face. "Not them! You can't mean . . ."

Bagsby held one finger up to his lips and made the *Shhhh* sound. "Dragons," he whispered.

Bagsby warmed himself in the huge bonfire he had fashioned in the open field on the downside of the ridge. Despite the light of the fire, his eyes could pick out the twinkling of the thousand points of starlight that adorned the glorious northern night sky. He clapped his hands and rubbed them briskly near the roaring flames; it got cold this far north, even on a summer night.

The fire was huge. It had taken Bagsby the greater part of the day to cut the wood for it, and he had built it as large as possible, working well after the setting of the sun. Then he had waited anxiously as the first smolderings of flaming tinder had passed the magic of fire onto the larger pieces of wood, and then on to the great logs he had managed to pile up, until the whole was a circular blazing inferno some twenty feet in diameter. The flames licked at the starlight, rising high into the sky, and the combination of black and white smokes rose higher still.

Shulana did not share Bagsby's joy in the accomplishment. Bagsby did not find it strange that she had grown somewhat sullen at the news that they had come north to find the two dragons that had hatched from the Golden Eggs. He did think it odd that his reassurances that he could handle the creatures did little to ease her mind.

In fact, Shulana had begun to work even before Bagsby had the fire blazing. Taking some curious white powder from a vial in her leather pouch, she had outlined the earth around the bonfire in a great circle. Then, making sure that she and Bagsby were both inside the circle, she had begun weaving her hands in the air in a series of strange, fluid gestures, and chanting in the musical tongue that Bagsby knew was her native language—a language of great magic power. She had continued her chanting far longer than Bagsby had ever seen before. What spell, he had wondered, was she weaving?

"Protection," she had answered simply when her casting was done and he had ventured to ask. "I do not intend to give my name easily when your 'friends' arrive."

"Give your name?" Bagsby had queried. "What do you mean? You don't want to be introduced?"

Shulana had hung her head in part mock, part sincere despair at Bagsby's human ignorance. "To an elf, to give your name means to die. When one elf slays another in fair combat, the victor must give his true name—not his common name—to the vanquished. It is considered the giving of a life for a life, so there is no blood debt."

Bagsby had shaken his head, still confused. "You mean, elves all have two names?"

"Certainly," Shulana had responded. "All things have two names: their common name and their true name. The true name is the name in the language of magic, the name that allows its possessor to have great power over the named thing."

"Hunnh," Bagsby had said. Useful bit of information, he thought to himself.

It was this useful bit of information that Bagsby was now pondering as he warmed himself by the great fire and gazed skyward. They would come, he knew. They would see the fire from their perch high in the mountains, and they would wonder who dared to come so close to the mountains which even the dwarves had abandoned years in the past. They would come, swooping down out of the night sky in all their power and majesty.

And, Bagsby thought, they would see an elf. But they would also see him. He was gambling both Shulana's life and his own that they would pause to listen to him before simply toasting a representative of the race that had nearly exterminated their own kind.

Shulana sat huddled near the edge of the circle, her head resting on her knees. This was insanity, she thought. Bagsby was so confident of his own abilities that he had doomed her, and very likely himself. Worse, he had probably doomed her entire race, for when the dragons had time to breed, to grow strong, they would seek revenge against the one race that had first challenged their virtual domination of the world and eventually driven them to extinction. No glib-tongued human could possibly overcome the power of a racial hatred so deep. Shulana fingered her bow, kept handy by her side. She wondered if one her arrows, enchanted as they were, could pierce the tough armor of a dragon. Perhaps if she shot for the eye. . . .

Her musings were interrupted by the growing sound of a dull roar that grew and grew in intensity until Shulana could feel the force of the winds.

"They're coming," Bagsby said, racing to her side and throwing himself on the ground. "Better grab on to one of these rocks. Their landings cause quite a ruckus!"

Shulana flopped onto her belly, grasped her bow tight in her left hand and, with her right, grasped one of the jagged outcroppings that dotted the portion of the field inside her magic circle. The wind, of course, might blow away most of the magic powder, but even then the spell would hold for a short time. If she could get one strategic shot, she thought, she could kill one of the things, or at least wound it horribly. . . .

The howling din grew too great to even think. Shulana's arm ached as the wind tugged at her light body; her fingertips began to bleed from the force with which she grasped her granite anchor.

"It's both of them, all right!" Bagsby shouted at the top of his lungs.

Shulana could see the movement of his lips, but could not hear his words.

"Oh boy! Hang on!" the little thief called again.

Shulana's hand could not hold. Reluctantly, she let go the bow and grasped the rock with both hands; even then, she found, she could barely hold on against the force of the violently swirling air. The fire behind her churned, swirled, and then, with a crash, scattered—the burning logs tossed across the landscape with the same ease that a child would toss seeds of grain.

Then, abruptly, the wind stopped, and there were two mighty crashes that jarred the earth so hard that Shulana and Bagsby both bounced up, only to have the wind knocked from their lungs as they flopped back down again.

Shulana began to tremble, experiencing the effects of dragonfear that Bagsby had already known. Bagsby, for his part, his lungs burning, was struggling to breathe. The fear of the dragons seemed not as great to him—in fact, he hardly felt frightened at all, so inured was he to their presence by his long association with them. *Next will come the voice,* he thought. *Poor Shulana. Bet she's scared stiff.*

"Who defiles the lands of Scratch and Lifefire!" the thundering, gravelly voice demanded. "Who attempts with the frail spell to keep Scratch from taking justice upon their person?"

"Scratch!" Bagsby managed to shout, air flooding back into his aching chest. "Scratch, it's me, Bagsby!"

The ground shook again as the mighty male dragon stomped it with one powerful hind foot. "Thief! Liar! Cheat! You dare come back to face Scratch?"

"I do," Bagsby shouted, finally releasing his grip on the rocks and staggering to his feet. "I wanted to talk to you and Lifefire," he said, deliberately lowering his voice to get the dragons' attention. "I remind you that you yourself agreed I was neither thief, nor cheat, nor liar, as far you were concerned. Did you not find your treasure where I said it would be?"

"I did!" Scratch thundered back. "But you were cunning, you tricked us. . . ."

"He was within his rights, Scratch," the slightly higher voice of Lifefire sounded. "You can always kill him, or berate him at your leisure if that is your will. Right now, why not see what he wants?"

"Ah, Lifefire, it is good to see you again," Bagsby called. "I, too, have a friend with me. This," Bagsby said, pointing to the huddling mass of fear that Shulana had become, "is Shulana, who has traveled here with me to meet you."

"Elf!" Scratch boomed. The mighty dragon's head reared back, the jaws gaping wide, the lungs sucking deeply at the night air.

"I come to bring you life for your race!" Bagsby cried. "Don't you dare harm my friend, who has risked her life to join me in this offer to you."

Lifefire, moving with a quickness belied by her great size, swung her head outward and upward, catching Scratch with a glancing blow to the neck that lifted his own head upward. As the male dragon exhaled, a gout of flame shot outward into the black night sky, its orange, red, and blue hues dancing with the dragon's own rage.

"Hear him out," Lifefire commanded. "Bagsby," she said, lowering his voice to a volume that no longer hurt Bagsby's ears, "your life depends upon your words."

Don't I know that, Bagsby thought.

"Lifefire, as always, is full of wisdom, even as Scratch is full of the awesome power of the great dragon race," Bagsby replied, bowing as courteously as he could. No doubt, he realized, some of the grandeur intended by the gesture was rendered comical by the bandage about his face, but then perhaps dragons didn't notice such things. "I willingly put my life in your hands so you may hear my words. And I tell you plainly, your lives as well as mine depend upon what I say."

Scratch bellowed in anger. "You dare to threaten us? You, who have seen our power?" the dragon roared.

"I do not threaten the great Scratch," Bagsby responded. "I simply state the truth that Scratch himself knows."

"What truth is that?" Lifefire demanded. "Be quick; Scratch grows impatient," she warned.

"You see huddled here this frightened elf?" Bagsby asked, pointing to Shulana, who only now was beginning to recover from the waves of fear that afflicted all beings who saw a live, adult dragon for the first time. "She is a mere slip of a female, a nothing, less than a tiny morsel for the great Scratch," Bagsby continued. He noted that Scratch, for once, nodded in agreement and began to puff up with pride. "Yet it was elves such as these that once destroyed the dragon race, mighty as it was," Bagsby declared.

"That is an ancient story," Lifefire said. "One whose outcome is still in doubt, as our presence attests."

"True, true," Bagsby agreed quickly. "By good fortune, by the power of magic and by the favor of the gods, the dragon race has gained a reprieve. You exist. This elf and I are here to offer you the chance to continue to exist."

"The elves are weak now!" Scratch said. "Their numbers are few. . . ."

"And yours are fewer, but I did not come here to threaten you with elves. I came to tell you of a greater threat," Bagsby said, stepping right up to Scratch's huge body and trying to look into one of the dragon's great eyes. "The threat of humans. They are coming, the humans; they are coming everywhere. It was the humans who defeated the elves and reduced their numbers, even as the elves defeated the dragons. And if a race of dragons could not defeat the full race of elves, what chance will two dragons stand against the entire race of men, whose numbers are greater than the number of stars in the sky?"

"I see how I could reduce the numbers of humans and elves, each by one," Scratch said, pawing the earth.

"It is you who threaten us," Lifefire interjected, "for you are human."

"I am human," Bagsby admitted. "And never did dragons have a greater friend, for I bring you great news that can be the salvation of your race, and the key to peace between elves, men, and dragons."

"Live long enough to tell me this news," Scratch replied, "while I cast the spell that will break this circle of protection, that I may enjoy the taste of your human blood."

"You see?" Bagsby said. "If the two of you must use magic to defeat the feeble spell of one elf, you will have no chance against the vile human wizard who even now directs his forces to the conquest of all Parona, including these mountains where you dwell. But my news is this," Bagsby quickly added, noting that Scratch was beginning to mutter something in strange gravelly tones. "The humans are divided into two camps. One would conquer all and either exterminate or make slaves of all dragons. The other, my camp, fights for the freedom of all races, and peace between us."

Bagsby paused. Was it time to ask the key question? Lifefire, he knew, was ready. Scratch must be interested, Bagsby noted, for he had momentarily stopped his mumbling.

The stillness was broken by the soft sounds made by Shulana as she slowly rose to her feet. The elf then silently walked to stand by Bagsby's side, gazing with awe, fear, anger, and wonder at the two huge red creatures whose bodies stretched out before her. How, she wondered, had Elrond ever slain a creature so powerful?

"On behalf of humans and elves, I have come to offer peace to the dragons, and security for their race. In exchange, I ask for your help in the great battle we must fight against those who would enslave both us and you," Bagsby said grandly. Then, putting on his sternest face, the one he had practiced when leading troops in Argolia, he demanded, "What is your reply?"

The two huge beasts turned face to face, staring at one another. Scratch's giant rear feet clawed at the earth in frustration. How much simpler to just eat these troublesome creatures. He had no intention of sharing a world with them. But Lifefire—Lifefire was always concerned about the future. What would she say? For who could live with her if her path to the motherhood of a new dragon race was blocked?

Lifefire answered first. "How," she queried, "would we begin?"

Bagsby exhaled slowly and with an enormous sense of relief.

"Well," he said, "to start with, we need to teach Shulana how to ride on your back."

"No!" Scratch boomed. Bagsby and Shulana staggered backward, the ground beneath their feet trembling from the deep bass vibrations of his enraged voice. "There can be no peace with the elves! With men—I do not like it, but I will permit it. But not with elves, not with the creatures who slew the mother of us all!"

"Yes, it must be," Bagsby said, leaning forward, then striding forward, regaining his ground. "For the elves fight with us. Nevertheless, I understand your ancient hatred. If you will agree to this alliance, I will give you one more thing, once the battle is fought. It is the one thing, Scratch, that you want more than any other thing."

"No gold can buy my honor!" the dragon boomed, and again the earth trembled, but this time Bagsby managed to stand his ground, clinging to Shulana to keep them both from falling.

"Not gold, Scratch," Bagsby said. "I will give you the life of the elf who slew your mother."

The huge dragon, Scratch, cocked his head toward his mate and muttered in the dragon tongue, "What are they doing?"

Lifefire cocked her head in return, so that the crests of the two great dragons scraped together. She studied the strange scene before her for a long while in silence, then she replied in the guttural rush of air that dragons call a whisper, "I don't know."

The two mighty beasts watched in amazement the puzzling behavior of the male human and the female elf.

At first it seemed to be a fight—strange behavior indeed for one coming to offer peace. The elf hurled herself upon Bagsby, her tiny fists clutched tightly, hot tears of rage streaming down her flushed cheeks. Her flurry of blows caught Bagsby off guard; he fell over backward, and Shulana threw herself upon him, her fists pounding into his face.

"No, Shulana, you don't understand . . ." Bagsby shouted.

"You would murder Elrond for the sake of dragons!" the elf shouted, her solid little blows striking Bagsby's nose, eyes, and cheeks until he managed to raise his arms over his face in self-defense. Still she pummeled him, striking his arms and shoulders.

"No, no, wait," Bagsby cried. "Let me explain."

Shulana plunged a fist sharply into his breastbone. The air rushed from Bagsby's lungs and his eyes bulged.

"Why," Scratch commented to his mate, "does he not fight back?"

"Perhaps they are frolicking," Lifefire suggested.

"Hmmm," Scratch replied. "Perhaps that is why she does not use magic to destroy him."

"Just so," Lifefire agreed. "See?" she added, nodding toward the continuing bout.

Shulana, her fury spent, had collapsed into a tearful heap on Bagsby's chest. The little man, sucking air furiously, moved his arms to place them around her back and shoulders, his bruised hands patting her softly.

"How could you? You knew I loved you—how could you?" Shulana gasped in tearful whispers, her voice muffled in Bagsby's shoulders.

"It is the only way," Bagsby managed to whisper back. "But I swear it will not mean Elrond's death."

"How?" Shulana asked in a voice breaking with grief.

Bagsby sat up in the dirt, pulling Shulana to a sitting position in front of him. He took her small face in his hands and raised it until her eyes met his.

"I have done all this so far for you. Now you must make a decision. You must choose to trust me—or not," he said calmly.

"But Elrond. . . ." Shulana protested.

"Will live," Bagsby replied calmly. "As will we all if this mad scheme of mine works. So far, I've had reasonable success with mad schemes, as long as you were there to help me. . . ."

Shulana stared long and hard at Bagsby. *Who was this human who had so captured her heart? Were there no young elves in the Preserve that she should be brought to this pass with a human?* Every ounce of her being told her that this was madness. She should flee, warn the elves, warn Elrond, and raise a force to destroy these dragons. And yet deep within her, an instinct older and stronger than survival flowed toward a different path.

"I . . . ," she began, then hesitated. She lowered her head, gently removing Bagsby's hands. She stared at the earth, then at the powerful beasts just beyond, who stared back with eyes of wonder. Finally she stood, extending a hand to Bagsby, who stood up beside her. She stared straight into his soft eyes, and said, "I choose to trust you. May the gods pity us both if I am wrong."

Bagsby encircled Shulana in his arms and drew her to him until their lips met.

"There," Lifefire announced, pleased to have been right. "You see, it is a frolic of sorts, though they do seem to take a while to get about the real business."

Shulana soared on Lifefire's back, high above the clouds that shrouded the mountain peaks. Bagsby was right; flying on a dragon was exhilirating beyond compare. It was different even than flying under a spell of magic, for in that case there is no great beast beneath one's body and within one's control. The sheer power was thrilling. No wonder Bagsby had chosen her—an elf—to share it. Few humans, she knew, could ever be trusted with such awesome force.

"Now, Lifefire," Shulana shouted into the winds, "let's try it again. Remember, the blast must appear chaotic but actually be controlled."

"You are demanding, elf," Lifefire growled. "But you are correct."

The creature flexed her shoulders ever so slightly, and a ripple of tension ran down her back toward her tail. An instant later, her wings tilted slightly, and the huge bulk of the beast began to dive downward, the angle becoming steeper and steeper until Shulana was forced to push off against the hand-hold of her saddle to keep from pitching forward. Dragon and rider plunged downward into the thick, white nothing of the clouds, lost in time and space with no sense of motion, until suddenly the mist parted and the granite earth gaped beneath them, littered with a forest of evergreens.

"Only the right half!" Shulana called, gripping the saddle of her mount even tighter as she felt the huge chest begin to expand beneath her.

An instant later, a stream of fire belched forth from the

dragon's mouth and, ever expanding, dropped earthward where it exploded against the tops of the trees, bathing almost exactly one-half of the copse in flames that, in a second, left nothing but charred, falling trunks and smoking black earth.

"That's it! That's it!" Shulana shouted. "You've got it, exactly! This is how you will destroy foes on the battlefield, but leave your friends unharmed!"

At last, Lifefire thought. The countless practices had tried her patience with this tiny creature with whom, however, the dragon sensed a strange kinship: the kinship of those who both are fighting for the survival not only of themselves, but also of their very race.

Slowly, the dragon descended the rest of the way to the ground, coming to an especially gentle landing for the elf's sake.

"I have learned. You have taught me as Bagsby said you would."

"Yes," Shulana answered. "But now there is Scratch. He must learn before the appointed time. And he despises me still."

"I think it best," Lifefire growled slowly, "if I teach Scratch. He still barely understands the terms of our alliance—terms that were difficult for you, too, to comprehend."

Shulana nodded. The dragon was correct. It would be best for Scratch to learn from Lifefire, even as both of them had learned the true meaning of their alliance and the true seal that would guarantee the peace between their races.

But time was pressing, Shulana knew. Soon would be the day of battle—and she would see Bagsby again. Somehow that thought was almost as exhilirating as flying on a dragon.

"Shouldn't we wait? I mean, until Sir John returns?" Marta gasped, her face flushed and her breath coming in short, surprised gulps.

"Why wait for some noble?" George replied. "Besides, Bagsby's okay; 'e'll understand 'ow it is. A man's gotta do wot a man's gotta do. And right now, I gotta do this."

They stood in the midst of the vast training field with the noontime sun streaming down on them. It glinted off the steam rising from plate of hot stew Marta had prepared and brought to the hard-working George.

George grabbed the plate and stuffed a wooden ladle of stew into his mouth. "Good," he declared. "You ain't given me an answer yet."

"Well, a woman in my position has to consider this very carefully . . . ," Marta began.

"Wot position?" George demanded hotly. "You're taggin' around wit' an army, that's wot you're doin'. And while you got me to protect you, that's all well and good. But wot about later? It ain't fittin', I tell you. A woman like you deserves an 'usband, and I may not be the best, but I 'ave one great virtue," George declared.

"What on earth is that," Marta teased, trying to hide the depths to which she was truly overjoyed.

"I'm available, and you already knows me. 'Ell, that's two virtues."

The wedding that evening was a simple affair. Marta chose to wear something other than full-battle regalia, which pleased George to no end. For his own part he had carefully chosen a day when his pants and tunic were both clean. A simple priest, originally from Clairton, officiated at the ceremony—which George found mercifully brief, unlike most of his previous exposures to religion. As the words of the final blessing were said, George and Marta released skyward one dove each, symbols of the love and peace between them, symbols that they offered to the gods in hope of their blessing. A cheer went up from the numerous low-level officers who had gathered to witness the occasion.

"Now lads!" George called out grandly. "A tankard of ale, or two if we need them, and we'll celebrate in a way that will make the gods jealous of our happiness!" More throaty cheers resounded under the star-studded sky, and four men came forward, bearing a great barrel of brew.

"I think not!" Marta shouted, stepping forward to place her substantial person between George and well-wishers. "You're a married man now and have better things to do than carouse with soldiers! And especially," she added more softly, "on your wedding night."

" 'Ere now, love, just a quick tankard, then I'll be straight. . . ."

"You'll be straight-off with me right now, George, if you know what is good for you," Marta growled, the glow of love turning to anger in her face.

George hesitated, but only for an instant. "Go ahead boys, celebrate all night!" he cried, sweeping his bride up in both arms. "As for me, I've got important business to attend to!"

The loudest cheer of all rang out in response as George carried Marta off toward a nearby tent.

"Oh, George," Marta whispered. "You've made me so proud."

"Thank you, love," George said, panting from his burden. *Ten thousand hells*, he thought. *Wot 'ave I got myself into?*

"Close it up there! Close it up!" George shouted. By all the gods, had these men never fought in battle before? It was bad enough that, even with the treasury of Parona to plunder, he could come up with pikes for only half the footmen. And that was with Elrond's help—the old elf seemed to know how to get the artisans of Parona to redouble their output of spear shafts and pike points—but even then it wasn't enough. Many of the men were still armed only with long bills, or worse yet, short spears. Most had little or no armor; many wore nothing more than a leather cuirass over their everyday tunic. They grumbled continuously about the drill George had imposed, and the Paronans, especially, seemed incapable of grasping the concept of keeping their ranks closed while they marched forward at a slow, steady pace.

"You see, Sir?" George asked, turning to Bagsby who had come to witness the day's activity on the drilling field by the great camp outside Parona. "You see? They won't keep in closed ranks, and I ain't goin' to be responsible for the result."

"You'll whip them into shape," Bagsby replied. "You can't expect them to learn the whole Heilesheim system in a week."

The commanding general of the Holy Alliance looked out over the drill field to see that the other units were doing about the same as the one to which George was currently devoting his less-than-loving attentions. The sun-drenched field revealed that the attempt to teach the men to fight in pike blocks had so far resulted in ragged square formations that fell apart when advancing. Still, Bagsby saw reason for hope.

"Look there, George," he said, pointing with his riding whip across the field to one unit that was drawn up in close order, the front two ranks kneeling with pikes extended, the ranks behind with pikes forward, set to receive a charge. "Those fellows seem to have the hang of it while they're standing still."

"Can't win a battle standin' still," George retorted. "An' what about them blokes over there?" George demanded. He jabbed a finger in the direction of a wedge-shaped formation of northern bowmen. "They won't even take orders, they won't. Won't give up them stupid bows for a trusty pike. Won't learn to march in any kind of formation. Won't . . . ."

"True, true, but that is at my order," Bagsby said. "I told you they were exempt from your training."

"Well, I'm cursed by all the gods if I see why," George answered. "Out there in the field, all in loose order like that, they'll get ridden down by the first cavalry charge, mark my words," the soldier predicted.

Bagsby smiled. That was exactly what he'd hoped George would think, and he hoped the enemy would think that as well.

Bagsby looked on as George went back to drilling his unit, cursing the men, kicking them, thwacking them with the blunt end of his own pike, which he handled with the skill of a seasoned veteran. As Bagsby had thought, promotion and a meaningful task had brought out George's better qualities. The title of Commander for Training of Footmen had flattered him, and the rich salary Bagsby had liberated from Parona's treasury for him had mollified his desire for treasure. Any time the man had left over for doubting what had happened to the Golden Eggs was taken up by Marta. She was more than gratified to see her new husband advanced to such a position of importance, and she would never allow him to breathe a word against dear Sir John who had made it all possible.

No, George was not a problem, Bagsby thought, as he watched his director of training kick a stumbling farmboy in the belly. The kings were a bit of a problem, though; neither they nor their nobles—which included the entire mounted force of the Holy Alliance—had the slightest grasp of Bagsby's plan. There were constant grumblings from them, and King Alexis in particular was spreading his own discontent with the enormous costs associated with Bagsby's plan—whatever it was. Then, there were the dragons. The timing of their appearance was everything. For the third time that day, Bagsby touched the small gold ring on his left fourth finger, a gift begged of Elrond which allowed him to touch the mind of Shulana.

Instantly, he saw before him the icy peak of a great mountain coming toward him with great speed. Suddenly the peak turned upside down. Bagsby staggered, dizzy. Then, as abruptly, he somehow passed over the peak—or under it, depending upon point of view.

"Shulana," he said "how is the training going?"

"It's wonderful!" A thought came back in Bagsby's mind, and a warm glow of elation and peace suffused his being. "It's wonderful!"

"George!" Bagsby called, disengaging his mind from Shulana's. "George! Come here."

George trotted across the field, curses raining from his lips.

"George, I want you to try the men in much larger formations. All the footmen we have in three mass formations, three huge blocks."

"Sir," George responded, his dark eyes widening, "they can't even drill in hundreds yet! 'Ow in ten thousand 'ells they gonna' drill in blocks that big? Look 'ere—there's thousands of 'em."

That there were, Bagsby saw with satisfaction. All in all, the footmen mustered from the conquered lands and Parona came to a force of almost thirty thousand men combined. If Bagsby's calcuations were correct, he would be outnumbered in the great battle by odds of less than three to one, which he considered quite good given the plan he had in mind.

"Never you mind, George. Just teach them to form huge defensive blocks that can take a charge, and all will be well."

"As you say, sir," George replied. He would have liked to say quite a bit more, but Marta wouldn't like it.

Bagsby walked from the field toward the great camp, past a sea of tents, fires, wagons, and all the other paraphernalia required by a huge army. He tromped across the muddy ground toward the greatest tent, a large white affair with three poles holding up the giant roof, and with the improvised banner of the Holy Alliance forces fluttering from atop the center pole.

Pikemen posted by the entrance saluted smartly at his approach. Those inside, he knew, would not. For awaiting him were the chief nobles of the Alliance, gathered to hear from his own lips the plan that justified their faith in him, and in the unorthodox training he was giving their footmen—men who should, as far as the Paronans were concerned, be at home working their farm plots, assuring the harvest and the continued prosperity of the kingdom.

"King Alexis," Bagsby said with a curt nod. "King Harold. Nobles of the Alliance. I pray you all be seated and make yourselves at ease." His curtness was calculated; these men had given him almost absolute power; he wanted them to know that he intended to use it.

Bagsby went to the head of the improvised camp table, and took his seat squarely between the two monarchs. He clapped his hands twice, and servants appeared from outside, bearing wine and delicacies for his unwelcome guests.

"I see you spare no expense in your hospitality," King Alexis said drily.

"We would not want to endanger the Alliance by offending any member with a lack of customary courtesy," Bagsby replied smoothly. "Please refresh yourselves, and then let us get to the business at hand."

"Yes, let us," a Paronan lord demanded. "We have done all you ask, and at great expense have allowed you to engage in training exercises that seem to have no possible outcome but disaster on the field," the man said bluntly. "Now we who are responsible for the welfare of our kingdoms and counties—whom the whole world opposed to Heilesheim looks to for leadership—want to know: what is your plan?"

Shouts of "Hear, hear!" went around the table, and mailed fists banged their approval of the speaker's words.

Bagsby rose. He waved a hand at a servant, and a large map showing the Elven Preserve, Argolia, and most of southern Parona was spread out on the great table. Bagsby waited a moment for the servants to leave. "No one in or out," he called to the guards, who closed the flap of the tent entrance. "What is said here stays here—and here alone," Bagsby said to his guests, eyeing them with his sternest gaze.

"Shown on this map are the current positions of the legions of the Heilesheim forces," Bagsby began. "Please observe them."

There was more muttering as the nobles stood, leaned, squinted, and gawked, trying to take in the information spread before them.

"As you can see, there are two full Heilesheim legions in the process of forming just south of the Elven Preserve. These, as Elrond has told us, intend to invade the Preserve itself from the southern end and advance northward."

"Quite right," Elrond said. "It is that eventuality that we hope to avoid by this alliance."

Bagsby nodded. "Here," he continued, indicating the length of the southern border of Parona with northern Argolia, "are the bulk of the enemy's legions, six in all, threatening to march into Parona. From Elrond's intelligence, we know that this threat is mere posturing; Ruprecht has ordered that once the invasion of the Elven Preserve has begun, these troops will shift to the west to overwhelm the flank of the elven line as it retreats north through the woods. The combined army, having defeated the elves, will pursue their remnants north and then emerge, still a combined army, into the southern reaches of Parona."

"That, we presume, is what this alliance will prevent," King Alexis said, provoking laughter from the Paronan nobles.

"Your presumption is correct," Bagsby said in a matter-of-fact tone, "although Elrond's is not. I intend to fight them here," Bagsby said, stabbing the map with a short dagger. "Here, one day's march south of the Parona-Argolia border and one day's march east of the border between Argolia and the Elven Preserve."

A ripple of dissent passed through the small crowd of nobles. "How will you get them there, where they have no intention of going?" one lord asked, a clear tone of derision in his voice. "Do you think they will conveniently march in a mass to the spot where you prefer to offer battle?"

"Yes, I do," Bagsby said. "Because they will believe it is in their interests to do so. When the Heilesheim Legions first attack the Elven Preserve," Bagsby continued, "the elves will offer no resistance beyond the show of a small skirmish line across the front. Even this line will rapidly retreat, moving north and east through the forest until it emerges into Argolia. The elven force will then march swiftly to this point, where I will join it with the main army."

"Thereby," King Alexis said, "taking in flank the six enemy legions that will be marching west toward the Elven Preserve! That is a good plan, but can our attack succeed with the strange tactics you are teaching our footmen?"

"No," Bagsby said. "We will not attack. We will stand our ground, allow the enemy to concentrate and turn toward us, and we will fight a defensive battle in very open terrain."

"Madness!" shouted a Paronan lord, and his cry was taken up universally around the table. Even King Harold, who for reasons of past history had been Bagsby's strongest supporter, was aghast.

"We will be slaughtered as we were at Clairton," King Harold cautioned. "We will be outnumbered, nearly three to one or more. Our infantry will never stand against their pikes, and our horses will be outnumbered as well."

Bagsby motioned with both arms for silence, then ordered it in a booming voice.

"Silence! Hear me out. Do you want this war to go on and on, or do you want it over, decided, once and for all?"

"No one wants the war prolonged," King Alexis commented, "least of all me. And from what I see of your plan, it will not be prolonged. We will lose it in a day."

"I think not, Your Majesty," Bagsby said. "I want the forces of Heilesheim concentrated, in one open place, so that they may be destroyed in one great blow. For I will bring down upon them nothing less than the fire from heaven of old!"

Stunned silence greeted this announcement.

Bagsby folded his arms in front of his chest and waited out the stillness.

At length, King Harold rose to address the lords, who were slowly beginning to whisper to one another and shake their heads in sadness.

"I think I speak for us all," King Harold said. "Sir John Wolfe, I have been your greatest admirer in this noble company, and I must tell you plainly. The fire from heaven is but a legend from the past—oh, yes, our priests can call down small strikes of flame when it pleases the gods—but the fire from heaven of which you speak was an all-consuming, endless, wrathful magical fire that was said to devour entire counties in a day's time. Clearly, such a thing does not exist—or if it does, its secret is a magic beyond the ken of any wizard. Even our foe Valdaimon, if he had it, would use it."

Nods of agreement came from all the assembly.

"Sir John Wolfe, I fear the power we have given you has led you into madness. You are deluded. You cannot have the secret of the legendary fire from heaven."

A brief scuffle and a call of voices from beyond the tent flap interrupted King Harold's speech. A guard reluctantly thrust his head in, catching Bagsby's eye.

"Sir, begging your pardon," the man began. "There's an old man out here, some kind of holy man, who insists on seeing the noble lords."

"Show him in," Bagsby called.

Mild astonishment gripped the assembled lords as a small, bent, wizened man with wrinkled yellow-brown skin stepped into the room. The little man wore nothing but a simple white linen breechcloth, and leaned for support against a heavy staff.

"I am much thanking you, my goodness. Those men would not let me being in."

"You are welcome, Ramashoon, Holy Man of the East," Bagsby called.

"Well," the little man stated, "I am here to be telling all of you that this man is not crazy," Ramashoon said, his lilting voice and smiling face spreading bemusement. "Oh, my gracious, no. He says he has found the secret of the fire from heaven. And I am being here to tell you that this is true, for I, Ramashoon the Holy, have seen it with my own eyes, oh my goodness, yes."

7

Trial by Fire

Rupprecht of Heilesheim sat upright in the saddle of his prancing black charger, his plain white blouse blowing in the gentle breeze of the summer morning, his golden coronet glistening in the early sunlight. Behind him, on a broad plain, were massed two legions of Heilesheim, their ranks now depleted by disease, hunger, and the endless of accidents of war to about ten thousand foot and two thousand mounted, armored men. The infantry was massed in pike block formations, three per legion, while the cavalry stood in two long ranks to the rear. Behind them, but ready to move to the front at an instant's command, were one hundred wizards of Valdaimon's League, armed with spells carefully crafted to set ablaze the vast forest that faced the king about a thousand yards to his front.

Culdus was mounted next to the king, on hand to command what he foresaw as a possible disaster. Valdaimon's plan was sound enough, but there were endless difficulties that weighed this morning on Culdus's mind. Once the blaze began, how could the infantry advance in its wake? It could take days to march through that scorched earth. And already, the troops selected for the attack were hungry. Despite constant patrolling to the supply lines, Culdus had been unable to prevent the loss of over three thousand wagons in the last thirty days to attacks from Argolian villagers who overwhelmed the supply convoys, burned what they could not loot, and then disappeared back into either the few remaining villages or the small woods that still dotted these southern lands.

162

"A fine day!" Ruprecht declared. "Is all in readiness?"

"It is, Your Majesty," replied the dreadful figure of Valdaimon, standing on foot beside Ruprecht's giant steed. "Your Majesty has but to give the word of command. I would, however, make one small suggestion," Valdaimon said, staring ahead at the thick forest which held more secrets of magic than even he had amassed in his many lifetimes of effort and study. The thought of the wholesale destruction about to be unleashed on such valuable magic was painful to the old wizard. "An infantry probe," Valdaimon wheezed. "Let us see where the elves have formed their first line. We can begin the fire from there."

Ruprecht's face scrunched up in annoyance. He turned to Culdus, who had listened intently to the old wizard's words. For once, Valdaimon was daring to give the king good advice, Culdus thought. He had always opposed the notion of simply blasting the woods with magical fire before probing it to learn the enemy's position, strength, and dispositions.

"Valdaimon's suggestion is well taken," Culdus said. "In fact, I had planned to send in a skirmish line first to determine the enemy's strength. Then," he added quickly, seeing the young king's growing displeasure as the pyrotechnics show he had expected was delayed, "we will have a very good idea of how many elves we have destroyed."

Ruprecht considered. He pictured himself recounting the tale of this day in the great banquet hall of Heilesheim. *And on that day, three thousand of the foul little elves were burned to death in the fiery trap I had prepared,* he heard himself saying. To Culdus he said only, "Very well. But make it quick."

Culdus nodded, turned, summoned his frontline officers, and spoke a few words of commmand. Less than a minute later three long, thin, widely spaced lines of infantry began advancing at a slow jog across the open plain toward the edge of the wood. They carried light spears, that Culdus had improvised, thinking they might be more useful in the wooded setting; and a few, who had the skill, even carried bows. The men wore light leather padding as their only armor; for skirmishers in a dense wood, freedom and ease of movement was of greater value than weight of armor. Culdus could only wish there had been time and supplies to so equip a whole legion for use in this dubious adventure.

The first line of men, about one hundred strong, reached the edge of the forest and paused only an instant before disappearing into its darkness. The second wave followed them seconds later; the third waited at the edge the forest for a good minute, then slowly advanced after them.

"Well, well, what's happening?" Ruprecht demanded. "Why isn't there any noise? Where are the shouts of battle?" The king's horse pranced back and forth before the massed troops, mirroring its master's impatience.

"Patience, Your Majesty," Culdus counseled, a frown crossing his own brow. Where were the sounds of fighting? Surely the elves knew they were coming; it had taken two days to mass the troops, and the camp had been less than two miles from the edge of the Elven Preserve. Not even elves could be blind to so large a force on their very borders!

A trio of runners began to emerge from the wood, hastening back to Culdus to report.

"My lords! Your Majesty!" the first one to approach shouted as he came nearer. "The elves are retreating! They are fleeing at our approach!"

His cry was echoed by the two more distant runners. "Light resistance—a few arrows fired, and then their line broke and fled on the forest floor," one man called. "No casualties—the enemy is in full flight," the third reported.

"Ahah!" Ruprecht exclaimed. "Where is the vaunted elven prowess and magic now? You hear, Culdus, they flee at our approach. The whole world trembles at my approach!" The exuberant youth spurred his steed forward, waving a sword in the air as his charger worked up to a gallop. "Forget the five! Let the whole army advance! After them! After them! Let not one of them escape the sword of Ruprecht!"

"Majesty!" Culdus exclaimed, but the king paid no heed. Behind the general, in obedience to the king's command, officers barked orders and the massive formations began a slow advance across the plain.

"Valdaimon!" Culdus cried. "This is dangerous! It could be a trap!"

"Have no fear," the old wizard croaked back. "My League will be at the rear of the advance. Say the word, and the flames will begin."

What great luck, Valdaimon thought. The elves are abandoning part of their forest. So long had that woods been enchanted that even the smallest part of it could yield secrets of magical power!

Elrond stood in the branch of a tall tree, his mind half melded with the flowing sap of the giant, green living thing, his eyes partly glazed, his consciousness a jumble of images. He saw a brother elf, crouched in the underbrush, loose an arrow in the direction of the advancing Heilesheim skirmishers. He felt the soft thud of the earth as the man's body hit the ground. He saw another elf, no weapons on him, high in a faraway treetop, gesturing, and pointing a finger into the distance. A scream came and went as a tiny bullet of magical force claimed yet another Heilesheim life. A body of three elves took careful aim and let loose three arrows, each striking its mark.

Caution, caution, Elrond's consciousness breathed to the tree. *Slow them, but do not destroy them—not too quickly, not yet.* And throughout the dense wood, elven warriors felt a sense of peace, security, and safety well up from all the living green things around them, urging them to slow their retreat, slow their firing, minimize the killing.

"We must keep them coming, coming after us," became the sole thought of a thousand elves, deployed in-depth across a mile-long front of the sacred forest. And so it was that little by little, step by step, the Heilesheim skirmishers advanced, taking light but acceptable losses, inflicting almost none, moving forward at a slow, steady pace.

Even then, Elrond noted, the humans had to slow their advance, lest they get too far forward of the main body of their infantry—great lumbering masses of men encumbered by their huge pikes, who slashed and scarred the plant life and the earth as they stumbled forward, one painful step at a time, through the underbrush and between the great trees.

Time and again, the old elf sensed the enemy formations losing their cohesion, and time and again they stopped, regrouped, and stumbled forward a few hundred yards more.

So it had gone for three whole days, as Elrond and his elven warriors lured the Heilesheim legions deeper and deeper into the Elven Preserve. Now, Elrond thought, it was time to begin bending the line back toward the east. Again, the communal thought went out. Throughout that day and into the night, the Heilesheim forces slowly discovered less and less resistance on their left, as the elven line bent back, back to the east, toward the edge of their beloved forest, toward the open plains of Argolia.

Thieves do have their uses, Bagsby mused, as the band of swarthy vagabonds was shown into his tent. Indeed they do! The war effort he was coordinating had involved the entire population of Parona, and all the refugees who could be mustered. Artisans, of course, were in high demand for the manufacture of weapons armor, and the various other necessities of war. Women were put to work over the camp's great cooking fires, preparing three meals a day from the endless parade of livestock and produce delivered to the camp for the thirty thousand footmen and five thousand mounted knights of the host of the Alliance. There was no segment of the population unused, Bagsby had realized only days before, except for the thieves. And these he had found good use for as well.

The thieves themselves were only too grateful to be released from their cells in Parona and set loose on the land. A goodly number of them did not return, as Bagsby had expected. But this handful had come back, lured by the promise of easy gold and a full pardon.

"Report!" Bagsby barked, to the leader of the small band.

The scrawny man stepped forward, his ragged hat in his hands, his small, dark eyes glancing this way and that in the characteristic manner of a thief—always searching for the quickest way out of a place, and anything that wasn't nailed down.

"Sir . . ." the man began.

"And know this," Bagsby interrupted at once. "Your words had better be true, for your reward, your pardon, and even your lives depend upon the truth."

"Sir," the man said again, "we went like you said, down to the border with Argolia. Went fast, like you said, took them horses you gave us."

Bagsby grimaced. The gift of horses to the more than two hundred thieves turned out from Parona's dungeons had brought more howls of protest from the nobility—and especially from King Alexis. "We rode real fast, fast as them horses could take us," the man droned on. "Right to the border, like you said."

"Yes, yes, man, get to the point," Bagsby said sternly.

"We seen them Heilesheim troops there, in Argolia, just like you said we would."

"How far from the border?" Bagsby asked. This much he knew from his own cavalry scouts, whom he had withdrawn from the area days ago to avoid alarming the Heilesheim legions.

"Real close to the border," the ingratiating man replied. "Not more than three or four miles at most."

So far, so good, Bagsby thought.

"What did you do then?" he demanded.

"Well, sir, we didn't do nothin'. What I mean is, we hid the horses and blended in—they's lots of people milling about with them troops."

"Yes, yes, and what did you see?"

"Looked to me," the man said, stepping forward and lifting his head slightly, assuming an air of importance, "like they had problems. A lot of them soldiers was taking food from whoever had any, and lots of the civilians was going hungry. They was drilling, too, but they didn't look very good," he added.

Culdus has supply problems, Bagsby thought. *And if the drilling is poor, he's filling in his ranks with green troops. Very good.*

"Then, sir," the man went on, "we done like you said. We waited until them troops marched off, and we come back here right quick. Left yesterday afternoon and rode all night, got here this morning."

Bagsby sat forward, his interest peaked.

"What direction, man? What direction did they take?"

"They went west, sir, by my soul they did."

"You all saw this?" Bagsby demanded.

The crew of thieves nodded to a man, fixing Bagsby with their most sincere looks.

"Very well," Bagsby said. "Captain of the guard," he called.

The guard appeared at the tent entrance.

"See that these men are well fed and cared for. And keep them under close arrest until further orders," Bagsby ordered. There was always the chance they were lying.

The thieves squawking protests were quickly silenced by the troops who took them from the commander's presence. Bagsby stood, walked over to his map table, and took a last look at his carefully drawn plans. So it begins, he thought, a chill running through his body. So it begins.

George looked out with great pride at the spectacle that stretched below him. The secondary road was narrow and rough going, but the vast procession of the army of the Holy Alliance was making as good a progress as any Heilesheim force ever had. George sat on the ground on the side of a small hill, overlooking the single road that wound its way through the rolling plains. He sucked on a blade of sweet grass as he marveled at the army and his own fate.

In the lead of the great procession, of course, was the contingent of priests. The priests of all the gods of Parona were represented, and there were priests for some of the other gods, too—gods from Argolia and from the conquered duchies, even gods from the cantons in the north. The priests were a pretty sight, George reluctantly admitted. At the fore, they carried the great banner of the combined army of the Holy Alliance— a huge, white square with gold fringe all around it. In the center of the square, a golden dragon flew upward toward a blue field of sky laced with white clouds. Pretty scene, George thought, not like most battle flags. And the priests themselves were colorful—all dressed in their fine and colorful robes. Couldn't be prettier, although what good they were George couldn't imagine. They had stayed away from the camp for the most part—except when it was time to get money, and then they'd showed in force. This morning they'd blessed the whole lot. Couldn't hurt, George guessed.

Next came about a thousand mounted knights, riding out with their high-spirited horses prancing, wanting to increase the slow speed of the advance, their armor clanking as they went along. Knights were necessary for battle, of course, but George had lost little of his antagonism toward the ruling class, and these men on horseback were the symbols of that class.

The bowmen—now there was a strange lot. They marched fast; they were tall, proud men in their white shirts, brown breeches, and good, solid boots—the same thing they always wore. Their lines were ragged and unimpressive, but there were a lot of them, and George had seen what they could do with a bow. Their bows were different; tall, long things, much longer than bows of Heilesheim. They took a lot of strength to pull—George had tried. But these men could get off six good arrows in a minute with those bows if the strings were dry, and most of them were dead-on shots. What's more, those arrows seemed to carry an unusual amount of force. George himself had seen one penetrate plate armor, something that only a crossbow bolt could do, and then at point-blank range.

George stood up, swelling with pride as his eye came to rest on the first of the footmen. Now, these men kept in ranks as they marched, and they held their pikes in the rest position just like he'd showed them. They didn't dawdle or fall out of ranks, and there didn't appear to be very much talking. It was a great sight, George thought. Less than four weeks ago, some of those men had been nothing but peasants, and now any one of them could wield a pike effectively—at least in defense, which was what Sir John had wanted.

George turned at the sound of an approaching horse.

"What do you think of our army?" Bagsby called cheerily.

"They'll do, I suppose, they'll do," George said, nodding.

"I'm glad you approve," Bagsby said, "because when the battle begins, you will be commanding them."

The long blade of sweet grass dropped from George's mouth.

"Me?" the man gasped.

"Of course," Bagsby said, chuckling. "Why do you think I had you train them?"

"But I . . . I ain't no general, sir," George said.

"I know. But as you may recall, I ain't either," Bagsby said, teasing. "Don't worry. The horsemen will all have their instructions from me before the fight begins. You will command the masses of the foot. I'll arrive at the battle at the crucial time, before the decisive moment," Bagsby said.

"Where you going?" George demanded. "Where you going to be?"

"Quit worrying. I won't leave until just before the fighting begins, and I'll show up at the right time. I'm going to pick up the treasure, as I told you I would."

"Why in ten thousand 'ells would you be bringin' a treasure to a battle?" George asked, bewildered.

"You'll see in good time, George," Bagsby said, his visage growing grim. "Now listen, this is important, and I want you to think hard about it between now and the time of the fighting. When I leave and before I get back, a lot of those men are going to be scared. Not of fighting—everybody's scared of that. But out there on that battlefield, they're going to see something they've never seen before, and it will scare them bad. You, too. Your job will be to hold them together, keep them from running. You do that by telling them that the thing that's scaring them so bad is on their side," Bagsby explained.

"I'm not sure I understand all that," George said, shaking his head. Sometimes he wished Sir John would just speak plainly.

"Don't worry," Bagsby said. "You will when the time comes."

Ruprecht, Culdus, and Valdaimon sat in the king's tent on the eastern edge of the Elven Preserve, poring over Culdus's great maps.

"I knew it was too easy," Culdus moaned. "I knew it had to be a trap!"

"I don't see the problem," Ruprecht shot back, plopping a fresh grape into his mouth. "Valdaimon," the king added, "step back from me, please. Your smell spoils the taste of my fruit."

Culdus stood up, his muscles twitching. There was nothing he wanted so much as to thrash this young, spoiled wastrel who happened to wear a crown. Ruprecht looked at Culdus's impressive armored bulk, at the angry scowling face, at the tension in the muscles that showed even beneath the coat of chain mail and livery that covered the old general's body.

"We said," the king repeated coldly, "that we do not understand why there is a problem. We expect an explanation."

My oath, Culdus reminded himself. My oath. I bound myself to this man for all time, no matter what. I am a man of honor. I will honor my oath.

"The problem, Your Majesty," Valdaimon intruded, "is quite simple. The army of the Holy Alliance is moving parallel and north of the advance of our flanking force. By now it has linked up with the elves, who are now driven from the Preserve. Their entire force sits on the flank of advancing legions. Were they to attack . . ."

"The military term is defeat in detail," Culdus snapped. "They could attack the flank of one legion, defeat it, then attack the flank of the next, and so on."

"I doubt that rabble can defeat anything," Ruprecht said. "They are peasants with bills and staves. We outnumber them, with superior troops. We have Valdaimon with us to deal with their magic and, if need be, he can . . . bring up a few extra troops for us," Ruprecht said disdainfully. He popped another grape in his mouth. "That might be kind of fun, actually, Valdaimon, if you were to bring up some of our undead things. Frankly, this campaign has been too easy. It begins to bore me."

"Your Majesty," Culdus said coldly, "in order to prevent the defeat in detail that we mentioned, it is necessary to concentrate the army, and quickly. I recommend that we concentrate here," he said, stabbing with a mailed finger at a point on the map about a day's march east of the Elven Preserve and a day's march south of the border with Parona.

"If we do that," Ruprecht asked, "will there finally be a big battle?"

"If we are able to do that," Culdus said carefully, "there will most certainly be a very large battle." He didn't add that it would be the largest he had ever seen, larger than any he had even studied, in terms of the numbers to be engaged.

"Then do it," the king said, waving his hand to dismiss his general. "Now, Valdaimon," the king said, turning to more pleasant matters, "have a few of the prisoners we've taken sent in for my amusement."

It was after midnight when Bagsby met with Elrond on a bare plain behind the army's camp, just south of the border with Parona.

"Well done, well done," Bagsby enthused as the elf approached him in the pale moonlight. "You pulled it off splendidly."

"I have only one question to ask you," Elrond said. "I did not ask it before, and I did not ask it in public, because I wished to do nothing to jeopardize our victory over Heilesheim."

The tall pale elf turned slightly away from Bagsby to gaze up at the pale light of the moon. The elf's appearance was even more magnificent, Bagsby thought—more magical, more charming—in the pale flood of light that danced across his fine features and bounced off his longish white hair, than it had ever been.

"I want to ask this," Elrond continued, quietly. "What did you promise the dragons to get their cooperation?"

"Hmm," Bagsby grunted. "Of course, you did know, didn't you?"

"That you would bring them, yes," Elrond agreed. "Why they would come, no."

Bagsby hesitated. Everything hinged on the battle in the morning. The battle could well hinge on the elves. There were so many small things that could wrong, so many little things that their magic could fix. . . . If he lost Elrond now, he would lose the whole world to Valdaimon.

"I promised them peace with men and elves," Bagsby answered.

Elrond nodded. "Yes. I can see how it must be so, though it will be hard for us elves. But hard as it is for us, it must have been harder for them. They have racial memory; they will know their history as well as you know how to walk."

"It was hard for them," Bagsby acknowledged.

"They must want revenge," Elrond went on.

"They do," Bagsby admitted. "But they see the values of cooperation."

"They must have demanded some token," Elrond pressed.

"I promised them the life of the elf who killed the Ancient One, the mother of their race," Bagsby said. "Of course, there are many ways for an elf to give his life."

Elrond stood still for a moment, gazing at the moon. Bagsby squirmed. He could not keep his feet still. Elrond finally turned to face him, a smile of gentle peace on his ancient face.

"It is a small price to pay for the gain to be had," he whispered. "But the elves as a whole must survive. There is a curse, cast by the Ancient One herself, that dooms my race. And now is the time of its fulfillment."

"I will do all I can," Bagsby said simply.

Over the next hour, Bagsby gave the orders for the final disposition of the army for the morrow's battle. He had chosen his position with some care, once arriving in the general area where he wanted the battle to occur. As he had expected, it took the Heilesheim forces almost three days to reorient and regroup—about a day longer, Bagsby noted, than crack, veteran troops would have required. There had been plenty of time to scout the open plain for the battlefield that would best suit the tactics Bagsby planned to use.

His army was deployed in a flat, open plain between two low hills, about a mile apart. His infantry occupied the center of the line, arranged in three great blocks, each with a frontage of almost five hundred yards and a depth of twenty ranks. Clustered on the flanks and in the gaps between these three massive blocks were groupings of the northern bowmen, in their own irregular wedge formations. The mounted knights, some four thousand of them, were deployed eight lines deep behind the infantry. Another five hundred cavalry each were posted in line on the crest of each hill as flank guards. The elves, who had borne the brunt of the battle so far and, had pulled off such a marvelous retreat and feint, were posted to the far rear as an emergency reserve.

The priests, who always kept to themselves, were deployed in their own lines behind the cavalry, but under strict orders to come to the front immediately if, as expected, Valdaimon used his dark powers to unleash the beasts of the undead world upon the Holy Alliance forces.

The few mages available to the Holy Alliance were deployed with the forward troops, ready at a moment's notice to try to counter the force of Valdaimon's mages.

Bagsby had seen to the dispositions of the troops before sunset, in the hours after the Heilesheim forces had finally advanced to within striking range of the field. His men were instructed to sleep in the open, in ranks; despite Valdaimon's penchant for the undead, Bagsby feared no attack during the night. His scouts had reported to him fully on the disarray in the Heilesheim ranks—the crossing of supply trains on the narrow, limited roads, the low morale of the troops, and the marching and countermarching that had been ordered to meet the threat to the Heilesheim flank. Culdus was a cautious general, Bagsby knew. He would make no move before morning, and Valdaimon dared not move without him.

Now, Bagsby stood on the southernmost of the two hills and looked out over the field at night. Tomorrow would be the test. He had done all that he could to ensure that the opening of the battle went well. Now he would have to do the only remaining thing he could do.

Sir John Wolfe patted the flank of the white charger provided for him, put his foot in the stirrup, and hoisted himself up. Then, with a final glance at his sleeping army, he turned the horse and galloped off into the dark night, leaving the army far behind.

A little after dawn, the sun was already burning off the morning mist that covered the fair, open plain on which the army of the Holy Alliance was deployed in full battle array. Culdus surveyed the field from the back of his favorite warhorse. He was puzzled by what he saw.

The Holy Alliance commander was showing only his infantry strength. That seemed massive enough; it stretched in three great, rectangular formations across almost a mile of front, with only two gaps. There appeared to be irregular formations of some sort in those gaps; these were of little concern to Culdus. What did concern him was that the enemy infantry seemed to be armed like his own, with the long, eighteen-foot pike. His thus far invincible pike formations had never faced troops armed and deployed in similar fashion; the pike formations of Heilesheim had been developed to defeat noble armies of mounted knights. Of these, there were few to be seen—a small group on each of the hills that delimited the enemy's flanks, that was all.

Culdus did like the odds. By his own rough head count, he had more than three times the enemy's strength in foot, and probably a superiority in cavalry as well. The old general thought about the problem for a moment, then ordered his dispositions.

"Well, Culdus, let the battle begin!" the king sang out as he rode forward on his own black steed.

"In good time, Your Majesty. The legions must be deployed to meet the enemy's dispositions," Culdus replied coldly.

"Well, then let's deploy. Who goes where?" the king asked eagerly.

"I plan a very simple battle using our numerical superiority to crush the enemy," Culdus explained. "We have eight legions, each of about five thousand foot. Two will be held in reserve. The other six we will form in a broad line, which will advance en masse. Our line will be much longer than theirs; our left and right legions will close on the enemy's flanks and destroy him in one great crush. Our cavalry, as always, will be used to counter the enemy cavalry, and for pursuit."

The king scowled. This was not the type of battle he had envisioned. "What about some wights or zombies or shadows? What about some magic attacks? I want to see some fireworks today, Culdus. This will be the greatest victory of my life— sadly, probably the last, for after today, who will there be to oppose me? I want it to be memorable."

"I do not doubt," Culdus said testily, "that the day will be memorable enough."

"Well, I do!" the king pouted. "I want Valdaimon to open the battle with magic and undead to terrorize the enemy!"

"Your Majesty, with due respect, that will only waste valuable time."

"I insist," the king screamed.

George watched the sun climb higher in the sky. He saw the forces opposing him across the plain, less than five hundred yards away. Their lines of pike formations stretched on forever; they would clearly wrap around his flanks. What puzzled George was why the enemy was waiting. It was almost midmorning, and still the enemy had made no move.

Finally George saw a short line of men dressed in colorful robes make their way toward the front of the enemy's ranks. No doubt about it, George thought, them there is wizards.

"Runner!" he cried. "Alert the mages. Alert all units. Stand by for magical attack."

George continued to scan the enemy front. Slowly one figure came to dominate the foreground. George squinted— it was Valdaimon!

"Runner!" he called again. Another youth sprinted to his side. "Go fetch those priests up here, and make them come double time," George ordered.

The order was delivered none too soon. Shortly after Valdaimon's appearance, the sky grew overcast, blotting out the brilliant morning sun. Then a vast mist began to form in front of the Heilesheim ranks, seeping out of the ground and rising slowly higher and higher, until at length it blotted out all view of the enemy forces. This mist began to roll slowly forward toward the center of the Alliance troops.

"Steady now, lads," George called. He moved himself laterally to the gap between his left and center blocks. With relief he saw the colorfully robed figures of priests hastening to the front, the robes whipping in the light wind that had come up, the various symbols of their gods in their hands.

"'Ere! Ere! Form a line 'ere!" George directed.

The priests seemed to keep their own counsel, ignoring George but nonetheless doing as he said, placing themselves in a line squarely in front of the advancing wall of fog.

The wall was less than a hundred yards away when the forms began to emerge from it.

Wails of despair went up from the front ranks of the Alliance infantry whose vision was not blocked by the priests. Prayers to a dozen gods soared upward as the hideous hodgepodge of undead began to slowly advance. The wights were the first to appear, bestial, stooped, brutish things, whose mere touch could freeze flesh and whose bite was fatal to the soul as well as the body. Behind them lumbered a host of zombies, and overhead a few bats began to soar—the more mobile form of the few vampires Valdaimon had seen fit to summon.

George grabbed a horse from a runner, sprang up on its back, and galloped along the front of the infantry line.

"Hold firm boys! The priests will get them!" he cried. "The priests will get them!"

Soon the chant of "The priests will get them!" arose along the Alliance front, and the priests slowly advanced, more than a hundred holy symbols held aloft, their deep voices chanting prayers to their gods and commands to the undead to return from whence they had come in the name of all that was holy.

The exorcisms had great effect. Of the three hundred zombies who had stumbled from the mist, all but a handful fled stumbling backward. About a dozen of the wights were strong enough to continue their advances, only to be hacked to pieces by priests armed with silver swords and spears for just such purposes. The few vampires, being intelligent creatures, were hardly affected by the priests' chanting, although they were discomfited, and thus chose not to launch themselves at hordes of increasingly excited, angry humans armed with wooden poles topped with iron and steel points. The undead attack evaporated more quickly than it had begun.

The sun peeped out from behind the clouds, which had rapidly began to dissipate, and soon the wall of mist was evaporating as well. George reined in his horse in front of his central infantry. As the fog lifted, he began to see the enemy front more clearly—which was now not more than 200 yards away!

The wily Culdus had chosen to launch his attack behind the cover of the undead and the wall of fog!

"Priests to the rear, priests to the rear!" George cried, galloping once more along the front line. "Infantry, prepare to receive charge! Prepare to receive!"

Unit commanders repeated the vital order, and the green peasant infantry of the Holy Alliance prepared to do the one thing they had been taught to do well. The front three ranks of the pike lines knelt, their long pikes extended forward at a low angle, making a hideous front for a mass of men or horses to break. Their comrades in the fourth and fifth ranks raised their pikes to shoulder height and held them extended frontally, adding to the death trap for any frontal assault.

But the Heilesheim pikemen were also well trained, and even their green men were a match for the Alliance troops. Pikes shouldered, they advanced to within sixty yards, where they paused, and then, the order given, advanced forward at the double-time step, their own pikes leveled. Those in front carried their deadly spears in both hands at waist height; those in the rear at shoulder height. At twenty yards the massed formation broke into a full run, and second later the impact occurred.

Hideous screams arose from the field as men in the front ranks on both sides were impaled in the mesh of pike points. Neither mass yielded; the Alliance troops held, and those in the rear ranks began stepping forward to fill in for their fallen comrades. In the frontmost ranks the few that had survived dropped their pikes, often made useless by the burden of an impaled body, and began the brutal hand-to-hand slaughter with swords and daggers.

George galloped down the gap between his center and right units. "Bowmen to the front and fire at the enemy," he ordered.

The sturdy northerners moved forward on the run in the gap between the units, the first to arrive near the front pausing to send a lethal volley of missiles into the few Heilesheim men who, trying to exploit the gaps, had moved inward toward the flanks of the Alliance block formations.

George galloped on toward the rear. He had to find a vantage point where he would see what was happening. How fast, he wondered, were the flanking forces coming? In seconds they would come crashing in on both flanks, and the battle would be lost.

Volley after volley of arrows poured forth from the archers as they whittled away the front ranks of the attacking Heilesheimers. But on the flanks, the archery was not enough.

George reached a very slight rise, just in front of his first line of cavalry, where the kings of Parona and Argolia sat watching with dismay as full legions of Heilesheim troops began to maneuver on the Alliance flanks.

Then the winds hit. At first it was just a roaring sound, like the howl of a tornado in the distance, but it grew louder and louder—though from whence it came no one could tell, for the mighty gusts blew in both directions across the field, along the length of the engaged fighting lines. A few seconds more, and the first men began to tumble over, unable to keep their footing.

George looked up to the sky, and terror struck his heart. For there, high above, coming one from the far right and one from the far left, were two seemingly tiny, winged creatures who were the source of this awesome wind. In his heart of hearts, George knew at once.

Dragons.

"By all the gods," George shouted to the kings. "Look! 'E's brought us dragons!"

All along the front, pandemonium broke out. Men began to scream in terror. Many fell to earth, hugging it, weeping with fear. Others tried to run, but the winds kept knocking them about so that they flew across the field like tumbleweeds in a storm.

George kicked the flanks of his horse and rode forward full tilt, struggling to keep his body on the steed as the winds continued to increase.

"It's fire from 'eaven, boys! Fire from 'eaven! And it's on our side. It's on our side!" he shouted, again and again, stopping now and then to scream his message into the ear of an officer, who could pass it along.

The fire came down.

Bagsby's mount swooped low over the field, heading straight toward the two legions that moments before had been about to embrace the Alliance only fifty yards away. Scratch opened his mighty jaws, and the greatest stream of flame the dragon had yet breathed came forth in an enormous, streaming gout—rolling and licking down the line of the Heilesheim pike blocks, incinerating everything in its path, spreading with the speed of lightning until, in a matter of seconds, the flames fanned by the intense winds had burned through the entire force of ten thousand men.

The Heilesheimers screamed in fear and panic, then they became silent as the flames sucked the very air from their seared lungs. Bodies burst into flames, and the stench of charred flesh, whipped by the winds, rose from the field and made its way toward the rear ranks of both armies where horses, spooked by the scent, began to bolt in panic.

On the Alliance right, Lifefire and Shulana dealt similar treatment to the enemy, until the two great dragons passed one another at a height of a mere fifty feet above the field.

Bagsby screamed into the din, with no hope of being heard, "The day is ours! The day is ours!"

"Valdaimon, you must do something! Do something!" Ruprecht cried in panic and rage as he saw the magnificent, fire-breathing beasts consume his legions.

"Retreat!" Culdus ordered curtly, waving back the cavalry.

"No!" Ruprecht screamed. "No! Wizard, kill those dragons! I know you have the power! Use it!"

Valdaimon stood silent, gazing in undisguised awe at the spectacle of the fiery field and soaring, red-hued beasts of whom he had, for countless centuries of his undead existence, only dreamed. They were, he thought, magnificent. They were beyond his wildest expectations. They were the secret of the Treasure of Parona, the fire from heaven, the source of limitless power. They were everything for which he had schemed and dreamed for centuries. It was only a matter of chance circumstance that they were, at the moment, arrayed against him. He could change that—he could make a plan . . . .

"Kill them!" Ruprecht screamed at the old mage.

"Kill them?" Valdaimon shouted back. "You stupid upstart pup! I will not kill them! They shall be mine! They must be mine!"

"How in ten thousand hells can those ever be yours?" Ruprecht cried.

"Make peace!" the wizard screamed back. "Make peace! We shall win them over yet!"

An explosion of brilliant light suddenly illuminated Valdaimon and his king, and from that light—teleported instantly from the Great Temple of Wojan in Hamblen—Sigurt the high priest stepped forth.

"Valdaimon!" the high priest called. "You have broken your oath to the God of War. Your healing is revoked."

"No!" Valdaimon screamed. His single, extended syllable becoming unintelligible as the wizard's arm withered and his face appeared to melt before the horrified eyes of the king.

"Ruuuuppp . . . ." Valdaimon called. "Oooomuss elll meee . . ."

"Now, evil one, learn the price of disobedience to the gods," Sigurt continued in a loud monotone. "Valdaimon of Heilesheim, in the name of Wojan, I command you . . ."

A horrible wail arose from the stinking disfigured form as Sigurt's hand reached forth to touch Valdaimon lightly on what was once his shoulder.

"Live!" Sigurt said.

Ruprecht watched in horror as the body of Valdaimon crumbled to dust before his eyes, to be scattered by the great wind still sweeping from the field, where Scratch and Lifefire, Bagsby and Shulana, were finishing the destruction of the army of Heilesheim.

Far from the continuing din of battle, on the field where the astonished Alliance troops consolidated their victory and their knights were at last unleashed to pursue the panicked, routing cavalry of Heilesheim, Bagsby stood by Scratch's side and watched Shulana slide down from Lifefire's back.

"I thank you, friends," Bagsby said. "I assure you, I will see that the peace I promised you is yours."

"As for the rest of your promise . . ." Lifefire began.

"It will be kept," replied the voice of Elrond.

Shulana whirled to see the old elf—the leader of the Elven Council, her blood kinsman, the oldest of his kind—slowly walking toward Scratch.

"I hear you are called Scratch," Elrond said, "and you are Lifefire."

"True, elf," Scratch grumbled.

Shulana ran forward, throwing her arms around Elrond.

"You can't," she said.

"It will be all right," Bagsby said lightly. "Tell me, Scratch, who was it that the elf killed? You know, the Ancient One she's called, but what was her real name? Bet you don't even know it!"

Scratch bellowed in anger, a word unintelligible to human ears. "There, you see, I do know it," the dragon roared.

"Thank you, Scratch," Bagsby said. "Now that we know the name, we can lift the curse she placed on the elves, proclaiming their destruction."

"Enough!" Lifefire bellowed, her voice for once even deeper than that of Scratch, and the volume so great that Bagsby and Elrond were thrown to the ground by the blast. "Scratch, be silent! The old ways will no longer do. We have a race to create—we need peace," Lifefire said.

The dragon turned her huge neck and lowered her head over Elrond's prone body. The old elf looked up into the dragon's eyes.

"Tell me, elf," Lifefire demanded, "how are you called?"

"My name," Elrond said, revealing this true name in the magical language of elves, "is Lelolan."

"Then, Lelolan, let there be peace between your kind and mine."

"Yeah," Bagsby said with a weary sigh. "But what peace will there be between us humans once we get this mess cleaned up?"

"Perhaps," Shulana suggested, "you can come up with some mad scheme that will help. You're usually pretty successful with those . . . ."

"Sometimes," Bagsby said, smiling. "Sometimes."

RETURN TO AMBER...
THE ONE *REAL* WORLD, OF WHICH ALL OTHERS, INCLUDING EARTH, ARE BUT SHADOWS

ROGER ZELAZNY

The Triumphant conclusion of the Amber novels

PRINCE OF CHAOS　　　　75502-5/$4.99 US/$5.99 Can

The Classic Amber Series

NINE PRINCES IN AMBER　01430-0/$4.99 US/$5.99 Can

THE GUNS OF AVALON　　00083-0/$4.99 US/$5.99 Can

SIGN OF THE UNICORN　　00031-9/$4.99 US/$5.99 Can

THE HAND OF OBERON　　01664-8/$4.99 US/$5.99 Can

THE COURTS OF CHAOS　47175-2/$4.99 US/$5.99 Can

BLOOD OF AMBER　　　　89636-2/$4.99 US/$5.99 Can

TRUMPS OF DOOM　　　　89635-4/$4.99 US/$5.99 Can

SIGN OF CHAOS　　　　　89637-0/$4.99 US/$5.99 Can

KNIGHT OF SHADOWS　　75501-7/$4.99 US/$5.99 Can

AVONOVA PRESENTS
MASTERS OF FANTASY AND ADVENTURE

SNOW WHITE, BLOOD RED 71875-8/ $4.99 US/ $5.99 CAN
edited by Ellen Datlow and Terri Windling

A SUDDEN WILD MAGIC 71851-0/ $4.99 US/ $5.99 CAN
by Diana Wynne Jones

THE WEALDWIFE'S TALE 71880-4/ $4.99 US/ $5.99 CAN
by Paul Hazel

FLYING TO VALHALLA 71881-2/ $4.99 US/ $5.99 CAN
by Charles Pellegrino

THE GATES OF NOON 71781-2/ $4.99 US/ $5.99 CAN
by Michael Scott Rohan

BESTSELLING AUTHOR OF
THE PENDRAGON CYCLE

STEPHEN R. LAWHEAD

In a dark and ancient world,
a hero will be born to fulfill
the lost and magnificent promise of . . .

THE DRAGON KING

Book One
IN THE HALL OF THE DRAGON KING
71629-1/ $4.99 US/ $5.99 Can

Book Two
THE WARLORDS OF NIN
71630-5/ $4.99 US/ $5.99 Can

Book Three
THE SWORD AND THE FLAME
71631-3/ $4.99 US/ $5.99 Can